NEW YORK TIMES and USA TODAY Bestselling Author

LORA
LEIGH

WHEN
Wizards
RULE

ELLORA'S CAVE
ROMANTICA PUBLISHING

What the critics are saying...

∞

5 **Ribbons** "The action is breathtaking and the love scenes are as hot at Garron's breath of fire, that's right our favorite dragon is back and he is more intriguing then ever... Ms. Leigh will lead you thru a maze of twists and turns with breathtaking heights that will leave you soaring. I thoroughly enjoyed WHEN WIZARDS RULE. Ms. Leigh has a true ! talent with writing fantasy, not an easy accomplishment let me tell you." ~ *Romance Junkies*

4 **Angels** "Ms. Leigh has woven a wonderfully wicked, erotic tale jammed-packed with sizzling, ultra hot passion and thrilling suspense. With her unique and powerful writing style, Lora Leigh is a dynamic, erotic storyteller." ~ *Fallen Angel Reviews*

An Ellora's Cave Romantica Publication

www.ellorascave.com

When Wizards Rule

ISBN 141995427X, 9781419954276
Edited by Sue-Ellen Gower
Cover art by Syneca

This book printed in the U.S.A. by Jasmine-Jade Enterprises, LLC.

Electronic book Publication August 2005
Trade paperback Publication February 2006

Also by Lora Leigh

About the Author

❧

Lora Leigh is a wife and mother living in Kentucky. She dreams in bright, vivid images of the characters intent on taking over her writing life and fights a constant battle to put them on the hard drive of her computer before they can disappear as fast as they appeared.

Lora's family, and her writing life co-exist, if not in harmony, in relative peace with each other. An understanding husband is the key to late nights with difficult scenes and stubborn characters. His insights into human nature and the workings of the male psyche provide her hours of laughter, and innumerable romantic ideas that she works tirelessly to put into effect.

Lora welcomes comments from readers. You can find her website and email address on her author bio page at www.ellorascave.com.

Tell Us What You Think

We appreciate hearing reader opinions about our books. You can email us at Comments@EllorasCave.com.

WHEN WIZARDS RULE

Prologue

Once, so very long ago, there was peace in the lands of Sentmar. A time when Cauldaran and Covenan did not exist. A time when it was only the land of Magick, ruled by the Wizard Twins and their Consorts.

But in the forgetfulness of the ages, and a search for power and standing, Wizard Twins and Sorceress Consorts forgot the first and foremost role of their hierarchy and that of their Joinings. That love must conquer the heart, that power meets and tender hearts mold, and in the joining, a union is born.

Power cannot be decided by the minds of men. Even men who hold all power at their fingertips. Power will dim and eventually cease when love does not heat the embers of lust and create a fire of endurance and compassion.

And so did this day come. A day when Joinings were decided by the depth of power gauged. Wizard Twins to Sorceress Consort, alliances built not on the tender emotions or the compassionate hearts, but on the less merciful basis of what can and must be gained.

And what had once been pleasure became pain. What had once been seen as a mating of hearts, souls and minds became but endurance, a basis for hatred and the chill of ice. And so this time continued, until both Wizards and Sorceresses no longer remembered why they strived to live within the same lands, or that their disharmony flowed from within.

Sorceresses whispered of love. Wizards dreamed of power. Daughters were contracted into Joining before birth, sons ordered to choose on basis of the material rather than of the heart.

And the magick began to falter, violence began to fill the castles. In one last desperate effort to force those who were blind to see, the Sentinel Select separated their children. To the land of Covenan, the Sorceress Select drew her daughters, women of great intuitive magick, of compassion and strength. Bequeathed to the Wizard Twins by the Wizard Select were the lands of Cauldaran, those lands which once held harmony, but were now torn with strife. For the Select believed their children to be wise, compassionate and would in time see the errors of their ways.

Instead the Cauldaran warred against Covenan, further dividing their races until finally there was no hope, no chance to realign the magick of their kinds. And the land settled, weeping for its lost children, as the humans of Secular grew in abundance.

And it was said the magick of the twin moons of the Select would weaken. That discord would result. That death and war would come to the lands as magick gave way beneath the hands of a darker alliance.

The alliance of Secular and the building tendrils of dark hatred.

And so this time has come. Violence builds as the humans strike. Betrayal, death and blood began to fill the lands that once knew only peace, only compassion.

The time has come to reunite. Wizard Twins to Sorceress Consort. Mercy, compassion and love to that of arrogance, power and strength. A gentling. A building of the foundations of harmony.

But the Seculars have found also an alliance of power. A dark strength that had built as the strength of Twins and Consort waned. And now shall it strike…

Chapter One

ഇ

There was such magick on Sentmar. The twin moons blazed overhead, the rings of power surrounding them casting a perfect illusion of serenity and peace above the land Marina so cherished. She leaned against the window, her hands pressed against the warm glass, her gaze trained on the rings, wondering if they appeared brighter, stronger than they had in the past. For so many years they had seemed so dim, just as the magick that flowed rich and hot in her veins had felt further out of reach than she knew it should have been.

Was it true that the magick increased from the bondings of Wizards and Sorceresses? That the mating of Wizard Twins to one magick female could truly heal the ills of their land?

If this were true, then her own future would be far more precarious than she had ever imagined it to be. Already the Priestess Select, the elders of feminine magick and truth were gathering together to discuss this matter. Her mother had been called away just this past night to attend yet another meeting called by the austere wise women.

Marina clenched her teeth in anger at the thought of such meetings. That so few would make decisions which would so affect so many of the sorceresses within their land. Already word had gone out that no bondings of Covenan Sorceresses and Sorcerers could be performed, that any promises of such pairing would be withheld until the meetings of the Coven were completed.

Her fists clenched as she pushed herself from the window, stomping across her bedchamber in a fit of pique.

"'Tis not fair," she charged, her fury rising swift and hot inside her as she pushed her fingers restlessly through the red-gold curls that fell about her face. "I will not heed their demands. My future is my own." She snarled the words, but in her soul she feared there was no chance of such an outcome. She was being waylaid at every turn, pushed back, hemmed in by the very fact that she was a sorceress, a daughter of the Ruling House of Sellane, and as such, possessing the promise of great power. Power which could be harnessed, could be used to strengthen the land against those who would destroy the magick forever.

Even now, within her home Wizards gathered, paying court to both her and her sister, Serena. Serena she could well understand. The heir to the throne of Sellane possessed great power. The strength of her magick, even in its immaturity, was often remarked upon. She was considered not just the heiress to the throne, but also the heiress of a power prophesied for centuries.

Marina's lip curled at the thought of the procession, which met her sister within the receiving rooms on a nightly basis. Wizard Twins by the dozens, declaring their suit, eager to test their powers to those of the regal princess, to see if they, through Rite of Reception, or Courtship, could claim her for their own. It was said Wizards and Consorts were chosen by the gods themselves, but Wizards had learned centuries ago, that alignments could be forced, no matter the will of the gods. They weren't as powerful, nor were the matches ones that the Sorceresses found harmony within. But those earlier Wizards had disregarded such warnings, just as they would now, Marina feared.

There had been no such gathering for her, though, and she knew well the reason why. Caise and Kai'el Sashtain. Damn their magick and their arrogance, they followed at her heels like great stalking beasts, growling and snarling at any other male who would dare to come to near her.

They gave her no peace. They gave her no chance to still the fears rising inside her, merely running over her objections, determined in their male superiority to claim her. And she could do nothing to fight them. That irked at her greatly. That there was nothing, no way to counter their suit for her body. And her magick had betrayed her the moment they had stepped forth.

Even now she could feel the crystalline spores of power surging through her blood, heating her body, and this was only at the thought of them. 'Twas worse when they were near, she could feel the heat pooling in her lower stomach, attempting to steal her breath as the harsh spasms tore through her abdomen. 'Twasn't painful, though the uncomfortable sensations were highly irritating. What truly enraged her was that only when those hateful Sashtain Twins were near, did this occur.

On the basis of this reaction, the Queen Mother and the Matriarch's Priestess assigned to the castle had suggested, rather forcibly, that she give the Wizards a chance to prove their suit, to determine if their male and her female magick could meld.

"I will not." She fought to push the heaviness in her limbs aside, to still the heat growing between her thighs, dampening the swollen lips of her pussy, sensitizing the once silent bundle of nerves hidden within her folds.

She paced her room, aware that the nervousness building inside her owed much to the determination of the wicked Twins. She found no ease, even within her dreams, there was no peace. There was only Caise and Kai'el. There was only the hunger that brought twisting shadows and memories of fear and of pain.

She pressed her palms to her stomach, fighting to hold back the fear churning within her. The long folds of her gown rasped against her flesh with each movement, raking her hardened nipples, wringing a gasp from her lips.

"I will not allow this thing to happen," she swore, her breathing ragged, her voice rough as she fought for control.

She could feel them. Bastards that they were, she was certain they were using their magick to draw her to them. No desire this heated, this uncontrollable could possibly be anything but of an evil design. Somehow, the Twins had learned the secret of control, of possessing another's thoughts and minds and forcing their wishes to be heeded. Such magick went against all the mandates of all magick holders. It was forbidden. It was punishable by death. Why, it was said there were wizards trained to search out such perverted users of power and destroy them on sight.

And yet, what other answer could there be? Her body and her magick reached out to the Wizards, despite her own wishes. They were stealing her mind, stealing her will. She would not allow it. She had fought back her fears for years, forcing herself to be the warrior she had always dreamed of being. She fought the Seculars, she defeated them, all male, and she laughed in the face of their cruel smiles and twisted confidence. Her blade tasted their blood and her vengeance found strength in their deaths.

She was no wanton harlot to be so easily manipulated. She was a Princess of the Ruling House of Sellane. Her magick was powerful. It was a part of her, and it would forever belong to her. Not to the likes of them.

She flung open her bedroom door, the fires of anger burning through her mind as she felt the heated surge of magick rising inside her, filling her mind, her soul as she stalked, she did not walk. She did nothing so weak as to move unhurriedly, she stalked through the silent halls, making her way about the castle until she moved into the neighboring wing that the Wizards had taken for their stay. She would tell them now, she would show them, she was no weak-kneed female to bow at their feet and worship the cocks they believed were so all-powerful.

She halted just before their door, enraged, the fiery sensations of her fury churning through her, making her feel flushed, powerful, confident. They were no more, no less than the hated Seculars. They would not control her.

Her fist pounded on the heavy door, striking it in demand as she ignored the harsh sting the motion brought. She cared not for the pain. She had endured worse. She would deliver worse before this week was finished.

The wide double doors were thrown wide by an unseen hand, magick pulsing in the action as her eyes narrowed in contempt at such laziness. She stomped into the room, enraged at the small slight. A real man, a true wizard would use no such displays. He would present himself accordingly, by welcoming his guests face-to-face and presenting them —

Sweet Merciful Matriarchs!

She heard the doors slam closed behind her, felt her breath lodge in her throat and her clitoris scream in excitement.

They were all but naked, wearing naught but snug loincloths as they battled in the center of the room. Naked, darkly tanned flesh gleamed beneath the glow of a hundred candles blazing from the walls as they stared back at her from their locked stance.

Thick muscles bulged in their arms and legs as they battled both physically as well as magickally. Gold and blue whipping strands of power pulsed around them, snapping, crackling small demons intent on destruction. Gold and blue eyes watched her with amused indulgence as hard, bare buttocks clenched as each fought to maintain their positions despite her presence.

"We should greet her," Caise, his golden eyes filled with laughter, taunted his brother as he strained within the grip each man had on the other's forearm.

"Why? She never greets us," Kai'el growled as he moved suddenly, his ankle hooking around his brother's quickly as he moved to flip him to the floor.

Caise countered in a surge of strength, flipping from his hold as his magick moved to block his brother, weaving quickly through the strands Kai'el sent to trip him up to strike against his powerful leg.

Kai'el moved not a moment too soon, jumping back and to the side as he sent his own magick to counter it.

Like lightning flipping across the sky in an age-old battle, one with the other, the powerful arcs of brightly colored power snapped and sizzled before the brothers were at it once again.

Such strength. Marina could only stare in wide-eyed amazement as they battled not just as Wizards, but as warriors. Powerful, magickal warriors, as timeless as the land itself, as strong as the mountain that birthed them. She could feel her own magick rising within her, streaking to her already hardened nipples, engorging her clitoris further, sending the hated, silky heat spilling from between her thighs as her pussy clenched in an instinctive response.

Desire.

Nay, she could feel no desire for such creatures. Surely, even amidst their battle, they were performing their dark magick against her.

"She could have changed her mind regarding our suit," Caise pointed out as he zapped his brother with a particularly strong bolt of golden power.

Kai'el grunted mockingly. "And the Seculars will lay down their weapons on the morrow."

Marina snorted silently. At least he was not a stupid Wizard. It was her greatest fear that his arrogance would be but misplaced ignorance. Which wasn't necessarily a good thing, she told herself with a spurt of concern.

"I don't know, Kai'el." Caise flipped out of the way as his brother's foot nearly connected with his chin. "It seems a bit impolite to ignore her. She is waiting patiently, after all."

Marina could no more than stare in bemusement at the impressive bulge riding between his spread thighs for the brief moment she was given the chance to glimpse it. Aye, she had been smart to refuse their suit, hadn't she? After all, that was no puny male, either in strength or in manly parts.

"Let her wait. We have waited weeks. And I will not...allow you...to distract me. Damned cheat." Kai'el cursed as Caise winked back at her audaciously a second before his brother's magick took supreme advantage of his distraction and snaked furiously around him.

Surprise and chagrin flashed across his face before he chuckled heartily as his own magick confined Kai'el as well.

"I believe we have once again ended this battle in a draw." Kai'el's voice was now amused as he stood still before his brother. "One day, Caise, you will falter in the face of your fascination for the wench and lose entirely."

Marina's lips opened as the insulting words left the Wizard's lips. Her arms crossed over her breasts as she glared back at them, no longer bothering to stem the rising ire filling her or the magick pulsing in her center.

"Princess Sellane." Caise bowed majestically, his arm sweeping before him in a completely mocking display of respect. "To what do we owe the pleasure of your fair visit. Dressed in naught but your nightrail and your beautiful, furious violet eyes." He straightened arrogantly. But at least he deemed her worthy of a greeting. His brother, the irritant that he was, merely laughed in the face of her displeasure as he moved across the room to the pitcher and glasses on the smooth, dark wood of the bar at the other side of the room, and poured himself a drink.

So why had she come to their room? She glared at Kai'el, her gaze slipping once again to his wide, glistening shoulders, the perfection of his muscular chest and tight, contoured abdomen.

"You are unnatural." She stomped her foot, her rage rising faster, hotter, searing her within its power as she felt her magick whipping through her.

It happened each time they were near. The weakness in her stomach, her thighs, the surge of power that left her shaking, unable to find the control which had once come to her as naturally as her own breath. It was insanity.

"Unnatural?" Kai'el lifted a brow in infuriating mockery as his lips curved upwards. Strong, full lips. Lips that touched her in her dreams…

"Think I know not what you are attempting?" she bit out, suddenly terrified of the power they were wielding against her. If she could not control something as simple as her own inherent gifts, then how could she ever escape their clutches? "I know you for what you are," she sneered. "You are using the dark gifts against me, stealing my mind and my soul. I will not allow such an atrocity. It is forbidden. It is beneath contempt, even for a Wizard Twin."

They stared at her now with twin expressions of shock.

"By all that is sacred." Kai'el slammed his goblet to the bar as he frowned at her darkly. "I knew not to open that door. I knew it was insanity." He cast an accusing glare at his brother. "Are you happy now? Now we are demons from the very Pits attempting to steal her soul. Shall we be stealing sweets from babes next?"

"Well, there was Harka's young daughter last season." Caise frowned with all apparent thoughtfulness.

"Merciful Sentinels, the little witch was slapping me with that overlarge stick of goo," Kai'el cursed in amazement. "I should have zapped the little gremlin rather than just taking the sweet."

"I would not put such past you." Marina could only stare back at them incredulously. Did they take nothing seriously?

Kai'el's eyes narrowed. "Use goo against me, my little temptress, and you will wear it as well, as she should have rather than losing her treat. Are all females so irrational?"

Or was she indeed losing her mind?

What was wrong with her? She was no shrew to rail at others, nor was she so stupid as to confront any that she believed could wield the dark gifts. Where had her sanity flown? She was in their rooms, dressed in only her sleeping clothes, her body humming, her magick whipping not just through her body, but through the throbbing depths of her cunt, aching, zapping her with a hunger which made no sense, which terrified her in the deepest parts of her woman's soul. She was not the weak child she had been years before. She was not without her own strengths. Why then did these two weaken her so?

"Marina." Caise's voice was a hard, irritated growl, the frown that creased his brow owed nothing to anger though and much to irritation. "This day has been trying, and as you can see, the night is growing late. Unless you have a reason other than such accusations for being here, then it may be best that you take your leave."

He spoke as though she were of no consequence, as though her anger, her confusion mattered not to him. She stared at him fully, only distantly aware of Kai'el moving to the side of the room, crossing out of her line of sight as she glared at his brother.

"I am no simpering fool to be so dismissed," she snapped. "I would know now what you have done to me. Why you must torment not just my days but my dreams as well. Stay out of them, for my rest is much needed and the sight of you only infuriates me, whether waking or sleeping."

He smiled, a wicked curve of his lips that set her teeth on edge.

"Such innocence," he sighed, his gaze gentling, his arms flexing with a hard ripple of muscle as he faced her with his fists braced on his lean hips. "Come to me, Princess, I will show you the cure for such wicked, evil imaginings as you seek your sleep." He held his hand out to her, his gaze hungry now, filled with deceptive warmth and wicked hunger.

21

She saw much more than that, though. She saw the tightening of the cloth between his thighs, the engorged length of his cock pressing against the tanned animal skin, appearing thick, long, a weapon to be avoided at all costs.

She backed up, desperate to escape him now, cursing her own foolishness in having come to them. The quick step brought her hard against the heated, lean, hard body blocking her exit.

Marina turned quickly, a cry on her lips, fear stealing into her mind as she faced the broad chest, rivulets of perspiration drying on the perfect bronze flesh as her face raised, her gaze caught, pinned by the flinty depths of blue surveying her.

He held his hands out to his side slowly as though willingly releasing her. Yet she was trapped. Held still by fear, she assured herself, though she knew it was indeed much more. It wasn't fear that had her deepest core warming, her womb rippling with a strange hunger she knew only when these two were near.

"I do not hold you here, Princess, just as I did not call you here. But know this." He lowered his head until his lips were poised just above her, his eyes holding her captive as she fought to breathe, to draw in air not tinted with a hint of sandalwood and spice and dark, hot male essence. "Do you come to this room again, unescorted, dressed only in material so thin I can see the sweet perfection of your hard little nipples and the soft red-gold curls of your woman's mound beneath it, then you will indeed find reason to chastise us. Now, do you not wish to learn that lesson this night, then I would suggest you *leave*." The last word was a husky, rough growl that caused her to flinch, to back away, only to be halted by what she knew was Caise's chest at her back. No arms surrounded her, yet she was immobile as Kai'el's hands reached out, the backs of his fingers rubbing against nipples that were indeed hard. Engorged and sensitive.

"Like sweet little berries," he whispered, his pale blue eyes lifting to hers as he caught one between thumb and forefinger, rubbing it sensually, heatedly, as her eyes widened further, sensation surging through her.

A whimper, sounding more of need than of the fear she knew it must be, left her lips as she felt hard hands cup her hips, steadying her, holding her close for but a brief moment before moving away once again.

"Run, little bird," Caise whispered seductively, the sound of his voice drying her lips, sending flares of response shooting throughout her body as she trembled before them. "Run hard and run fast before the smell of your sweet cunt tempts me further than the caution my brother preaches at me daily. He may be willing to wait, but I grow hungry..."

"Enough." She pushed away, sidestepping the hard, hot bodies as she faced them once again, her lips trembling, confusion mounting within her mind, her body. "I will not be manipulated by you. Nor will I allow you to so deceive me. Leave my dreams be. Leave my mind be. In the name of all that is merciful, leave me be."

She would not shed tears, she swore. She would beg no further. She would not go to her knees before these two, she would not give in to their demands. She rushed from them instead, betraying the vow to herself that she would never run in the face of their arrogance or the threat of their touch. But run she did. As though the demons of the Pits were at her heels, snapping with greedy ferocity at her tender flesh. Just as the Twins snapped at her soul.

As the door slammed closed behind her and the walls of the castle flew by her, in her soul Marina knew, she may never truly escape.

Chapter Two

ഔ

Caise Sashtain lifted his brow in mocking amusement as he glanced at his brother, knowing Kai'el felt the wisps of female power still edging toward them, clinging to the faint threads of their own magick as though in reluctance to part. Ah, but if only the holder of that power felt the same reluctance in storming away in such fear. The clash of passions would surely make for a much warmer night than the one they would undoubtedly spend alone instead. It was not exactly proper to take a lover within the castle of the Sorceress you were currently courting, he reminded himself with a silent sigh.

"At least she did not curse us again." Kai'el flexed his shoulders against the tension still wrapping about them, a small frown creasing his dark face as he paced back to the bar to refill the goblet he drank from.

Caise grunted as his comment. "She is as receptive to our suit as ever," he growled, anger simmering in his gut as he glared at his brother. "We are wasting precious time in this infernal castle on this fool's errand the Sentinels have sent us on. She is no more willing to allow a bonding now than she was upon our arrival. I grow weary of chasing that which hides from its own needs."

He reached back, releasing the leather that held back the long strands of his blond hair as he felt the tension in the room elevating as well. It was the same, each time she was near. As fair of face and body as she was, he would have been surprised if he had felt no arousal, but what did surprise him was the brooding anger that filled him each time she found reason to heap yet more accusations upon their heads. Not that most of it was not correct. Still, though, it rankled.

"Unnatural magick," he snorted at the accusation, feeling the prick of conscience with a frown.

Kai'el still stared at the door, his expression reflective rather than angry. It was clear he saw the challenge in the woman, where Caise could only imagine the consequences of actually taking her as a consort. Unnatural magick would be the least of her accusations then. She would likely run home to her Queen Mother, screaming in horror at their desires rather than sighing in bliss as her sister often did when her Wizard Consorts were near.

"She would be the perfect playmate, should we get past her fears." Kai'el finally shrugged, obviously ignoring Caise's look of horror.

"You must surely be joking?" Caise snarled, amazed that such words could come from his brother's lips. "She has already branded us as deviants and has yet to even know our touch. Gods forbid she should actually learn of our more extreme practices. She would become catatonic from sheer terror alone."

But the thought of it, he must admit, tempted his lusts. With her brilliant violet eyes, sun-kissed red-gold locks, and a body that would tempt even the strongest of warriors, he forgave himself for his lust. But he never forgot the all-important fact that the Princess Marina must be always handled gently.

It was enough to cause a grown warrior to whimper at the thought. She was not just a virgin, but a virgin scarred. One whose body and mind had known nothing but terror at the hands of Twins. Wizard Twins those assailants were not, for no noble son of the Sentinels' line would dare to so mistreat a woman. But they had been magickal Twins nonetheless, and the horror she had known during the misadventure had forever branded her woman's soul.

'Twas a shame, he thought, saddened by the knowledge. Each time he saw her, he could see the bruises, the soul-scars she carried and the dark edge of shadowed pain that followed her aura. She was a woman tormented by the past, and he feared the depth of that torment would never allow her to know true pleasure. At least, not the darker pleasures they could have shown her.

"I believe that perhaps our lovely Marina could be coaxed into experimenting a bit with the darker desires," Kai'el informed him, his voice soft as he lifted his goblet to his lips for a sip of the less than potent wine. "If she were approached properly."

Caise could not believe his brother would dare suggest such a thing, not here, within the sanctuary of Sellane Castle. The magick wards were strong at each remaining princess's door. The heir apparent, Serena, had included her own personal guards at her rooms, but the Princess Marina, whose powers were still yet unfocused, pushed beneath the barricade of her fear, still depended much on her mother's magick. A mother currently residing in the mountains within the temple of the Matriarchs.

"It would be a risk," Caise murmured. "If I remember correctly, there were several objections sent to the Sentinel Conclave in regards to the Veraga invasion of the Princess Brianna's rooms during their courtship."

"The Sentinel Priests did no more than shrug off the arguments the Queen Mother presented," Kai'el pointed out. "As stated, no magick could slip past the wards of protection unless the Princess wished it. They are wards meant only to defend against those who would harm the royal daughters. We wish her no harm." The reckless hunger reflecting in his brother's eyes was worrisome.

Kai'el had been certain Marina was the sorceress they had seen in visions for the past decade. Her features shadowed, her body lissome, they saw little except the exceptional hunger flowing from her as she lay bound before them, arching to their touch.

Caise felt his body tighten, his cock engorging with lust once again. Sweet Mercy, but to see her helpless before them, crying out in need, her body and her hungers pliable beneath their demands.

"'Twill not be easy," he warned his brother then. "The Queen Mother will have set wards against such magick slipping past her guard once again. She is incredibly protective of this daughter."

But the thought of such passions unleashed, unrealized... He could feel his lusts rising like a gathering storm, whipping through his body, accelerating his passions, his power.

"The Queen Mother can only protect against that which she knows," Kai'el pointed out then. "She cannot protect her little lamb against that of which she has no knowledge."

Caise frowned back at his brother as he voiced the suggestion. The implication was clear, but could it work? They had not, as she had accused, used the darker powers to invade her dreams. Had they done so, she would have never found the courage to face them with such fury surely?

It was, without doubt, an unfair proposition.

"There is a risk," he murmured, turning to pace to the wide, long windows which dominated the suite of rooms. "Her scars run deep, Kai, as do her fears."

"There is much more risk in continuing as we are," Kai'el sighed, weariness apparent in his voice, in the vibrations of his hunger. "She fears male force and strength, Caise. She does not fear her own capitulation. Perhaps we should begin there. She did not ask to be attacked, to be held against her will as her magick and her woman's soul screamed out in agony. There is no agony, no pain when the powers are aligned, and you must admit, her magick very much suits our own."

That was more than clear. Even now, long minutes after her hasty exit, they could feel the faintest presence of her lingering power as it melded with those stray threads of their own. It was an unusual occurrence, one that reportedly even the Veraga Twins had not experienced until after the bonding with their consort.

Caise ran his hand over his jaw, seeing his own reflection in the window as he stared into the darkness beyond. His golden eyes were odd, even amid the less than traditional Wizard Twins. The reflection of unique powers were often commented upon, but never delved into. The inherent sense of privacy each Wizard felt in regards to their magick extended to their curiosity involving others.

Likewise, Kai'el's pale blue eyes were indicative of his own powers. Should their secrets be revealed, then they would be viewed only with fear, with trepidation. Gold and pale blue blending among the magickal sects had not been seen in so many centuries, surely even before the separation of Sorceress and Twins, that the powers inherent in them had been forgotten as well, but for a select few. Those select few were even more interested in keeping the Sashtain secrets than the Sashtains were themselves.

"There would be no way to trace the power," Kai'el pointed out. "We could slip in, beneath the Queen Mother's guard, and see what tempts our little Princess. I am not suggesting we molest her. Merely that we give her the chance to…choose pleasure?" Wicked, reckless, Kai'el's dark suggestive smile had Caise grinning in turn. They could only get so lucky that she would feel the need to do such.

"She will, of course, suspect us," Kai'el continued. "Just as she has these many weeks. But covering our tracks should be a simple enough maneuver."

It was glaringly obvious that his brother had been giving this much thought, which surprised Caise very little. Kai'el was forever testing the boundaries of their magick, often more so than Caise did himself.

"You do not have to convince me," he finally growled. "It is obvious that means other than our charm and status as

Wizards and warriors will be needed to win over the Princess Marina. I worry only of her fears. I see the scars that fill her soul, Kai. They…disturb me."

Unlike many Wizards, certain powers they possessed were their own, and not easily accessible by the other twin. It was nothing they had set out to accomplish, merely one of the vagaries of their personalities, distinct, yet sharing certain traits. They were individuals, despite their bonds. Unlike the Veraga Twins, they could not interchange with their powers, using the other's as though they were their own. They were confined to only those powers they possessed. But that magick was deeper, darker, and in many, many cases, stronger than the average Twins. There were only two others stronger than they, and Caise did not envy them the responsibilities of such gifts.

"We are, then, in agreement?" Kai'el asked carefully.

Caise could feel his brother's tension, his hunger to touch the fair Marina however possible.

He drew in a deep, fortifying breath. "I am in agreement," he murmured, weighing the advantages as well as the risks of this venture. The satisfaction to be gained could be great, as long as they did not cross the line and tempt her powers out of her control. Otherwise, they could strip her of the strength her magick possessed.

"We will proceed with caution," Kai'el assured him. "She must come to us to find her true female satisfaction. But there are ways, brother, to tempt that journey without marring the sweet vintage she alone holds. We will merely seduce the unseduceable. Surely this is a quest we can triumph in?"

No doubt. They had done it well before.

Caise nodded sharply. The stakes were much higher than ever before, just as the risks would rise each time they tempted such extreme use of their magick. Delving into the darker sides of passion, or lust, was never without payment due.

"We will prepare her then." Caise would reserve judgment as to the merits of this journey until the first step had been completed. "When shall we begin?"

Chapter Three

🙰

'*Twas a garden paradise. The dream, the colors, even the scents were sharper, clearer, as though she existed within reality rather than a dreamscape of unimagined beauty. Deep within a valley sheltered within the Whispering Mountains, she found the Valley of Dreams. It could only be there that such beauty existed. It was said that only within that special glade did the soul find its deepest desires.*

And within it, she found the Garden of Nirvana.

She inhaled, a slow inhalation, drawing the scents deep within her as she closed her eyes and listened to the soft song of the tweeterlings, the whisper of the caws, the deep baritone call of the sharp-billed macanar. They were all there, the fantastical creatures only told of in legend, their brilliant feathers flowing in the breeze as the sound of their songs filled her ears.

Sweet Mercy, what pleasure there was to be found in the sounds. She had known of no other to have ever found this place, either in their searching journeys within the mountains, or within their unconscious journeys. It was said that only the most deserving was given a glimpse of the Sentmarian paradise. Only those that the gods favored could find their way into the joyous fields of blooms.

And such blooms. Deep, rich flora abounded. Tall, feathery stalks of gold phermona grew in abundance, deep petals of the palest blue pansy carpeted the floor of the field. Small trumpet-shaped carlies grew in multitudes, the sweet sound of their unique inhalation of the lands magick filling the air. Trees sheltered the little glade, growing low, their branches caressing the top of her head, bringing a smile of joy to her lips as her eyes opened, and a startled gasp left her lips.

There, within the center of the grassy, bloom-strewn valley was an obvious bed of blooms, shaded by the phermona, cushioned by the pansy and carlies. Peace. A night of sleep undisturbed by the nightmares that had haunted her for so many years, the shadows of fear absent. These were the gifts the gods had brought to her.

She stepped closer, then stopped in confusion as she stared around the warmth of the valley. Why? Why would the gods open this place to her, allow her within its beauty when she had done nothing to be deserving of its peace. She had not stopped a great war, nor saved one of great power or promise. She was but a woman, frail, and in the past weeks clearly not in possession of all her wits. Her chastisement of the Sashtain Twins within their suite had been proof of that.

Why then would the gods bring her to this place of rest?

She stared around the sunny warmth of the valley, feeling the humid press of the heat against her bare flesh and reveling in the caress of the invisible steam over her skin. It was so rare she could endure even the softest caress, that the natural kiss of moist warmth sent a shiver racing up her back for but a second. The pleasure far outweighed any danger which could lurk here.

It did not answer the question of why she was here, but the temptation of it was more than she could deny herself. Within the Garden of Nirvana, only peace existed, only the greatest wish of the one invited to sleep within its protection was granted. And the sleep, undiluted by fear and shadows, was her greatest wish, her most enduring need.

As she moved for the soft bed of blooms, she recognized with distant surprise her nudity. It made no sense that she would come to this place unclothed. She would have never done so if she had been given a choice. But the rules of the Valley of Dreams were said to be much different. Perhaps this was why she entered it as naked as the day she had been birthed.

As she stepped to the bed of blooms, the delicate, silken spears of grass tickled at the soles of her feet, bringing a smile to her face and carefree warmth to her heart. How long had it been since she had allowed herself such simple pleasures? The smell of fresh blooms, the feel of the warm grass, the whisper of a breeze on her naked flesh. It had been too many years since she had known such things, since her heart had opened enough to even realize she had indeed missed them.

But now, she reveled in it. The soft, sweet scents enveloped her, enclosing her senses in a comforting warmth as alien as it was familiar. Honeysuckle, a perfume so rare, so evocative of innocence and joy, teased her nostrils as she moved to the thick bed of blooms, lying back against the sun-kissed warmth with a muted groan of pleasure.

Tiny, tiny pale blue and gold blooms caressed her back with a rhythmic motion that had her eyes closing in bliss. Ah, such pleasure would only exist in dreams, she thought in regret. If she could but find this when she awakened as well, then she would know true peace whenever the touch came. True pleasure.

The feathery phermona rustled at her side, bending against the delicate breeze wafting over her flesh as heated warmth wrapped around her, inside her. Relaxed her. She could feel each muscle falling victim to the magickal caress of each bloom. Like tiny fingers, calloused at the tips, smoothing over her.

They reminded her of Caise and Kai'el's touch. She frowned at that thought. They were forever stroking their fingertips along her arm, her shoulder, touching her hair if she wasn't quick enough to jerk away. But she didn't have to move from this touch. This touch knew no design, only pleasure. What harm could there be in enjoying the tender motions of the blooms?

She stretched against each touch, raising her arms until they curled above her head, her breasts lifting to the breeze, her neck arching as the soothing warmth washed over her tender nipples, ruffled the soft curls between her thighs.

Insidious heat filled her, a slow, sensual wash of pleasure that she refused to allow to intrude upon her relaxation. She would rest here, nap for as long as the gods would allow her. She wondered if they would allow her to stay.

A whispering brush of silk over her nipples had her eyes flying open. A surprised laugh trickled from her throat at the sight of the phermona, its featherlike branches brushing over her breasts, bent in half by the breeze cooling her. She allowed her lips to curve in pleasure as a trembling moan left them.

How completely sensual. There was no need to fear, no pain to expect. There was only the tenderness, the warmth surrounding her, *the sensual beckoning pleasure beginning to overtake her. Like firelight on a clear night, heating her first on the outside, then sinking into her bones. Effervescent, a hint of sizzle as it beckoned, the welcoming touch of the phermona tickled her nipples, hardening them further as others brushed over her body.*

Beneath her, the blooms massaged, reaching muscles she had not known were tense, tired from her vigilance, even in sleep. Marina drifted, only half aware as the blooms and the feathery strokes of the soft branches shifted beneath her, raising her arms further, spreading her thighs, moving further along her body as the stalks of the phermona wrapped about her wrists and ankles, massaging those muscles a bit deeper while fingers and toes relaxed as they bid.

How incredible, sprawled beneath the sun's warmth, hedonistic delight sizzling in her veins as the blooms began to manipulate the insides of her thighs, brushing against the dewy curls on her aching mound.

Aye, her mound ached. She could feel the slow clenching within her pussy, the heat springing to her clit as her senses awakened to the sensual pleasure beginning to fill her. What heat, what extreme sensation. She moaned again as the blooms moved further, working against the lips of her cunt as they stroked the sides of her breasts. Like soft kisses, the trumpet-shaped blooms suckled at her flesh as the pansies kissed with a ghostly caress until she was undulating beneath their touch, the heat moving inside her now, tempting her to erotic thoughts.

What danger was there here? No Wizard Twin could follow her into the Valley of Dreams. Only the Sentinels could bring her here, and only they could watch over her. Here she could safely fantasize of the Sashtain Twins. Why she chose those arrogant males over the warlocks she could have chosen, she was uncertain. But now was not the time to think, now was the time to feel. And ahh, such sensation in the feeling.

The feathery phermona brushed over her pussy, parting her swollen lips as the silken brush of its lighter than air stalks began to probe and stroke the moist folds within. Marina licked her dry lips as they parted, a whimpering keen of need surprising her as she felt yet another bloom, she knew not what, cup over the swollen knot of her clitoris, even as others attached to her nipples.

The stems holding ankles and wrists stretched her further, opening her thighs wider as the lips of her pussy parted more so. Mercy, the thought was but a hazy plea as she felt the air-light stalks caressing her as the blooms suckled at her. Her nipples, her clit, slow drawing movements that had her arching, gasping, then writhing as the velvety stalk slid further below, probing at the tender opening of her anus.

Mother Sentinel! It was entering her. Slow, precise movements parted the hidden entrance as another branch moved to the rapidly slickening portal of her vagina. There it probed, teased, never entering, never bringing an end to the torturous pleasure suddenly filling her, whipping through her like strokes of lightning crashing over her nerves. Heat enveloped her, stretching her on a rack of pleasure so intense she could not but help to fill the glade with her strident cries for ease. There must surely be an end to the tension tightening her body.

Or was there?

A soft, heated strike of a branch at her rear had her bucking, rearing up as an electric thrill of forbidden sensation shot through her mind. The next wrapped about her thigh, a heated lance of pleasure striking into her pussy at the hot slap. Then she was being moved once again, turned to her stomach as the blooms cushioned her, pouting against her flesh until it seemed a thousand mouths suckled her at once as the stems began a heated series of sharp little taps over her buttocks and thighs, as the one probing at her anal entrance began to slip inside her, opening her as she tightened on it, swelling marginally within her as she gasped in pleasure-pain.

Intense. Blinding. Perspiration began to coat her body as she gasped against the careful slaps of the feathery stems, the stroking caress of its wafting limbs, the overwhelming sensations, the heated fury of arousal unlike anything she could have imagined. Was it possible to even imagine pleasure such as this? Pleasure that sent a wicked heat burning through her senses, filled her mind with images so dark, so erotic it left her writhing against the suckling pressure of the blooms at her nipples and her clit. The lancing eroticism of the feathery phermona stretching her anus with delicate strokes was yet another caress. One she did not wish to delve into, for the very darkness of the act pricked at her conscience and incited fear, she wanted neither of those to intrude upon the incredible pleasure controlling her.

She was bound to the bed of blooms, legs and arms spread wide, the sun bearing down on her with merciless heat, just as the flora of the valley ate at her with greedy delight and probed her anal recess with curious thrusts.

It was too much. She was crying out hoarsely, the tension tightening in her womb, building, so close… Whatever awaited her at the end of this journey was so close… And then it was gone.

Her eyes flew open, her gaze meeting the candlelit warmth of her own room and the knowledge that she was naked, as she had been in her dream. Her arms and legs were spread wide, her body heaving against the quilts, her dew slick and hot upon her thighs. And she ached.

A whimpering cry left her lips once again as she rolled to her stomach, pulling the quilt with her, wrapping it around her sensitized body as she choked back a desperate, despairing moan. Sweet Mercy, what was wrong with her? She could feel magick burning in her blood, pounding at points where she should feel no such desire, no such hunger.

But she ached. Sweet, white-hot hunger of a sort she could not explain clenched in her pussy, pinched her nipples into tight hard points and had left her anus, that forbidden nether-hole, aching to be filled.

It was sexual hunger. She knew it for what it was, for what her sister Brianna had described with such a self-satisfied, intent look in her violet eyes. Bri had not lied, as Marina has suspected, that such impossible to imagine desperation could fill a body until it was writhing for release. But how did one attain such release? She could not imagine how to go about it, how to end the ache searing her senses.

Bri would know, surely. But she was no longer on Covenani land. She had returned to the Veraga castle, taking her place as Queen Consort between her ruling Twins. And Marina dared not attempt to reach out to her. Even though her sister's magick was now by far stronger than any sorceress known, her Wizards were still yet more powerful. They would know the needs striking at her helpless body and inform those infernal Sashtain Twins of her weakness.

God help her if they ever realized it had been their image that came to mind within the Valley of Dreams. That it had been their fingers, their touch, their suckling mouths possessing her. Should they ever learn the truth, she would never escape them.

* * * * *

Kai'el's eyes flew open as he jerked himself from the dreamscape he and Caise had built for Marina. His flesh was covered in sweat, a chill racing over his body as a hard, near-violent shudder racked his frame. His fingers were clenched around the width of his cock, holding back the silky semen demanding release. Vibrant pale blue and violet swirls of power licked over him, drawing his mesmerized gaze as the misty threads of feminine power curled along his chest and scrotum like a lazy lover.

Marina's power. And still it had not yet dissipated. It was faint, hazy, but the visions she had built in her mind of her lovers' caresses had sent her power winging out to them.

Blessed Sentinels, but the touch of her magick was like liquid fire. Like the lava that trickled from Fire Mountain. Should she actually find the courage to lay her hands to him… A grimace twisted his face as he moved carefully from the bed, the hard ache in his balls sending waves of uncomfortable sensation shooting up his spine. Mercy. Had he ever known such sexual agony? Surely he had not.

Muting a hungry growl, he unwrapped his fingers from his erection and jerked his robe from the bottom of the bed. His teeth clenched as the ultrasoft material caressed his flesh. Still the whispers of Marina's power clung to him, torturing the marble-hard erection rising from between his thighs. Why in the Blessed Sentinel's name did she not retrieve her magick upon waking? Why continue to torture him with it? Was his power still caressing her? Hell no. He pulled back. He played fair.

The fact that inducing the dream to begin with had been less than fair was only a distant thought as the wispy magick clenched over his tight sac and gave a single hungry lick to the base of his cock.

He jerked at the touch, feeling the moisture of his semen leaking from the wide crest as he groaned in torture.

"Merciful Sentinel take her," he heard Caise curse from his adjoining room, his voice rough, as tortured as Kai'el felt.

He smiled tightly at the thought. What miserable company they would make for each other this night. It was obvious there would be no sleep, not as long as her unconscious caresses continued to torment them. And there was no stopping it. To block against her power would be the most effective means of betraying the forbidden journey they had given her.

The Valley of Dreams was a gift only given by the Sentinel Select. The power to give such gifts had been taken from Wizard Twins eons before. Until he and Caise had found the way during their magickal journeys and their flirtatious expeditions along the darker perimeters of magic.

Sighing in resigned misery, Kai'el moved from his room back to the sitting area of the suite the Queen had assigned them. There, his brother, robed as well, poured himself a healthy measure of the less than strong wine the Sorceresses produced on their lands. He knew he should have slipped in the bottles of Wizard Elixir he had threatened to bring along.

"The next time you come up with such a foul scheme, leave me ignorant of it," Caise cast him a furious glare. "Still her magick enfolds me like a hot little mouth, sucking my sanity through my dick."

Caise's robe was tented, just as Kai'el's was. The engorged fullness of their cocks beating at their brains in the plea for release. A release they could not attain, unless they allowed Marina hers. Sentinel knew he had not expected quite this reaction from her.

"Come dawn's light, I send my warriors back to Cauldaran," Kai'el sighed. "I will not survive this venture on this weak water the benevolent Queen Mother dares to call wine. I will have something far stronger to dull the ache in my loins."

"Insanity," Caise muttered again, swallowing down the drink before pouring another. "We were insane to attempt this. She took to the touch like the owls to the air. Blessed Sentinel, we nearly did not pull free from her in time."

Had they allowed her peak to reach its zenith, the flesh would have been flayed from their backs, and rightly so. Should she find release without their presence, without their possession, then the strength of her magick would be forever diluted.

Kai'el shot back the wine in his goblet, before following his brother's example and pouring yet more. The taste of her still tempted his senses. The sweet honey of her woman's cream lingered on his lips, in his nostrils. The silky slide of it upon his tongue had been a paradise all its own.

The Valley of Dreams was forbidden for a reason, he now knew. They had never attempted to bring another into its treasured dimension for fear of discovery. And never, not once had they known such heat and the promise of paradise within that particular garden. Nirvana. It was called such for a reason.

As the blooms had taken the nectar of her passion, it had touched his and Caise's lips, tempted their tongues. The slap of the reeds on her pearl-kissed buttocks had been their palms, the silky feel of her flesh a sharp reminder of their need for so much more. And inside the fisted, tight depth of her anus, stretching her with the lightest touch, his fingers had itched to fuck her in truth.

She had taken their caresses easily, naturally. No taint of fear or pain had marred her dreamscape, or her vision...of them. That had been by far the most satisfaction he had known in his life, despite the tortured length of his cock. To have her hips rise as the reed parted her buttocks, the tiny opening easing apart at the penetration, had taken his breath.

"Would you stop in the name of Mercy," Caise snarled, fury building in his tone as Kai'el stared at him surprise.

"Mother Sentinel, in all the years since we have been birthed, never have I felt your thoughts or your own sensations until this idiotic scheme of yours unfolded. I tell you, brother, it is most vexing." Caise glared at him with dark gold eyes, his magick glittering like small candle-points within the color.

Kai'el grunted. Aye, it was most vexing, and a problem he was sharing. They had never known the bonds most Wizard Twins knew. From the moment of conception, they had been isolated in that regard, knowing a freedom of movement, of thought, that the other could not intrude upon. Until now.

Until this journey with the willful, stubborn Marina.

He clenched his teeth as the faint caress of silken fingers at the base of his cock had him tightening in longing. She still thought of them. Still, even outside the Valley of Dreams, she imagined their touch. Imagined touching them.

"That woman shall be the death of us." Caise threw himself into a large, well-cushioned chair with a glower, his dark blond hair falling over his face in disarray.

Or their lives. Should their vision come to fruition, then she would be their souls. He suspected it was such already. He could think of no other woman, had been unable to touch any other since the moment he first caught sight of her. With her long, sun-kissed reddish curls, similar but still unique to her sister's darker red locks. Her deep, deep violet eyes, nearly black, rather than the lighter shade of the Consort Veraga.

There was no doubting Marina shared much blood with Brianna Veraga, but so much was different.

Her laughter was shy, her skin like the softest cream kissed by the rising sun. Her soft little body was compact, lightly muscular, for her social life owed little to parties and frippery. Ho no, this little Princess thought herself a warrior true, battling Seculars and slipping from the castle at each opportunity to spy for the Queen's guard and her secretive heir-apparent sister, Serena Sellane.

"Brother, I beseech of you, still your thoughts," Caise groaned, his dark voice vibrating with latent threat. "Perhaps if you think of other things—slugs in slime, the putrid waste of the dacar—then our wayward dicks will surely soften."

Kai'el grunted. "Order her. 'Tis her thoughts holding her magic about our flesh, not mine. I refuse to be held accountable for that vixen's hand in this."

"Had you not been so determined to tempt her, I would not be in such misery," Caise growled between clenched teeth, his sun-darkened expression brooding, though absent the anger in his voice.

Kai'el shrugged his shoulders in negligent disregard. "The choice was made, 'tis far too late to cry foul. And were I given the choice, I would not change the event in any way. Consider this, Caise. Even now, her magick torments us. It would not do so were her thoughts not with us. It would be my suspicion that our tempestuous little Princess is even now lying with thighs clenched, reliving her heated imaginings. That would not be the actions of a frigid maid. But rather those of one whose passions run hot and deep, and whose hunger will soon rise past her own control."

Caise opened one eye, watching him warily now.

"You are plotting." He snarled the accusation before groaning with resigned displeasure. "Kai'el, Sentinel's truth, should you be the cause of this torturous agony ever again, I will kill you myself. Cease. For in truth, I would as soon face a dark sorcerer as to face that woman's wrath should she learn what you have done."

Kai'el laughed at his brother's misery. Caise searched tirelessly for dark wizards and sorcerers, so the lie falling from his lips was such a blatant untruth as to be worthy of Sentinel despair.

"It should ease soon," he finally sighed, sinking into a matching chair and laying his head back along the cushions as he frowned up at the ceiling. "Perhaps next time..."

"Next time?" The shadowed promise of violence in Caise's voice had Kai'el clearing his throat in an attempt to cover his laughter.

"Be at ease, brother." He shrugged dismissively, his lips quirking in amusement. "I will perfect the plan, you shall see. Trust me..."

Chapter Four

ಐ

Marina rushed through the tunnels deep beneath the castle, her brow creased into a frown as she buckled her short sword about her waist and checked the strap to her thigh that held her dagger in place.

She was late, she knew. The meeting her sister had set for long minutes ago would have commenced by now. Which meant Serena would be most displeased. There was too much ground to cover, too many farms to protect for Marina to be lazing about the bed until after dawn.

Not that it had truly been lazing, she assured herself as she rounded the corner that led to the inner meeting hall. The delay had been beyond her ability to control. Damned Wizard Twins crowding the halls and the serving tables for their breakfasts before heading out with their warriors had found any number of reasons to waylay her.

"About time you arrived." Serena looked up from the rough sketches laid out on the rough wooden table, her deep, velvet-blue eyes watching her in concern.

"What in the Mother Sentinel's name is going on upstairs? Have we suddenly acquired every bedeviled Wizard Cauldaran possesses?" Marina threw up her hands in despair. "On my word, Serena, I know of at least a dozen pairings who stopped me for one reason or another. Do you have any idea how long the serving hall is? Mother truly needs to do something about this."

"Our Queen Mother has been delayed at the Temples of the Select." Serena frowned as she moved closer to the table.

Marina fidgeted under her sister's close regard, barely keeping the flush of embarrassment from mounting beneath her cheeks. Her sister was amazingly intuitive and she prayed the other woman could not glimpse the sleepless night she had just spent, and the reasons for it.

"Is the delay serious?" Rarely was the Queen required to attend meetings which lasted for more than a few risings. The Sentinel Priests and Priestess were well aware of the troubles brewing within Covenan.

"I do not know," Serena finally sighed, the sound filled with concern. "The message reached me last night that it would perhaps be a few more risings before she returned. They are currently in meetings with other Priestesses to divine the reasons for the Secular uprising. An ambassador from the human capitol arrived just this past evening, and is lending his aid. It appears the dacars are bedeviling even their own."

Marina's lips twitched. The dacar was a long, slimy serpent whose putrid waste acted as a layer of slime beneath the creature, giving it a protective base to slither about on. They were the most vile of creatures, incredibly poisonous and avoided at all costs. Thankfully, their numbers were quite small, for the female of the species often killed her mate before copulation and fertilization was completed. Tragic, the end those males received, she thought mockingly, thinking of two Wizard Twins she would not mind to see suffering such fates.

Gathered around the room were a dozen other sorceresses, their expressions harried as they sipped at dark, heated javal, an energized, sweetened brew made from the beans of the java plant. It was apparent even they had not escaped the Wizards above.

"Are there no tunnels accessible from another route?" Marina asked her sister with a frown. "Moving through the serving hall is not going to work, Serena. Those Wizard and warrior twins are enough to drive even the Mother Sentinel insane."

"I may have to see about having one of the upper tunnels unblocked." Serena propped her hands on her slender hips as she considered the option. "Damned Twins. They are making my work less than comfortable."

That was clearly evident. Her sister was dressed as the reigning heir apparent rather than the warrioress she truly was. Her long, dark auburn curls had been pulled to the top of her head, secured by pearl and emerald combs before cascading in a rain of silk down her back. The matching tiara with its three emerald points was securely in place and gleaming in hues of gold, the palest cream and dark greens. Her gown was a traditional receiving gown. Pale cream to match the pearls and emphasizing the pale and peach tones of her translucent flesh. It was caught at one shoulder with a brooch emblazoned with the crest of the Sellane Sorceresses, draped over her full breasts, smoothed to her thighs then fell to her feet in soft, cloudy folds. Misty colors of soft green threaded through the fabric, teasing the observer with the swirl of color.

Before the arrival of the Wizard and warrior twins, she would have dressed in leather breeches, a plain tunic and carried her sword at her thigh. Her hair would have been tied back in a braid and her eyes would have glowed with excitement. Not for the first time, Marina thanked the Sentinels that she had not been the firstborn.

As her sister began to direct the Sorceress teams for their scouting areas, Marina moved to the warming pot of javal and poured herself a cup of the rich brew. As she sipped at it, her eyes closed as she awaited the end to the drowsiness that still plagued her. Finding sleep the night before had been near to impossible. The ache between her thighs had been tormenting, but her thoughts even more so. She should have been horrified by the complete sexuality of her dream, but had instead found comfort in it.

Not that there was comfort to be found in the fact that it had been the Sashtain twins whose images filled her mind, even after waking. That was irking her to no small degree. But at least for once her dreams had been of pleasure, rather than pain and fear and the memory of darkness overtaking her.

As the Sorceress teams cleared slowly from the room, heading to the tunnels that led to the sheltering hills beyond the castle, Marina turned to her sister once again.

"What would you have me to do this day?" She tilted her head, watching as Serena glared down at the sketches of Covenani land.

"Here." A delicate finger pointed to an area of farmlands just past the forests. "Take a unicorn and scout the area. Be certain to stay within the forests. Mother's protection only extends so far while she is at the Temples. But this area bothers me. I fear the Seculars will attempt to find a way into the forests. Without the landholders there to strengthen the area, they could gain ground we cannot afford to lose. Sentinels save us if they truly find a way through our forests."

Marina nodded as she sat the cup back to the sideboard, still watching her sister's worried frown.

"Is there something more, Serena?" She seemed more concerned than it seemed there was need.

Finally, her sister's head lifted, her lavender eyes dark, shadowed with intense worry.

"I received word today that The Veressi will arrive within a week's time. I am to prepare to receive their petition of courtship."

A chill raced through Marina at this news. Should the forces of magick align during reception, then her sister's fate was sealed. With a set of Twins whose very name sent horror quaking even throughout their own realms.

"This cannot be, Serena." She gasped. "We must contact Mother..."

A bitter laugh left Serena's lips. "The message was sent by our Queen Mother, just this night past," she spat furiously. "She swore to me, before her departure, she would not spring such a thing on me. And The Veressi..." She swallowed, a tight movement that gave proof to the upsetting emotions racing through her. "The Veressi followed up the message this morning with their courier. They are preparing to leave their lands even as we speak."

Serena turned from her, moving gracefully across the rough stone floor as she paced the confines of the meeting room.

"I am the heir apparent. I have known no other life," she whispered, her voice soft, regretful. "It is my duty, some would say, to follow the dictates of my Queen Mother." She lifted her shoulders in a gesture of bitter acceptance as her gaze filled with regret. "'Twill no doubt be my luck that the magicks will align, giving me no choice then in the Joining or in my destiny. 'Tis my duty," she whispered once again.

The Sashtains had not yet demanded a petition to court, and for that Marina thanked the Mother Sentinel daily, but grief welled within her now for her sister.

"Can you be certain our Queen Mother sent the command? She has groomed you to rule in her stead, Serena. I cannot believe this would be her wish." In times of court, or commands issued for state obedience, Amoria Sellane ceased to be their mother. She became instead, their Queen Mother. It was a rather childish way to still view their parent, but one they had not grown out of, it seemed.

"Until she answers my summons, I can be certain of nothing." Serena shook her head at the uncertainties now plaguing them. "I have received an answer neither to my psychic calls, nor to those I have penned. Until such time as one or the other comes, I can only wait. And if The Veressi arrive before she returns, then I can do nothing but receive them as commanded. The official Sellane seal accompanied the command, as did the adjoining request from the Sentinel Priestesses. I can not disobey it until I speak with her."

"It could be a trick of The Veressi," Marina pointed out. "They are feared even by their Kings, the Veraga."

Serena laughed bitterly. "According to our beloved sister Brianna, this is an untruth. The Veressi have impressed her as being Wizards of honor and truth, and reminds me of the rumors she believed of Wizard Twins in general when I attempt to warn her of the deceit. I do not know, Marina, what is coming of our world. But this smacks to me of a grand deception on The Veressi's part."

They were not referred to as The Veressi Wizards for a reason. For years they had heard rumors of The Veressi—Wizard Twins who were mirror images of the other. Even their eye color was the same, whereas other Twins were different. A deep, bottomless black. As dark as the Shadowhell. And rumor abounded of the reason why Wizard Twins, born a pure blond, with eyes of green and blue, had slowly darkened as they matured, and became a reflection one to the other, with hair as black at the pits and eyes just as dark.

"I say we send a courier to Mother." Marina's eyes narrowed thoughtfully. "It must be one we trust. One we know will not betray us."

Serena breathed out roughly before she nodded. "I will do this when the sun sinks this evening. I have one I can trust. And we will pray she answers in time."

Marina nodded in a sharp, decisive motion. "I will head out to the farms then. I should return before evening and I will accompany you to dinner." Her mouth twisted at the promise. "Bedamned Wizard Twins."

Serena's look of surprise was ignored as Marina stomped to the tunnel, heading for the exit. She wanted to make no explanations for the promise. She did not understand herself why she felt she could now tolerate the presence of so many forceful males when just this evening past she had forcefully railed that it would never happen. It made no sense to her, and she was certain it would make even less sense to her sister.

As she entered the hidden stables, she chose one of the unicorns lazing in the soft hay and munching on oats from within the sheltered caverns. The creatures were fearless, magickal, and reveled in the spoiling attention they received as the mounts of the secretive Sorceress Brigade.

The soft halter she slipped over his long head was taken easily, as was the tooled leather saddle strapped to his back. He pranced before her, flipping his long white mane as though in pride, his dark blue eyes glittering in excitement as she mounted his back and headed through the exit to the forest.

This was what she loved. Protecting her land, overseeing it as she had been born to do. As they had grown, they had believed certain duties would be theirs. Serena would rule, as was her right by birth. Marina would oversee the land, and Brianna would be the caretaker of the people.

So much had changed in such a very short time.

Brianna now ruled in the land of Cauldaran beside her Wizard Twins, and Marina feared that soon The Veressi would reside within the Sellane Castle. Serena would no longer rule as she had believed she would did this happen. The Veressi would never allow such a thing. And the land? As the unicorn raced through the forest, Marina grieved for the land, wondering who then would oversee it. The house of Sellane was slowly falling apart, all that she had known, had believed to be true was being overshadowed now.

The loneliness that engulfed her at the thought had pain clenching her heart, tears dampening her eyes. Soon, the house of Sellane would be no more. As Keepers of the powers of Sentmar, The Veressi were more than just Keepers of the Cauldaran powers. They were the Keepers of all that was magick upon the planet. Should they decide it, her bond with the land could be broken by the simple means of moving within it themselves.

She would fight it, she knew. She would never rest should such dark beings decide to rule as well as hold the secrets of the magick. Unless... There were rules of magick with Covenan that denied a Keeper the throne. Could such be true of The Veressi as well?

There were no answers for now. Asking the Wizards who courted her so earnestly wasn't to be done at this moment, and there was the chance they would not know. No one outside the ruling house of Sellane knew the secrets of Keepers and Rulers, they were closely guarded. Even the Verega Twins, Brianna's Consorts, did know the identity of the Keeper of Covenan.

She turned her attention to the land they raced over. Fertile, well beloved ground that she would gladly give her life for.

Here, the farmers held their land in stewardship, growing vast amounts of crops to provide to the castle and sell in the small towns of Covenan. As she drew closer to one of the smaller farms, she felt a chill of foreboding chase down her spine. Fast on the heels of that icy sensation was the horrified female screams that sent terror racing through her.

Marina knew those screams. She had voiced them herself. Urging the unicorn to a faster speed, she knew she would be too late. Knew there would be no way to save the innocence being taken, or the lives being changed forever.

Chapter Five

ဢ

There seemed no place to hide, neither from herself, nor from the Sashtain Twins. There was no peace from the desires which had begun invading her body, no ease for the conflicting emotions that wrapped around her mind. In her more lucid moments, Marina admitted that she well understood that once Wizards and Sorceresses had lived in harmony. That she understood that they had been created, one for the other.

She had read the old records, the ones written by her foremothers of their journey from Cauldaran and the reasons they had separated themselves from their natural counterparts. Their males had forgotten the rules of their magick. In their quest for power and yet more magick, they joined on the basis of alliances rather than the basis of emotion and alignment. The alignment of the magickal forces was most important. With that, all love was possible.

Brianna had assured her this was true, and Marina didn't doubt her sister in that regard. But she doubted the Wizard Twins had given up their grand plans of power. The announcement of The Veressi's intended arrival proved this. Only The Veressi could hope to be strong enough to control Serena once she reached her zenith and the forces of magick bloomed within her. Even now she was strong, not as strong as Brianna when aligned with her Twins. But still yet, stronger than any other Sorceress reaching back centuries.

What role did the Sashtain Twins play in this fair game? she asked herself mockingly as she stood within the shadowed corner of the great ballroom, watching the couples now mixed with units, whirling about the floor. Units consisted of Wizard

Twins and the female they were silently courting, testing the magick and its alignment before declaring suit.

Few Sorceresses deigned to enter into the dance with the Twins, which had caused Marina to smirk more than once. Wizard and warrior alike were being turned away by the stiff expressions of the Sorceresses forced by royal summons to attend the nightly balls.

What was her Queen Mother thinking to order such a thing from afar? It was so unlike Queen Amoria that Marina was tempted to travel to the Sentinel temple herself to question her. The only problems with such a venture were the dangerous paths into the mountains and the risk of being caught. Especially by the Wizard warriors now patrolling the lands.

How had this farce occurred? She could not countenance it. In the space of months, Covenan had been overrun by a few dozen Wizard Twin sets and their damnable warriors.

"Ahh, I see once again that the fair Sorceresses are proclaiming their injustices far and wide."

Marina turned with a gasp, staring in astonishment at the great dragon who had materialized within the arched exit beside her, which led to one of the many balconies. The dragon's voice, rather than bitingly sarcastic as she knew it could be, seemed shadowed with curt anger.

"Perhaps we do not enjoy being forced, Garron," she said, keeping her voice soft, allowing her regret to color her words. "We are not playthings for the Wizards. We are not children to be ordered to play nicely."

"No, you are but compassionate, strong women who have so lost the understanding of your foremothers of the Wizards' ways, that you hide in shadows, or stare past their forms in fury, rather than seeing they are men as well, perhaps?" It was voiced as a suggestion, a question, but Marina sensed much more.

She sighed deeply, moving closer to the dragon, feeling comforted as he allowed her to nudge against him, tucking her head against the smaller forelegs he had crossed about his huge chest.

Garron was strength, safety. Over eight feet tall, with massive legs and arms, and a powerful build. His sharp face seemed to evermore reflect his mockery, or biting humor. Were he a man, she had no doubt the women of Covenani would have risen against him ages before and relieved him of his head. But he was just male. A dragon of fierce strength and undivided loyalty where the Sellane was concerned. He may mock their femininity or female ways at times, but she also knew he would give of his last bit of strength to protect them.

"Eh. You cuddle against me like a babe," he growled, though he made no move to push her away.

"'Tis your fault, Dragon." She laughed low. "You have spoiled us for many a year now. Then rail at us for accepting your meager kindnesses now that we are grown."

She remembered the moonless night when his howls had cut through the darkness, the flames of his fury descending to wreak vengeance on her assailants. Blood had flown around her as screams had turned to silence and death had scented the air. And Garron had been there, lifting her from the dirt, his great voice grieving, rough with his shame as he had begged forgiveness for allowing her to be harmed.

She had never blamed the dragon. It was not his place to guard her every move. She had blamed herself and her own ignorance of men and of twins.

"My meager kindnesses?" She could hear the amusement in his voice above her. "Did I forget once again to bow at your delicate feet, my Princess?"

His mocking voice was sharper perhaps than normal. It seemed the influx of Wizard Twins was straining not just her own patience.

"Your Queen Mother will unfortunately be absent a few more days yet," he said then. "She has asked that I return here, to ensure you do not cut these young pups down too severely."

"You were with Mother?" She stared up at him in surprise.

A leathery brow lifted. "Your mother is my first priority, child. Her protection outside her own lands is never assured until she reaches the Temple grounds. Where else would I be?"

Of course. Where else.

"Is it true she bade Serena to prepare for The Veressi's declaration of courtship?" she asked then. "I cannot fathom the reason for such an order."

He stiffened against her.

"She told me no such thing," he growled then. "Who delivered such a message?"

"Her personal courier." Once again, Marina wondered who to trust, even within her own home.

"Sentinel's blood." The curse had her jumping in surprise as anger filled his voice. "I cannot say the message was not given, but I can say she told me nothing of it." He set her from him carefully, looking out to the candlelit ballroom as though seeking some answer there. "Where are those Sashtains when I have need of them?"

"Those dacars?" she snarled. "Who knows where they hide. Do not seek them out, for Mother Sentinel's sake. They are vexing enough without calling attention to the fact I am here."

"Oh, settle down, Princess," he growled. "They have duties other than sniffing after your royal rear."

Marina's eyes narrowed in anger, her lips parting to reply with heated emphasis when a hand suddenly shaped one side of the rear in question.

"But what a tempting rear it is," Caise Sashtain whispered at her ear as he deftly slipped past the elbow she would have slammed into his tight stomach.

Shadowhell. He should never look so tempting. Tall and broad, dressed in dark leather breeches and a shimmering white short tunic tucked into the waistband. A ceremonial sword was strapped to his thigh and what a powerful-looking thigh it was.

His dark gold eyes sparkled with amusement while his teeth flashed in the darkness with a rakish smile.

"What did you wish, Dragon?" he asked of the creature as his brother moved to his side. Both of them together were too impressive by far.

"I will leave and allow you to talk…" Marina turned to do just that, or she would have if Garron had moved his arm a fraction. "Dragon…"

"You will stay put." The order was neither cutting nor mocking. It was very un-Garron-like in its commanding tone.

Marina stiffened in surprise, her eyes narrowing as the Sashtain twins watched Garron silently.

"You will watch over this one," the dragon grunted as she slapped at his arm.

"Are you insane, Dragon?" she snapped in fury. Who was to say she needed protecting? She protected herself fine.

"Some days, after dealing with sorceresses, I do wonder," he replied drolly before popping out of sight in the blink of an eye, leaving her to deal with Wizards. Which she decided was definitely worse.

The feel of a fingertip, lightly calloused, reminding her too much of a dream of flower petals, had her gasping and turning to face them in irritation.

"Did your parental unit not teach you to keep your hands off what did not belong to you?" she questioned them archly, directing a tight, cold smile toward their shadowed expressions. "I would advise you, did they not, to learn. Or lose a finger?" she continued with the mocking suggestion before stalking to the staircase, and she prayed, the safety of her room.

"Well, that worked beautifully," Caise murmured as they followed behind the tight, bouncing little rear of the Sorceress ahead of them. The smooth line of her emerald gown flowed down her back, to a short train behind her quickly moving feet. She was holding the front nearly to her knees as she raced up the stairs. Sweet Mercy, what a vision she was with all those sun-kissed curls pouring down her back to her hips, emphasizing the bouncing butt below it. It was enough to make a Wizard's cock threaten to burst from his breeches. Just as his was doing now.

"Suggestions?" he questioned his brother from the side of his mouth as they followed her.

"Well, the dragon seemed quite irate, and not a little concerned." Kai'el's tone was filled with laughter. "I say we do exactly as he says, we watch her. I assume he would mean until he returns to tell us better."

Caise smothered his bark of laughter. Devious. It sounded like a plan to him.

They lengthened their stride, making certain to stay close enough to her to keep her from barring the door to them as she gripped the handle and raced to do just that. It was Kai'el's hand that hit the panel first, pushing it slowly open despite her heated curses.

"This is my room." She faced them furiously, her eyes flashing violet fire. "You will leave it immediately."

"Sorry, your highness," Caise sighed, following his brother into the room and closing the door carefully. "The dragon said to watch you. We are sworn to do just that."

"A dragon commands you?" she sneered mockingly. "How pitiful. 'Tis the other way around here."

Evidently she had no idea the power of the dragon she spoke of.

"It is a chore." He shrugged dismissively, controlling the smile that would have curved his lips. "But some Wizards must bear the brunt of such onerous tasks."

She snorted at the reply. "Move from the door and we will return to the dragon…"

You will keep her where she is. The Princess Serena is no longer in the ballroom and the warriors and their Wizards are now on alert. And if you please, you will keep this information to yourselves. There was a world of sarcasm in Garron's thought as it echoed through their minds.

Shadowhell, just what he needed. A dragon talking in his head.

"I think perhaps we will stay here, until Garron calls for us." Kai'el pulled a wing-backed, cushioned chair from the side of the wall, placed it in front of the door and then sat back comfortably. "Have a seat, Princess. I'm certain we can find something to discuss. Do you like flowers?"

Marina stared back at Kai'el silently, holding fast to her control, refusing to allow the heat filling her body to stain her cheeks. It was not possible that he knew of the dream. Were it not for the fact that even the Sentinel Select, the Priests and Priestess to the gods, swore that only gods themselves could offer shelter within the Valley of Dreams, she would swore he knew.

Coincidence, she scoffed at her imagination.

"I enjoy flowers very much, Wizard Sashtain," she sneered openly. "Though flowers have little to do with your actions at present. I demand that you leave my room."

The frilly room was her place of peace, of serenity. Long filmy curtains surrounded her large bed, the quilt turned back to show the rich burnished tan of her sheets. The quilt itself was a patchwork of varying colors that pleased her eyes.

The mantel over the fireplace held small keepsakes. A crystal rock her father had given her as a small child. The first tiara she had been presented with at her fifth birth-year. A small pair of silk slippers, barely large enough to fit into her palm. Her father had fashioned them himself when she was a babe.

Flowers graced her room. Proof that his comment had been mere chance. Tall vases filled with blooming branches, smaller ones of stems of colorful flowers placed strategically on the low chest, beside her bed and to the sides of the fireplace.

Two forgotten gowns had been tossed over the low settee Caise was heading for. He brushed their folds of cloth back carefully before sitting down, leaning back and for all the world appearing as though he were enjoying himself.

"Did either of you hear me, or did your warriors forget to clean your ears this morn?" She tilted her head and regarded their expressions of mock innocence.

Caise lifted a dark blond brow in mockery as Kai'el chuckled.

"Tell me, Sorceress, why were you seen patrolling the forests this morn? Several warrior units glimpsed you on that unicorn you ride, dressed in breeches and sneaking through the forests as though on some mission. What mission could you be about?"

She opened her eyes wide, affecting wounded confusion.

"The lands are mine to oversee, as by my Queen Mother's command, just as Serena is heir apparent and Brianna was to oversee the needs of those within the towns. The farms are in my trust and I visit them often." Which was the truth, as far as that went.

Kai'el relaxed further in his chair, watching her broodingly now.

"You are in league with the Sorceress Brigade, are you not, Princess?" The question was voiced so casually, so easily that she nearly betrayed herself with the surprise shuddering through her. He spoke as though he had proof, as a high justice would speak in matters of the law.

"You have lost your senses." She spread her hands innocently before her. "Do I appear to be a warrioress, Wizard Sashtain? Really. That would be much too dangerous for a Princess."

Caise gave a surprisingly mocking snort as Kai'el lifted his brow again in cool mockery.

And where was her fear? Marina searched inside herself, feeling trepidation, nerves, but the fears she had known for so many years where men, especially Twins were concerned, seemed to have receded. When had this occurred? Surely it could not have happened and she was unaware of it?

"She affects innocence so perfectly," Kai'el drawled, his voice dark, vibrating with some emotion she could not quite put her finger on. "I wonder how innocent she would proclaim herself were we to petition for courtship?"

Her heart moved to her throat, nearly choking her on the near paralyzing sensation, not of fear, but definitely extreme nervousness.

"That would be unwise, and the joke is poorly given." She turned on her heel, pacing to the large window before turning back to them with a frown. "Is this why you continue to haunt my every move? Because you wish to convince me to accept your suit? It will not happen." She shook her head forcibly as she crossed her arms beneath her breasts, ignoring the sudden heated longing echoing in her nipples, and farther down, between her thighs.

"We could petition courtship, as The Veressi have with Serena," Kai'el pointed out then. "Or the Rite of Reception. Should we formally kneel to you, Princess, what think you would happen?"

Her heart was racing in her chest at that question. She remembered well what happened when the Veraga Twins presented themselves to Brianna. Sentinel's teeth, she had orgasmed right there in the reception hall. It must have been humiliating. Marina could not imagine such a thing.

It had also sped up the zenith of Brianna's powers, creating a conflict of riotous emotions inside her as her magick built quickly to its apex.

"You would not," she whispered, backing slowly away from them, watching them warily. "Why would you do such a thing?"

Merciful Sentinels, her emotions were in conflict enough—risking the alignment of her magick with these Twins was the last thing she needed.

"Perhaps because you refuse to allow us to court you in a more traditional means?" Kai'el asked then, his pale blue eyes watching her with curious intensity. "We have been here for many days, Marina, and still yet you refuse us even a small amount of your time. You do not allow the natural progression of the alignment. Why would we not wish to be certain if we are leaving behind our natural Consort before giving up entirely on the venture and returning to our own land?"

Oh, he should have been a Justice, Marina thought, impressed with his words, if not with his argument. He made it all seem quite logical, she had to admit. But she was staring into eyes that had no shame in showing his amusement, an expression creased with mockery.

She snorted in derision.

"You think me a fool." She crossed her arms over her breasts, staring back between the pair of them. "I am no toy to be tugged at, Sashtain."

Kai'el's amusement cleared as sober intensity overtook his gaze and he leaned forward in his chair, bracing his arms on his legs as Caise watched silently.

"You are wrong, my little warrioress," he growled. "It is no toy I see standing before me, but a woman grown and hiding behind her sword. And I, Princess Marina, am growing tired of lazing within this castle awaiting your consideration on this matter. Do not mistake my patience for foolishness."

The deepened tone was warning enough that this situation was rapidly growing out of her control. She watched the two men warily, feeling the shadows of fear rising within her. They were two. One she could battle and defend herself against, two would overwhelm her small amount of magick as well as her defenses.

"Ahh Princess, what unfounded fear." Caise spoke then, the gentle chastisement in his tone making her chest clench in despair.

How she wished she could trust them. And it wasn't just her innate fear of their strength and their power that held her back. But her distrust of their motives. She could sense much more going on with the arrival of the Wizard Twins within Covenan than just a desire to find their natural Consorts. Much more.

"Who is to say my fears are unfounded?" she asked him then, swallowing against her regrets, against needs she did want to feel. "You do not know me, Caise. You are concerned only with your own needs, your own purpose. What of mine?"

She had no desire to leave the land she had accepted stewardship over. She was tied to Covenan, and to the power that fed it. To leave it would be to leave a part of her very essence behind her.

"And you know this how, Princess?" Kai'el's voice was soft, throbbing with a passion she did not have to sense, for the magick that filled it throbbed within his voice. "This is the first chance we have had to even speak of wants, needs, or purposes. And it was a time forced upon you, rather than one you willingly chose. Perhaps you should give thought to the fact that we have not forced the Rite of Reception, but have tried to give you that choice instead. Does that not leave us worthy of at least your smallest regard?"

How sincere he sounded. Marina stared back at him, feeling the hunger inside her to believe his words. No, he had not forced the Rite of Reception, nor had he demanded a petition to Courtship. They shadowed her every move, mocked her desire to run from their presence, and stole every opportunity presented to them to fill her time. But they had forced nothing. They had demanded nothing.

And oh, how they did fascinate her. All fears and wariness aside, she could admit to that.

"What would you have me do?" She spread her hands wide then, staring back at him the question plagued her. "If, and I say if with great prejudice, I were to be part of the Brigade, what would your reaction be? To go to my Queen Mother, demanding my confinement? Demanding I cease? And were I to give you leave to court me, who is to say you would accept my word when I declared your suit not to my liking? How, my good Twins, am I supposed to trust that which gives me no reason to trust?"

"Let us make a trade instead." Kai'el's expression cleared, becoming serene, calm. Despite that, she had the strangest feeling some trickery may soon be evolving.

"And what trade would you propose?" She was interested, despite her misgivings.

"Something we would desire, in exchange for something you would desire, if you were a warrior sorceress, that is."

"Kai'el," Caise's voice was suddenly warning, intriguing her further.

"Go on." She nodded sharply, her eyes narrowing as she watched Kai'el.

He did not glance in his brother's direction, despite the muted, resigned groan that came from him.

"You will choose one of us, now. On that bed..." He pointed to the bed. "You will lie with him willingly, fully clothed, and allow his touch."

Marina could feel the color leaching from her flesh.

"I am not asking for the sexual act, Marina," he said. "I am asking you allow touch. No more. Whatever touch you do not wish, you will simply say 'no', your wishes will be heeded. But you will allow touch."

"In exchange for?" She was trembling. She could feel the small tremors racing over her flesh, fear rising within her mind.

They were large men, strong, powerful men.

Kai'el smiled. A slow, disarming curve of his lips, filled with laughter, filled with a sense of pending excitement.

"Tomorrow, on the sun's rising, the Twin you did not choose this night to touch you will take you to the air on his Snow Owl."

Marina's eyes widened. No Sorceress had ever flown. It was unheard of. The great Owls heeled only to the Wizard Twins. Even Brianna had not flown upon the great beasts, despite her Consortship with the Veraga Twins.

"She would allow it?" Marina whispered in awe. "You would not lie to me, surely? Were I to announce your words were false, Wizard, then no Sorceress in the land would so much as aid you were you bleeding in the streets. Playing me so falsely would not be to your best interests."

Kai'el grunted at her words. "The Snow Owls would gladly allow you to ride with one of us." He waved his hand negligently. "And we do not lie, Marina. I assure you of this now."

She glanced then to Caise. "You would fulfill this bargain as well?"

Surprise reflected in his golden eyes.

"Twins do make pacts separate of each other, Marina. Surely you have heard of this? I will fulfill his promise, just as he would fulfill any I would make."

She shrugged at the question.

"Who is to say what is true and what is false of the rumors we have heard in regards to the Wizard Twins. I merely wish to be certain."

Sweet Mother Sentinel. To ride on the back of the Snow Owl, to stare down at the land below, and know the freedom of the wind rushing over her. It was a dream, one that had followed her since she had first seen the great birds flying above the Snow Mountains. Pure white, graceful in their flight and majestic as they coursed the currents above. Even her griffons were not as graceful as those lovely owls.

But first, she would have to submit to the touch of at least one of them. She would have to choose.

"What of the one I do not choose?" She licked her dry lips as her nerves rioted. "What will he do?"

The tension in the air thickened. Magick sizzled just beneath the surface and hunger, deep and filled with lust, swirled around her.

"Watch," Kai'el whispered with sizzling heat. "Much pleasure can be gained in observing, Marina. More than you could ever imagine."

Chapter Six

❧

Marina swallowed, feeling the constriction of fear that tightened within her throat as she laced her fingers together nervously and stared back at the Wizards. They watched her. Caise with his eyes of molten gold. Kai'el, his gaze the palest blue, eerie as it seemed to sear her soul.

Could she do this? Could she trust either of them to lie upon her bed with her, to touch her as a lover and not feel the shadows of a nightmare past pressing in upon her? It had been years, she reminded herself, since that horrifying attack. She was stronger now, she had grown in her own confidence, in her own strengths. Her magick was still much weaker than theirs, but she could feel her mother's powers encompassing the room. Here she was sheltered, protected, as she was in no other part of the land.

"Why?" she asked them both then. "Why must you attempt this courtship of me? What is it, Wizard, that you seek, that only I will do?"

She was no fool. They had not declared the Rite of Reception, nor petitioned for courtship, but it was a courtship all the same.

"We seek our true Consort, Marina, nothing more," Caise answered her, his voice dark, throbbing with hunger. "You are that Consort. Whether you wish to admit this or not, it is true." He held his hand up to ward back the objection rising to her lips. "Wizards know their mates when their magick touches them. They search endlessly, tirelessly for that alignment. We understand your fears, Princess, as we understand your suspicions. We ask only for the chance to prove the truth of our words to you. To prove that you will not be mistaken in placing your trust with us. Nothing more. But nothing less."

It was no more than she had suspected herself.

"Why not merely petition for the Courtship?" She shook her head in confusion.

"Do you believe we wish to force anything upon you?" Kai'el seemed to snarl the words. "Did we want a forced mate, my lady, then we would have merely gone the quickest route and demanded Rite of Reception. We would want acceptance, not forced compliance. Now, do you accept our bargain, or do we fly alone come morn?"

She propped her hands on her hips, facing him with a frown.

"You are as impatient as a child," she scoffed, covering her attempts to hide her fears by chastising him instead.

"And you are withholding my treat," he grunted in reply. "Make your mind up, woman, and put us out of our misery."

"Fine." She flounced to the bed, throwing herself on it, forcing herself to stare back at them, holding her body stiffly. "For that, you may watch. Your brother may touch."

Sweet Sentinel, was she insane?

Her heart jerked to her throat as Caise rose slowly to his feet, his erection outlined clearly beneath his leather breeches.

"She will not go through with it," Kai'el warned him as he stared back at her, a smirk on his sensually full lips. "Look at her, laying as stiff as our cocks. She will jump and run before you ever have the chance."

"You are without decency." She flushed at the explicit language. "Did I not give my word?"

"We must place a time limit on it." Caise paused at his brother's words as Marina stared back at him in horror.

"Have you lost your senses?"

"As much as you may have wished your beauty dims my senses, I must say, I have not." He smiled mockingly. "I know you, Princess." He shook his finger at her chidingly. "You will allow the most meager touch, hoarding the pleasure like a miser does his gold do we not watch you carefully. So I say, for every moment you allow touch, that is the length of time you are allowed upon the owl's back. A moment for a moment you may say. Are we still in agreement?"

She thought little of his wagering, but could find no argument to counter it.

"I control which touch I receive," she further bargained. "It is at my discretion."

He inclined his head with a slow sigh. "Unfortunately, that shall I agree to. Though I fear you intend to cheat us greatly."

Aye, so she had intended to until she glimpsed the regret in the gazes of both men. This made no sense to her. Why beget a bargain they knew they could be so easily cheated within if there was no intent to force their will upon her? Not that she would have actually cheated, she assured herself, fighting desperately to distract herself as Caise neared the bed. But, there was complying with the rules and then there was...

"Lay on your side, Marina." Caise paused at the side of the bed, the length of his erection appearing huge as she stared up at him. "Turn your back to me, I will but hold you. Nothing more unless you wish it. Allow me to hold you, little one. This is all."

Marina bit her lip though she did as he asked. And she thought of owls. Huge Snow Owls that would carry her above the land, allow her to gaze down in wonder... Merciful Sentinel. Her gaze clashed with Kai'el's where he sat in the chair, leaning forward, watching with such hungry intent, such envy for his brother she forced herself to still the words which would bring him to her bed as well.

Was she insane?

She couldn't close her eyes against his as she felt Caise lowering himself behind her. She couldn't fight the demand that she share that small connection, despite her repeated, desperate insistence that she owed either of them nothing.

"Shhh," Caise whispered behind her, forcing her to still the unconscious whimper that left her as she stared beseechingly back at Kai'el. What was she thinking, to believe she could do this? She could feel her chest clenching with terror, her eyes dampening with the struggle to rein in her emotions, despite her body's insistence that the warmth at her back was most welcome.

"Kai…" Regret shimmered inside her. She could not.

"The Snow Owls have the softest feathers," Kai'el whispered as Caise settled at her back, his broad chest cushioning her, his hand lying lightly on her hip. "They are softer than the finest silk against your flesh, Marina. As you fly, they enfold you, wrapping you in warmth…"

She wanted to fly. How desperately she had longed for such adventure.

She forced herself to breathe deeply, evenly, holding Kai'el's gaze, seeing the compassion, the heat in his eyes, as well as the envy as she felt Caise's fingers in her hair, testing the feel of the curls.

"Unlike most Wizards, I do not feel Caise's emotions. Neither his anger, nor his pain," Kai'el sighed as he watched. "I cannot feel the silk of your hair, nor smell the scent of your sweet flesh. But I can watch, see his fingers tangling within the mass, and I dream of silk softer than even the feathers of the Snow Owl. Watch him inhale the scent of you, and imagine a field of flowers in riotous array, and know even that scent is incomparable to what he knows at this moment."

Her lips parted. There was no artifice in his words, there was no deception nor deceit. There was hunger, blazing and intense instead.

"I see him against you, Marina, and I ache with such hunger, but 'tis an ache far better than any I have known in my life. It is a gladdening ache, for if I cannot smell your flesh or touch the softness of your hair, then there is none other I would wish to know it rather than Caise."

The bond of the Wizard Twins went deep she knew, but to hear it throbbing in his voice touched a chord inside her. To be a part of such a bond would be, as her sister Brianna had said, a paradise unsurpassed. To know something was hers and hers alone, that someone walked this land who belonged to her soul and no others.

"Kai..." She whimpered his name as she felt Caise smooth her hair behind the shoulder left bared by her dress. His fingertips glanced her flesh, their calloused rasp bringing to mind the dream of flowers and a pleasure unlike any she had ever known before.

"How brave are you, Marina?" he asked her then. "Brave enough to soar above the land, to feel the wind whipping through your hair? Brave enough to endure the touch of one who would give his life in exchange for yours? To find pleasure rather than pain?"

Her lips parted in a gasp. Behind her, Caise stilled, and she wondered if he were watching his brother as well.

"I don't understand." Her voice was ragged, her breathing choppy.

"Let me direct your play, Marina," he growled. "Allow me to direct his touch. You will know then what is coming, be prepared for each caress. And then, little one, we shall see how brave you can be." There was just enough mockery in his voice to have her watching him in suspicion.

"You think I cannot do this?" she asked him. "That I must be led as a child into uncharted waters?"

He chuckled, though his expression held little amusement and much arousal.

"Prove me wrong." He shrugged. "That or allow me what satisfaction I can find in the fact that you did not choose my touch as well. What say you, Princess?"

What say you?

Her eyes narrowed.

"I do not trust your direction in the least," she snorted. "But go ahead, Wizard Sashtain, let us see how well you ply your intuitive powers. What touch will I accept, which will I not. We can even raise your wager. Each time you go too far, and I am forced to call a halt, doubles the time I have gained upon your great Owl."

He laughed. Throwing his head back, gleeful amusement gleaming in his eyes, he inclined his head in agreement. "It will be as you say and I will wager for nothing in return. Now little one, let us see how well we do together. As you lay there, you will watch me. I will give Caise the command, you will have two seconds to decline or touching commences. Agreed?"

"Agreed," she spoke rashly, and knew well she did.

"To begin, Caise will first show you the differences between his flesh and your own. As you watch me, his fingers will caress but your bare shoulder."

She waited the two seconds, her gaze holding his easily until she felt the touch of Caise's hand on her bare flesh. She could not halt her flinch, but she did not object. Curiously, there was no pain, no fear. The roughened pads of his fingers smoothed over her as she felt his breathing become rougher at her back.

"You should see his face." Kai'el's voice was low, his gaze reflective. "He gains much pleasure from the feel of your skin, Marina. Have you ever known pleasure from touch alone?"

She had, but never sexual pleasure. And never had another's touch heated her as this one did.

Caise's fingertips slid over her skin, from shoulder to neck, sending shivers of sensation racing through her as she watched Kai'el's hands clench on the arms of the chair.

"Very good." His voice was rough, guttural with the hungers suddenly whipping through the room. Not just those of the Wizards, but she realized hazily, her own.

"Is the feel of his hands upon your flesh pleasant, my Princess?" His voice was low, rasping across her senses even as Caise's fingertips rasped across her flesh.

"Yes." She could not deny him, no matter how she wished to. Answering him was imperative, seeing the flare of response darken his once pale eyes filled her with an ache to see them darken further.

He licked his lips slowly, his gaze moving from hers to the sight of Caise's fingertips playing across her shoulder.

"His lips now," he growled. "He will caress your arms with his fingers, your shoulder with his lips. Can you bear such a touch, my Princess?"

She shuddered, not in fear, but in longing. She should be screaming against such caresses rather than lying submissively beneath them.

She waited the two seconds, steeling herself against the coming touch. In years, no man's lips had touched her, not since that night. Not since fetid breath had filled her senses as her attacker forced his kiss upon her.

"Such fear I see in your eyes," Kai'el crooned as she felt Caise's fingers trail down her arm.

Like a whisper of the phermona, a bit rough, like unbrushed velvet sliding over her. She could feel him behind her, his head lowering.

"He's hungry, my Princess," he whispered. "As hungry as I. His eyes are like brass, rather than gold, dark, filled with his need of you. Sweet, hot need." His voice throbbed as a shudder raced over her flesh and Caise's lips touched her flesh.

She gasped, her gaze holding desperately to the naked need and the compassion in Kai'el's eyes. No pity there, no mercy, but emotion, as thick and as hot as the hunger that filled his gaze.

"Such courage." His voice gave her strength as her fists clenched at her sides, her body held stiffly as heated male lips pressed to her flesh.

She expected the wet feel of slobbering lust, as she had before. Instead, his lips were heated, though dry, smoothing over her skin in a gentle kiss before they opened, and his tongue tasted her quickly.

Marina jerked at that touch, feeling a heaviness invade her limbs. Her heart was racing in her chest now, her breasts becoming heavy, her nipples sensitive as the flesh between her thighs began to slowly awaken. Sentinels have mercy on her, but his lips were nibbling at her flesh now, his tongue stroking a heated, moist path across her shoulder that had her fighting for breath against the pleasure. True, unshadowed pleasure.

"Kai..." She whispered his name beseechingly, not for cessation of the touch, but something unnamed, some need she knew not how to give voice to.

"Such beauty." The chair floated closer to the bed, drawn by her, pushed by his magick, she wasn't certain and didn't care. Suddenly he was at the edge of the bed, leaning close to the mattress, his gaze following each stroke of Caise's lips. "I would wager your taste is more intoxicating than that of the finest Elixir," he groaned as Caise's lips settled at the indentation between neck and shoulder, his lips suckling at the area with the utmost gentleness as his tongue tickled at the flesh.

She breathed in harshly, her eyelids becoming heavy, her body tensing. What strange sensations. Her mind felt hazy, yet so alert that it immediately responded to the slightest touch, making her flesh so hypersensitive that the lightest touch was an agony of pleasure.

"'Tis magick," she gasped. "'Tis not natural." She couldn't help but tilt her head, to allow him greater access to the nerve-ridden area.

"No magick," Kai'el growled. "See you even the faintest thread of power, Princess? Nay, not so. We will not force the alignment, we swore this to you. This is pleasure, nothing more."

There were no trails of power, no threads of magick reaching out from them. How then were they were bringing such sensations? Surely this could not be natural?

A ragged cry left her lips then as she felt Caise's teeth rake over her shoulder, heard his muted groan behind her as his fingers settled more firmly against the flesh of her arm, stroking with long, heated motions as his tongue tasted her neck.

"Sentinel's teeth. His eyes are closed, Marina, his senses immersed in the pleasure of touching you. Such pleasure must surely be paradise."

He was stroking himself. She couldn't see his hand to be certain, and knew he had not released his male flesh from his breeches, but she was certain of it. Rather than being repulsed, her palm itched, causing her to clench one in the quilt beneath her, the other in the folds of her gown.

"Would you kiss him, Marina?" Kai'el asked her then. "Turn and part your lips for him, allowing him to possess the sweet taste of you?"

She stared back at him, her breathing harsh, her lips parted, as his gaze demanded either a denial or submission.

"I see your lips, and all I can think of is the sweet taste of paradise," he groaned, his expression tightening into lines of extreme hunger, blistering need. "Of feeling them part beneath mine, your shy little tongue peeking out to welcome me in, licking at mine in invitation. I do not know if I can even bear to see my brother possess that which I am denied. But I will, Marina. I will watch him, and when I retire to my lonely chamber I will close my eyes in dreams that it was I, rather than Caise, tasting paradise."

Her tongue peeked out, swiping at her dry lips in nervous need as a groan shook his large body and his gaze centered on the action.

"Will you allow the kiss?" He was demanding, needing.

Marina fought to breathe as she fought to break contact with his gaze. She would turn to her back, give him what he wished for, but she could not break his gaze.

"Merciful Sentinel," he whispered as a longing whimper left her lips.

What was she to say, to do? Tremors of sweet agony raced through her body. She ached, she needed and knew not what she ached for. She knew she could not turn from him, even to do as she longed to.

When the two-second mark passed, she felt Caise move as he drew her to her back, his shoulders rising above her as his broad palm cupped her cheek and turned her face toward him.

His eyes were molten gold, hot and intent as they locked with hers, his expression tight, the angles of his face thrown into stark relief from the hunger filling it.

Marina felt her fingers gripping his wrists. One to the hand cupping her jaw, the other to the hand at her hip. She needed something to hold onto, needed an anchor amid the chaotic sensations tearing through her.

"I fear..." Her breath hitched as she stared back at him helplessly, remembering the darkness of that night long past and the smothering moisture of lips that stifled her screams, teeth that bit at her lips, bringing the taste of her own blood to her mouth.

"You are as precious as sunlight," he whispered then, his lips fuller, sensual as he stared down at her with nothing but tenderness and hunger. Stark, unrelieved hunger that sent conflicting needs crashing through her. The need to flee, the need to taste the sensuality pouring from him. "I will share but a taste with you. No more than you wish, my love."

A taste and no more. She shook in his grip as she stared up at him, feeling her lips tremble as his head lowered, hearing her own whimper as his lips touched hers. And there he but lingered, staring back at her, his eyes so filled with regret at her fear as she gasped beneath the heated warmth.

His breath was scented with mint, fresh, clean, with but a hint of wine. His lips were not overly wet, but rather a warm, barely damp sensation as they rubbed against hers, tempting her to take him, to accept more of his kiss.

She had never been kissed, not truly. Her hands tightened on his wrists as she fought to show him she would take more. Despair filled her now at her own inexperience. She would kiss him fully, revel in the taste and the touch if she but knew how.

Regret filled his gaze as his head lifted.

"No." Her hand flew from his wrist, tangled into the golden strands of hair that curtained over the sides of his face. "I do not know…" She swallowed tightly. "I have kissed no other, Caise. I…" She licked her lips in a quick, nervous movement that immediately drew his gaze. "I do not know what to do…" She was on the verge of tears, could feel the dampness filling her eyes as despairing need whipped through her body.

His gaze heated further as understanding filled his expression.

"I could show you." His grin was rakish, wicked. "Do you wish me to teach you, my love?"

There would be no taming this Wizard nor his twin, she knew that then, but with such pleasure as a reward, what sorceress would wish to?

"Slowly?" she asked, staring back at him as she fought back the demons within her own mind. "I would know your kiss. Slowly."

"Aye, slowly it is." His smile was more tender than wicked as his head lowered once again. "Part your lips for me, beloved. Let us explore together."

Explore. That was no word for the inferno of heat and pleasure that tore through her body as Caise's lips took hers. Slowly. The fingers of one hand threaded into her hair as his head tilted, his lips sipping at hers, nibbling, stroking, sending arrows of longing straight to her womb where they clenched that weak muscle violently. How fickle was her feminine flesh to come to glorious, blistering life with so small a caress? Or was it truly such a simple touch?

But the pleasure. It was unlike anything she could have imagined. It wrapped her in heat, in trailing fingers of sensation that seemed to caress her entire body. It sensitized her, pushed back the shadows of fears and the demons of darkness which had kept her hesitant to allow any other male near. But this touch, this caressing, challenging, rakishly wicked kiss he was bestowing so slowly, rubbing against her lips, his teeth taking a second to nibble, to open her lips wider, was more pleasure than even the dreams of flowers.

His tongue stroked at her lips before slipping inside, teasing hers to play, a sensual challenge she could not help but to accept. A dare that she eagerly met as her lips opened to his. Like pieces of an interlocking puzzle they fit, lip-to-lip, tongue-to-tongue as muted moans began to fill the room.

She was intoxicated on his taste, his touch. It sank into her very pores, spreading throughout each inch of her flesh, overwhelming her with pleasure. Her senses were on fire, the heat building throughout her in ways she could have never known existed.

Kai'el's voice was but a distant murmur, easing through her senses, his explicit words, rather than shocking her, spurring her to greater hunger.

"The day shall come, as his lips possess your kiss, mine shall linger between thighs of the sweetest alabaster in a kiss filled with passion's nectar..." Her pussy spasmed at the image his words conveyed. Caise, his lips nibbling at hers as Kai'el's kiss possessed the secrets of her womanhood. Could she bear such a touch?

Her clenching pussy assured she could. She felt empty, aching—gods, how she ached deep within her vagina as her clit swelled and pulsed in a silent plea for ease.

Aye. She could bear it. Shadowhell, she was beginning to crave it.

Distantly she realized her hands were now locked in Caise's hair, her nails pressing to his scalp, holding him to her as Kai'el seduced her with his words.

"Your nipples like ripe little berries, hot beneath my tongue, Princess. As hot as summer's riches..." Her nipples ached, grew harder. "Your cream flowing to my tongue, liquid passion, searing my senses as your sweet syrup flows for us..." Her thighs clenched as she felt her juices ease from the tortured depths of her cunt. Sweet Mother Sentinel, she needed such caresses.

And still Caise's lips possessed hers, eating at her, licking at her as he consumed her with pleasure. She arched into him, feeling his hands as they smoothed over her waist, to the sides of her swollen breasts, to the thighs clenched against the pleasure tearing through her. Against her hip she could feel the hardened length of his cock pressing against her, thick and hot, she could feel its demanding throb through his breeches and her gown. And she needed more.

"We would feel you, Marina..." Kai'el's words were broken, his voice hoarse, weaving through the arousal as pleasure overtook her. "Your sweet tongue against us, your hands caressing as we caressed..."

She could hear his arousal building in his words, just as hers built in her body. She imagined them both beside her, her fingers caressing warm, naked flesh, her lips opening, not just for eager tongues, but for the hard, burgeoning length of a cock as well. The need to taste them brought a shattered cry from her lips as Caise's kiss deepened.

"Gods, Marina…" Kai'el's voice was hungry, his words shaping the visions filling her mind. "Would you touch in such a way? Your lips opening, your tongue curling about my flesh, destroying the last of my control?"

Aye, she would. She whimpered with the need as the kiss she shared with Caise turned desperate, their ragged moans filling the air around them.

"There, love…" Kai'el's voice was strained, his breathing hard and heavy. "Ah gods, I will lose what little control I possess this night."

She arched slowly, turning more fully into Caise's arms, the pleasure astounding in its richness, the sensations rioting through her overtaking her mind. She wanted, nay she needed, to rub against him, to feel him breast to chest, hip to hip, caressing the most sensitive areas of her traitorous flesh.

His arms surrounded her as she turned to him, a fractured groan filling her ears as his kiss deepened. She could not have imagined it deepening, becoming hungrier, but suddenly, it did just that. Her neck was arched, his lips slanting over hers as his tongue thrust forcefully against hers. It probed and licked before withdrawing, tempting her to follow. And follow she did. She demanded then and he gave. Her tongue licking at him, battling with his for supremacy as his body shifted, and she felt his erection notching into her thighs.

Marina froze, a whimper of hunger tearing through her chest as she felt a blooming heat rising within her. She was flying and needed no owl to carry her. As the heat and hardened length of his cock pressed against the fiery knot of nerves at the apex of her thighs, she sensed the flight beginning.

"Gods..."

Suddenly Caise's lips were no longer upon hers, his body no longer pressing tight against her. One hand gripped her hip, the other her shoulder as he held her from his touch, denying her the sensations lifting her from within herself.

Marina struggled to open her eyes, to part her lips and force the beseeching words from between them when she saw the surprise on his face, the direction of his gaze. She turned slowly, blinking, staring up at Kai'el.

His fingers were buried in his brother's hair as though to tear him back, his face twisted into a grimace of sublime pleasure as threads of violet magick whipped over both men. They swirled through thick strands of hair and over broad, heaving chests. Most frightening, though, was the fact that the magick was devoid of blue or gold power — it was her power only. And it was thickest between Kai'el's thighs, obviously milking the broad erection, suckling, stroking it. Just as she had imagined doing.

Her magick. Her power.

Alignment.

"No." She struggled between them then, jerking quickly away as she stared in horror at the phenomena.

The power was not returning to her. It sang through the air, whispered in shades of incandescent light as it sizzled over their bodies just as pleasure still whipped through her veins.

"Enough. Make it stop," she gasped, stumbling from the bed, fighting the need to return between them, to give them whatever they wished. To see forever the agony of pleasure twisting their expressions.

Kai'el released his brother's hair slowly, his jaw bunching with the effort it cost to move, but his head was still tipped back, the magick, though dimmer, still racing across his body.

She had done this. She blinked in shock, uncertain, confused as the power refused to move back to her. It lingered, because her hunger lingered, her needs. A whimper left her lips as Kai'el's eyes met hers, the darkening depths filled with an agonized pleasure, a satisfaction which terrified her.

As she stared at the Twins in horror, she knew deep inside the meaning of the sight. Her magick racing over them, tempting their own, though they held it carefully in check. Had they released their own powers, then she would have had no choice... No choice.

Marina trembled at the thought. Had they allowed the alignment her magick was so obviously seeking, then she would have been forced to submit to the Joining, then and there. There would have been no question of it, no matter her fears, no matter her needs or her secrets. They would have possessed her. Not just her body, but all that she was would have belonged to them. And in that instant she realized the betrayal she would have dealt those she fought with had she done so. She was part of the Sorceress Brigade, the backbone of the power they wielded. Should her magick align into a joining with these Wizards, then her secrets would be theirs.

She stared at Caise and Kai'el, her needs, her desires pounding within her as they eased slowly from her bed, staring back at her silently as she clenched her hands in her gown to force herself from touching them, from pleading with them to do the unthinkable.

Caise sighed, his molten gaze watching her in disappointment.

"Trust is built, Princess." His voice was rough, his breathing still harsh. "Trust, like love, like magick, cannot be betrayed when it is true. You have no need to fear us."

But she did. They suspected her already, suspected her participation within the Sorceress Brigade. Gods help them all if the Wizard Twins learned just how many of the women they sought as Consorts had sworn their lives and their protection to Covenan. With the vows to the land that many of them had made, they could not be taken from it, no more than she herself could be taken from it, and survive. But how would she survive if she gave her heart to these men, only to have them leave?

"Leave." She forced the word from her lips, forced herself to deny what she knew she could not yet have.

Kai'el shook his head pityingly. "For now." He nodded sharply. "We fly at first light. Should you be within the courtyard, you may fly patrol with us. If you are not there..." His shoulders shrugged negligently. "So be it. You shall have to wager once more to gain another chance. Good eve, Princess."

They left. Marina watched in surprise as they stalked from the room, the door clicking too quietly behind them. Anger echoed in the near silent sound, vibrating around her, stronger for the sheer control the Wizards had exerted in reining in their emotions.

"Well, Princess, you erred on the side of idiocy."

Garron's voice had her swinging around, staring back at him in shock.

"Dragon, you should announce yourself," she snapped, her own anger rising now, her loss of control stinging her pride as nothing else could have. "These rooms are private. You do remember the meaning of this word, correct?"

Mockery gleamed in rich black eyes as he stared back at her, a leathery brow arching in sarcasm.

"And do you remember the meaning of caution?" he questioned her then. "You do not play with Wizards in such a way, child, or you may find more than your fingers burned when the night draws to a close." He shook his massive head as he breathed out wearily. "The children of Sellane shall be the death of me. For now, my dear, you have nearly aligned yourself with your Wizards, at the very moment when you must hold your secrets closest. Tell me, which is more important? The childish games you play with your friends, or the Wizards who just left this room? Choices, choices, my dear. Have fun making them."

81

She had never accused Garron of delicacy or of tact. Mocking, condescending, forever butting his nose into business not his own, yes. Tactful, no. Why though did he suddenly seem more mocking, less comforting than normal? The sarcasm in his expression was deeper, his black eyes appearing angry.

"Be gone with you," she snapped. "I have no time for your male machinations nor your riddles." She sighed wearily.

"Keep up this idiocy of playing with these Wizards and you will find yourself in much more trouble than you imagine," he grunted. "Beware, Princess, they will not be controlled as you seem wont to control them."

And in that second Marina knew the choices she must make come morn, would never be easy for her to settle within herself. She and her warrioresses had hidden for too long. Perhaps now was the time to show these arrogant males that they did not fear them, and that they would not allow themselves to be taken from their lands. Nor their lands taken from them.

It was now time for the Sorceress Brigade to be revealed.

Chapter Seven

ഔ

Sweet Mercy, the children of Amoria would be his downfall, Garron thought with a sigh as he watched the vulnerability, the indecision that filled young Marina's expression. A flash of fear in violet eyes, a sense of strength building within her. One he knew would have no choice but to fall. The time would come when she could do nothing but trust the Wizards courting her for reasons less than exemplary. 'Twas not emotion that pushed the dark seers of magick, rather than their own desires for the greater good, perhaps, but still yet, their own greater good.

And how easily they were being trapped within their own plans. It was enough to make a dragon roar with laughter. If he had any laughter left inside him of course. Laughter had been taken ages ago. Eons ago. It had been washed away by a mother's cruel deceit, a father's hatred and the lash laid upon his back. And to this end, here before this Princess who meant so very much to him, was where it had evolved. He who had sworn he would know no love, he who would have no bonds to chain him to any female's side, had lingered far longer within the castle of Sellane than he had lingered in any other land or dimension.

"They would trick me so easily," she whispered, an answer to her own thoughts surely, for none could read the minds of dragons. For that, he most blessedly thanked the Sentinels.

"And are you so certain they trick you?" He harrumphed. To his knowledge the Sashtain Twins had not exactly lied to her. Perhaps withheld small amounts of the truth. That was but a small transgression. It was an entirely male thing to do, of course. Sometimes, females did not exactly understand the full picture where the greater good was concerned.

"What else could it be?" A short, bitter laugh accompanied her words as she stared back at him.

Her fiery curls fell around her delicate body as she trembled still yet from her Twins' touch. Her eyes were saddened, darkened by shadows as her expression became forlorn, nearly lost. And how that winsome face could touch his heart.

He had taken her from those who would have destroyed her years ago. Their blood stained his scales, the sounds of their screams still haunted his nightmares. Twins, not Wizards, born of Covenan and secretly recruited to the ranks of the Seculars, they had sought to destroy the magick that would one day be hers. A magick that would guard the land as no other had.

How had they known this? Just as Garron wondered how the Seculars knew the weakest points within Covenan to strike. They targeted the daughters of the castle and had come much too close to destroying this one.

"It could be many things," he growled. "It could simply be their infernal male desire for their Consort. Aye, this is quite a sin, such hunger for the one created for them by the Sentinels themselves. Shall we flay them to the bone, Princess, for this transgression?"

She glared at him with such self-righteous anger that he was hard-pressed to hold back his mirth.

"You are in fine form this eve," she snapped in reply. "Should I have need of your particular brand of humor, Dragon, I shall call for you. Until then, you can return to wherever it is you gained your gentle bearing to begin with."

"Shadowhell is quite boring this moon," he sighed in reply, knowing it to be true. Even the demons were cowering in fear at this time. "It would appear the Princesses Sellane are the only amusement to be had in this fair plane. And amusing, my dear, you can be."

She crossed her arms over her breasts, her face flushing with her anger. Better her anger than the desire that had been there before. He had raised these girls, it was all he could do to keep from roasting the carnal Twins for touching his babes. Or those he considered his, he thought painfully.

"I do not care to be considered your amusement, Dragon," she informed him waspishly. "You can leave now if you do not mind. I am weary of dealing with the less than logical male intellect tonight. I believe I shall retire."

Garron snorted at that declaration. "Perhaps if you are a very good girl, your Wizards will take you to the Valley of Dreams once again," he suggested smoothly, pretending to ignore her shock as he gazed toward the window. "Aye, 'tis nearly mid-night. I would guess their powers are peaking due to their lust and the added stimulus of your magick sinking into them." He turned his head back, affecting innocence. "The fields there are quite nice, and most adaptable to certain magicks."

Her lips parted as fury lit her gaze.

"Only the Sentinels can so gift you," she whispered, her voice harsh. "It is written that only they have the power."

"And where, dear girl, do Sentinel Priests and Priestesses originate?" He questioned her softly. "The Sentinel Select, those gods who hold life and death within their palms choose the bearers of their gifts at an early age. Who is to say..." He shrugged as though he had not the answers to even the questions he invoked. Truth to tell, he knew more than he had ever wished to know.

She stumbled backwards as he watched her, hiding his compassion, the prick of conscience at the tangled web he was carefully unweaving. But if the daughters of this castle were to triumph in the times quickly approaching, then he could not allow deceit, even something so trifling, to stand in their way.

"They deceived me?" she asked, her voice thick with betrayal.

His eyes widened. "Did you ask them if they had given you the gift?" he asked her, knowing well her answer. "I was unaware of this. If they have denied the adventure, then true, they have deceived your gentle heart."

But she had not asked. He saw the answer in her face, yet it was one he had already known. He had felt the journey into the Valley—aye, he had helped to clear the safeguards into it himself.

Marina shook her head, turning quickly from him as she hugged her arms about herself, pulling back into the fragile shell she had used to defend herself for so many years. A shell which had already cracked. What was the saying of the egg once fractured? Like trust, it could not be repaired? He had simply ensured that trust was not broken, since the egg had indeed fallen first.

"No," she finally whispered. "I had not thought to ask."

"Perhaps you should think in the future, Princess," he pointed out. "But, I am not here to discuss Wizards or their faults. I would ask that you gather your Brigade close in case they are needed, until such time as I have learned the true purpose of The Veressi's arrival before your Mother's return."

"It is obvious the men of this world have lost their senses," she suddenly mused as though to no one but herself. "Perhaps the water is not agreeing with them in some odd way. It is something to ponder. Why else would The Veressi dare such a move at this time?" She stared back at him thoughtfully.

Garron lifted his brow. Aye, this one was much like her father, her sense of humor quite wicked, her strength that of the soul. She was one who would fill her Wizards' days with laughter, their nights with heat. She would do, he thought then, realizing that he had worried more for her than he had thought. But, she would do.

"Perhaps this is something you should investigate with your Brigade," he grunted, thinking of the reckless, foolhardy Sorceresses who lived for the battles they fought. "That would keep you out of trouble."

"Or find a cure," she pointed out, before frowning fiercely. "Go away, Garron, I have much to consider this night, and you only infect my mind with your male insanity. 'Tis no wonder the Sorceresses abandoned the mighty Wizard males. Their insanity is contagious."

But she was no longer lost, no longer forlorn. And she was preparing herself in case the heir apparent, second in charge to the Queen Mother, should be absent as well. It would fall to her to lead, to comfort her people and to control the unruly forces of Wizard Twins seeking Consorts. He chuckled silently. Now that one, he would give gold to watch.

He nodded to her sharply, casting her a mocking smile before popping out of her room as quickly as he had popped into it.

Marina stared at where the dragon had stood, a frown creasing her brow as she began to weigh the problem she was now faced with. Wizards who knew their way into the Valley of Dreams, and could slip ignorant little Sorceresses in with them, were definitely Wizards to be wary of.

She lifted her hand, tapping at her swollen lower lip as she began to pace her room, attempting to solve this unique problem facing her. The men she had faced in the past since her attack had been easily controlled. For the most part, her position as Princess and Guardian of the lands protected her from their designs. She could only Join with a male whose magick complemented hers. There were few of those within the land. Unless she Joined with a Wizard. Even the weakest Wizard was stronger than the most powerful male born of Sorceress and human blood.

She feared the Wizards Sashtain had more on their minds than just a Joining, though. Their suspicions of her place within the Brigade and the careful questioning of her roused her instincts. They were not men to tiptoe about a question. So why did they in this instance? But shadowhell, she had known that all along. The question was, how did she learn their plans without allowing an alignment, thereby forcing a Joining?

She groaned in irritation. This Wizard business was beginning to irritate her. They filled the damned castle, invaded her land, patrolled it, and thought they could overrule the Guardian of it, duly appointed by her Queen Mother. Namely, herself.

She paused, pulling her lower lip between her teeth thoughtfully. The Sorceress Brigade had worked in secrecy because the threat against the lands had been in secret. Now that Wizard Twins were slowly overtaking what was not theirs to possess with the absence of her Queen Mother, perhaps it was time for them to reveal themselves. A wicked smile curled about her lips. They could show the Wizards they would not take such measures lying down. Her Queen Mother would have no choice but to accept those she had appointed as overseers, as was her right as Guardian of the lands. A right she had held in shadow in an effort to keep the delicate balance between female strength, and male ego, within Covenan. It was not easy for some of their males to realize that their women were stronger than they themselves were, perhaps not in physical strength, so much as in magick. A strength they did not understand.

And the Wizards, oh ho, would it not be a surprise to them to see the Sorceresses who truly ruled this land showing themselves? The very women they believed they could outwit, and steal their birthright from beneath their noses because they were *weak. Helpless.* Needed *protecting.*

A true spurt of laughter left her lips as her arms uncrossed and her hands propped upon her hips. It would take a bit of work before daybreak, but there were still several hours yet to work with.

Stalking to her door, she threw it open, startling the Covenan guard who waited at the end of the hall. "You will call the Ladies to my rooms," she demanded coolly. "Tell them I have need of them this night and to come prepared." Those stalwart females would know exactly how to prepare themselves.

The burly guard nodded quickly before moving to the staircase to carry out her demands. The Wizard Twins were adept at their magick, there was no doubt. To be strong enough to enter the Valley of Dreams was unique enough, but to be able to bring another, and to still their suspicions, was another thing entirely. Outmaneuvering them would not be so easy. But this was Covenan land. It was infused with Sorceress magick and would aid them well before it aided the Wizards. They may have the great Snow Owls, but the Sorceresses had the unicorns and the griffons, true fighters, and as protective of them as they were of the land itself. It was time the Wizards learned a very valuable lesson. The Sorceresses were not children to be protected and patted kindly upon the head. The Wizards may find a hand missing were they to try.

* * * * *

The first rays of the sun kissed the twin moons of Sentmar from the sky as the castle doors opened upon the courtyard to reveal a sight Kai'el admitted he had not expected to see. After the events of the past night, and Princess Marina's obvious discomfort with it, he had been convinced she would not dare to show come morning and risk herself further.

She was a woman with secrets, that one. A woman determined to control her life and the position she had set for herself. She would not easily relinquish her control to a man, especially to a Wizard Twin. And perhaps, he amended his thoughts, she still had no intention of doing such a thing. Because the Princess Marina was not alone.

Dressed in the dark tan leather breeches of the Sorceress Brigade and the matching vest that gave freedom of movement and tempted any stalwart male's control, all she lacked was the face-shielding hood it was said the Sorceress warriors wore. Leather boots, flat-soled and snug, covered her feet and lower legs, and on her shapely hips she wore her sword. Behind her, two dozen ladies followed, all dressed similarly, carrying their weapons with a confidence born of experience.

Kai'el stemmed his smile, merely leaned against the side of the resting owl and watched the procession in curious amusement as Caise moved slowly to his side. Around them, Wizard Twins watched in varying degrees of disapproval and outright displeasure, many of them certain that the Brigade had been no more than a figment of the Seculars' imagination.

As they watched, a thunder of hooves were heard clattering along the stone paths from several directions. Within seconds, unicorns, pure white, their horns glowing a pure sweet gold, moved into the courtyard. They chose their mistresses, going to them, butting against the small women as they laughed and rubbed at their sides affectionately.

The beasts were outfitted with saddles, but no bridles were needed. It had been rumored that the unicorns knew their riders so well, that often no direction was needed. They rode as one, weaving through the forests and often battling by their Sorceresses' sides. Amid the seeming chaos stood Marina, her red-gold locks tamed into a braid that fell like a silken rope down her back.

She stared back at them, amusement gleaming in her eyes as a sun-kissed brow arched in question as the Sorceresses rode from the courtyard without so much as a final order, until she stood alone, the rays of the sun piercing through the light cloud cover above to wash her in shades of gold and russet.

"Are you ready to bend over, brother?" Caise murmured from the side of his mouth. "This Princess is out to fuck us both, and I for one do not think we will enjoy the event."

Kai'el chuckled at the analogy.

"Nay, 'tis not a fucking she's out for," he replied, holding his laughter back as he realized the others watched them closely. "She is content to hide no longer. She believes she can best us at our own game."

"Shadowhell, the way she's dressed, I believe she can best us," Caise growled. "Do you think that vest is tied well enough? I would guess several of our warriors are wagering on whether or not those sweet curves stay covered."

Kai'el glanced around the clearing. Wizards and warriors alike glared at the Princess as she approached them lazily.

"Did you keep time?" she asked quite matter-of-factly as she neared them. "I would know how long we will be in the air before we return. I have much to do this day."

Wizards and warriors stared at Kai'el now, shock and disapproval clearly filling their gazes. It was unheard of to take a female on the Owls. The great beasts were made for battle, not for play. Unfortunately, as far as Kai'el was concerned, this Joining/Consort thing was more a battle than many he had fought involving blood and death.

"Ah, Princess, I fear I forgot to keep time," Kai'el admitted with a crooked smile. "What say I allow you to set your time within the air this day. Next time, we shall wager a bit more seriously."

"Definitely more seriously," Caise muttered.

Marina paused before them, staring up at the yellow eye of the owl staring back at her.

"She is a gorgeous creature," she crooned, though she did not reach out to stroke the pure white feathers so obviously tempting her. "I have it heard it said they are quite fierce in battle when Wizards ride upon their backs."

"This is Tamaree." He patted the owl's short neck fondly. "She is indeed fierce in battle, but as gentle as a babe otherwise. And quite friendly."

Tamaree was shuffling softly, inviting Marina's touch, which was unusual enough. Never had Kai'el known of the creature to do such a thing. The owls were amazingly loyal, bonding with but one male, never a set. Caise could not ride Tamaree, just as Kai'el could not ride his Minera unless Caise were upon her back as well.

"Hello, my beauty." Marina's voice lowered, becoming a silken whisper of delight as her hand disappeared within the thick feathers that lifted for her touch.

Tamaree was shameless when demanding affection, preferring her softer, satiny hide to be petted rather than the outer covering of feathers. The owl's eyes drifted half closed as she watched Marina, an expression of sublime pleasure entering her gaze as Marina scratched delicately at her underskin as the distinctive whispery *who* sounded from the large black bill.

"Do they connect with your magick as the unicorns do with the Sorceresses?" Marina asked. "I notice you use no bridle or harness."

"We are indeed bonded," he answered with a slight smile. He had a feeling that did he allow this Princess to ride upon Tamaree's back for long, then the great owl would bond with her as well. They were amazingly intuitive creatures, and Kai'el could sense the owl's knowledge of the alignment of magicks between himself and Marina. Just, he was certain, as Caise's owl would sense were she to ride with him.

"I take it I am to fly with you this morn then?" She turned back to him, her brow lifting again, mocking amusement glittering in the dark violet depths.

He inclined his head in agreement. "This was the wager," he agreed.

"Very well. I need to patrol the western boundaries of Covenan. That area has been difficult for the Sorceresses to reach due to the rough terrain. Until our griffons are fully grown and trained, it is an area well out of our reach."

Her words carried among the courtyard, the early morning silence of the clearing giving her a large audience to overhear her claim.

"Not possible." Drake Dulorne stepped forward, his Twin, Vander, watching curiously. "Griffons heel for none— either Twin, Sorceress nor human. They cannot be tamed or flown."

Marina inhaled in a slow, patience-gathering motion as her expression became a trifle more superior than it had been moments before. She glanced to the Wizard, taking in his tall build, his arrogant bearing.

"Shows how much Wizards truly know, does it not?" she answered as though speaking to a child. "Just because they have hidden these centuries from Wizard magick does not mean the Sorceresses have not known of them. Nor that they do not trust us. I believe they much prefer a gentle hand to a dominating force." The words were kindly delivered, but did not lack the sting they were meant to have.

Dulorne's gray gaze became shuttered, polite as he declined to engage the matter. Of course, the sudden defensive set of Tamaree's large body had much to do with it. No Wizard dared to disregard such a move from the great owls.

"Easy lady." Marina reached up to pat the fierce speckled face, a gentle smile creasing her face as she turned back to Kai'el. "So, do we fly, or do we argue?"

"It would appear, my Princess, that we fly." He waved his hand in invitation to the double saddle the owl wore. It was a practice used when battling off Cauldaran land. There were often injuries, and at times, the owls were too injured to carry the additional weight of a rider. For that reason, the Wizards often used the double saddle rather than the smaller single. "You will ride before me, and direct our flight. Let us see how a Sorceress adapts to the winds."

"One moment." She nodded abruptly before leaving his side and stepping back to the wide steps where a human guard stood ready. He extended a small bundle rather stoically as he glanced at the owls.

The bundle was a leather coat, falling to mid-thigh and lined, it appeared, with ultrasoft rabbin fur. The small, simple creatures were a staple of the Covenan meals. Unfortunately, they were not common to Cauldaran. The lucky little witch.

"Let us fly then."

His little Sorceress was much smarter than he had given her credit for. He had deliberately not mentioned the cold in the higher altitudes to allow himself the chance to wrap her in his own extra leathers and hold her close to his body.

As she neared the owl, Kai'el moved to aid her into the high stirrup of the saddle. She ignored his silent offer, jumping high to grip the pommel before swinging her leg into the stirrup and mounting herself efficiently.

Impressive.

Kai'el followed suit, settling in behind her as she gripped the high arch of the seat and awaited his order to fly. There was no way to muffle the order that went out from The Veressi's warriors at the head of the line.

"Fly to protect those women, Wizards," the Talgaria warrior called out in resigned tolerance. "If Sorceress blood is spilled, our Kings will have our heads."

Marina stiffened before him.

"Yes, do protect your ultimate goal," he heard her mutter, her voice low, throbbing with anger. "If you can find them."

Chapter Eight

℘

Kai'el had to admit, at least to himself, that Marina had managed to surprise him. He hadn't expected her to show up in the courtyard, let alone followed by the two dozen Sorceresses rumored to be part of the Sorceress Brigade.

At least they knew now who the ladies involved were, and a stop could be put to their dangerous underground activities. They had no idea the danger they were facing in seeking out the Seculars themselves and battling with them. The fact that none had been harmed so far was a testament to their luck.

The Seculars were gaining ground within Covenan, and even branching into Cauldaran. They were bloodthirsty and determined to ground all magick on Sentmar beneath their heels.

As though that could be done, he thought with a silent snort as he gave Tamaree the signal to fly. Sentmar power was weakened, there was no doubt, but the magick of the planet itself could never be defeated.

"Hang on, Princess," he murmured in her ear, bracing a palm on her hip as Tamaree rose to her full height, spread her wings and began to move. Three large steps and a hard, smooth flap of her wings and they were ascending.

Kai'el leaned into the high leather back of the saddle, his hand continuing to grip Marina's hip as he used the stirrups at the side to guide the huge feathered bird. The saddle sat high to the creature's neck, clearing the wings enough to allow the rider to stare down at the land below.

As usual, they could see very little through the thick covering of the forest. The small towns and farms inhabited the grassy clearings, but the thick forests were predominant in Covenan. Unlike the Cauldaran, the Sorceresses did not allow forest clearing, neither for homes, nor for farming.

This made patrolling the land difficult at best. Below, the Wizards and warriors were vulnerable to attack on foot. Above, their view was hampered by the trees and brush below. Not that it appeared so thick when on the ground. For weeks now, The Veressi warriors sent ahead by their Wizards swore the forests closed their view deliberately. Kai'el intended to find out.

"The forests are too thick in the west to patrol," he called out above the breeze rushing over them as Tamaree dipped along on the currents of the air. "We would have better luck in the East."

"Luck has naught to do with it, Wizard," she answered with a quick shake of her head. "You are neither Guardian of this land, nor are you a Protector. To the forests, you are an alien magick, it will not whisper its secrets to you no matter where you patrol."

It was the same answer the Queen had given them. Though as yet, the Wizards had not learned who guarded the lands. They knew only that the Protectors were said to be the Sorceress Brigade.

"How do you know when and where to patrol then?" He paid careful to attention to the tenseness of her body, feeling her stiffen at the question.

"The land will let me know," she answered again. "It is connected, bonded to each Covenani Sorceress born within it. The land will tell me what the humans will not."

The land would tell her what the humans would not. Kai'el wanted to growl at her response. She was as forthcoming as ever.

"Princess, how can we protect you if you do not cooperate with us?" He caressed her hip, enjoying the feel of her leather-clad flesh, firm and warm beneath his grip.

"We would first need your protection, Wizard." She turned her head, glaring at him as he stared back at her in surprise.

"The Seculars are not playing a game, Marina," he snapped, his brows lowering as he fought to find the delicate words to assure her of his sincerity. "They will not spare you simply because you are a female. You have seen this already."

"We have protected ourselves and our lands for a millennium, we can continue to do so."

"The Seculars have only grown in strength, and you have done nothing to combat them," he pointed out, staring into her raging eyes.

"Neither have the Cauldaran," she sniffed. "They plague your lands as well. They only amass here, now, believing we will be easier to defeat than are the Wizards. This is where they are wrong, and they will soon see the error of their ways. Now, I ask again if we may fly west to assure the farms there are secure. I have been several days getting out there because of the interference of the big tough males blocking my movements."

She turned, presenting her back once again.

"You have no business in battle," he growled. "You are not built to fight. You are built for warmth and caring, not for blood-letting."

"I was created to protect all that is mine," she replied then, her voice as cold as the Winter Mountains. "I do that however I must."

Kai'el ground his teeth together at her reply. No wonder the other Wizards were suffering from such vast irritability. If the other Sorceresses were as bedamned stubborn as this one, then the alignment of the powers between Wizards and Sorceress were in grave danger.

Unfortunately, he had heard that the Princess Marina was the most timid of the royal sisters, and those of the ladies inhabiting the castle. She was to have been the meekest, the most pliable. It went only to show him that Brianna Veraga did not know her sister as well as she believed she did. This was no meek, timid young woman. Nor was she was the frightened little rabbin she was rumored to be. She was a manipulating little minx instead.

"Very well, we fly west." He gave Tamaree the direction by the shift of his foot against her side, leaning into the saddle and holding Marina close as the great owl changed course and headed for the mountains beyond.

He was very interested to see how she intended to patrol her land above the canopy of leaves below. She seemed not the least worried. Instead, she relaxed marginally, her body flowing with the owl's movements, as contentment seemed to surround her. She enjoyed the flight, he could feel it in the subtle shifts of her body, in the ease in which she finally rested against his chest rather than forcing the small amount of space between them.

The warmth of her sank into his chest, causing him to wonder at the strange feelings welling within him as it did so. Did Caise feel this the night before? he wondered. The surging need to protect her, to forever wrap her in what comfort and security they could provide and keep her far from the battles she seemed intent to engage in.

It was terrifying, he admitted, the knowledge that she was as they had suspected, part of the Sorceress Brigade that sought out the small groups of Seculars moving across the borders between Covenan and the human lands of Yarba. Since the attack on the Princess Brianna before her Joining with the Veraga Twins, the Brigade had been rumored to be growing in strength. Led by the heir apparent Serena, which Kai'el did not doubt, they had become quite adept at ferreting out the Secular movements into Covenan lands and reporting them to their own warriors.

It was only a matter of time before one of them was harmed, though. Bruises healed, as did anger—rape and even death were quite another matter.

"These lands are inhabited by a mix of Covenan and Yarba humans," she spoke as they neared the sheltered valleys at the base of the Whispering Mountains. "Even Covenan humans possess some small magick. An apprenticeship with the land, the ability to direct minute threads of the magick in the air. They are our best farmers, the most productive and caring of the land. The Yarba humans have no ability in those areas, but make up for the lack in hard work and dedication. The land accepts them, so do we."

Below, the land cleared from forest to a patchwork of farms and pastureland. Cattle grazed in lazy herds beneath the bright sun as crops lifted their ripening plumage to the heat above. Tamaree's shadow dipped and spread out over the valley as they flew in a lazy pattern, Caise and Minera moving in parallel as Marina gazed down in wonder below.

He could see the side of her face, watched the play of emotions, the possessiveness, the joy that flooded her that all was well within the valley as she waved to the scattered few who gathered below to stare up at them.

Kai'el maneuvered the owl through sweeping turns, allowing her to survey the wide gorges, and lower slopes of the mountains, flying from farm to farm where she waved and narrowed her eyes to sense the land beneath.

He knew well what she was doing. It wasn't an unknown gift, though it was rare that one who battled, even in a measure as small as Marina, would have that connection as well.

"Harvest will be coming soon." She nodded in approval as Tamaree lifted her wings and ascended once again. "I'll have to send a unit of Covenan warriors out to ensure their protection. The Seculars have been hitting the border farms pretty heavily in recent months."

Interesting.

"We could assign a few warriors to cover this area daily," he offered. "The land is more open here, making it easier to patrol by air than by land."

"You would anyway." She shrugged at the offer. "Our warriors will be assigned in any event, they are as able as your flyers, Wizard Sashtain."

"Kai'el," he reminded her of his name as the owl climbed high above the valley. "You had no problem using my name during the night past."

It was perhaps not exactly nice to remind her of her previous night's play, but it infuriated him each time he heard her use the title Wizard Sashtain.

She tensed before him again, her shoulders straightening as that minute amount of space separated them once again. It infuriated him, the distance she was so quick to place between them. He should allow the alignment, he thought, glaring at her graceful back as he turned the owl toward the forest.

"Are we returning to the castle?" The faint thread of wistful regret in her voice did things to his insides that he would have preferred to ignore.

Returning her to the castle would be advisable—as long as she flew in the saddle before him, she was a temptation he found hard to ignore. Watching Caise touch her the night before, his lips eating at hers, had shredded his control. Forcing his brother away from her as the threads of her power wrapped around them had been near impossible. Especially considering the fact that her magick suckled at his dick like a hot little mouth, licking tongue and all. A second more of the torture and he would have lost all control and come in his breeches.

Had he expected it, he could have delayed the moment they were forced to leave her. But he had not anticipated her loss of control, nor the effect it would have on himself and Caise.

"Only if you wish to." He reached out with his free hand, running his fingers down her braid, longing to see the long, fiery curls free and trailing around his body.

His cock was now spike-hard, the hunger for her tightening his scrotum until he could barely breathe for the pain of arousal. All he could think about was the sight of her with Caise, her lips opening beneath his, welcoming him, inviting him. Would she welcome him? Would her lips part, and her tongue peek out to tempt him?

His fingers curled around the thick braid at the thought of so touching her, pulling her back to his chest as her head turned and she stared back at him hesitantly.

"No fear?" he asked her then.

"Should I fear?"

His lips kicked up in a grin at her question. "Aye, Princess," he growled. "You should fear for my sanity when you stare at me just so, equal parts passion and suspicion. Have I not yet assured you of my noble designs? I would have the alignment given willingly, the Joining freely. I will force nothing from you, nor myself on you."

"And perhaps it is not the fear of the hungers riding you, or even those you call forth within me that are your downfall," she said then, her hands curling around the large forearm now wrapped around her waist.

"Face me," he asked, refusing to touch upon the comment she made. She was leading this discussion into areas that would force her to place distance between them again, and that, he would avoid at all costs. "Turn within the saddle and face me, allow me to feel your lips upon mine, your body against me. Show me it is not those fears that hold you back from my touch."

Foolish courage glittered in her eyes a second before she moved. Kai'el kept close hold of her hips, aiding her in the movement as she turned herself until her legs draped over his, her breasts nearly touching his chest, her sweet pussy so close to his cock he swore he could feel its heat.

He and Caise had chased her for weeks, fighting for a look, a touch, despairing of finding their way into her trust. Not that she trusted them with all she was, but the emergence of the Sorceress Brigade, and her presence in his arms now he took as an all-important step.

"Tell me, Princess," he said then, his fingers reaching up to smooth over her silken cheek. "What would it take to allow the alignment, the Joining, as I know your body and your heart desires? What would convince your mind?"

She stared back at him solemnly, the sad curve of her lips tugging at his heart as he watched her.

"My freedom," she whispered then, and he saw the glittering determination in her eyes to have no less. "Just that, Kai'el. My freedom."

The freedom to fight. The one thing he knew his heart could never survive giving her.

Chapter Nine

ɛɔ

Kai'el felt the heated silk of Marina's hands pressing against his chest, felt the throb of his heart into her palm as lust beat a heavy rhythm through his veins. Her eyes, such a pure intense violet, filled with mystery, and a vulnerable hunger, heated and innocent, tore at his chest. She tempted every dark desire that raged in his soul. And yet, he wanted nothing more than to show her the utmost gentleness as he guided her through the storm of hunger building inside him.

He could feel her magick whispering through her, demanding the Joining just as he could feel his own and Caise's. How unusual, never had he felt either his brother's pleasure, or his pain, yet in this, he could feel the bond growing and knew Caise could feel the pleasure now, even as he did. It had begun the night before, subtle, whispering through his mind as he began to sense the heat, the wild pleasure Caise found in touching her.

Each second that she stared back at him, he could feel it growing. Sweet Mercy, how he needed her, ached for her. The combined arousal, his and his brother's, tempted his control as nothing else had in his lifetime.

"A taste, Marina," he growled then, his hands framing her face, his fingers tunneling into the taut strands of hair, loosening them from her braid as the feel of silk greeted his flesh. "Let me taste."

He could feel the magick building in them now. The three of them, bonding, connecting on threads of magick so slight, as to be invisible, yet stronger than any he had known before.

His thighs clenched as his scrotum tightened, his cock throbbing in near violent demand for release. Release from the breeches holding it back, a release into the tight, silken depths of her body.

"Would be most dangerous." Her breath hitched. He watched her battle to deny him, to deny herself, as it raged in her expressive little face. Her eyes were darkening, sparks of magick glittering within them as her breathing increased.

"Trust me, Marina." His thumb smoothed over her lips, the ever-darkening hunger pushing him to force her to admit to this pleasure if nothing else. "I can hold back the alignment, I'll not see you forced into a Joining, no matter my need for it. We will but kiss, a touch perhaps, a taste of the passion I see in your beautiful violet eyes."

She swallowed, he groaned. Her soft pink little tongue peeked between her lips to lick them with a nervous little flick that had his dick tightening further. Bedamned, if he didn't fuck her soon, he would be mindless with lust.

"I can make you wet and wild, Marina," he promised with a masculine, wicked smile. "If you feel the need for release, I will release you. We will but play."

"And this is what I fear." She smiled tremulously. "You are determined to win, are you not, Wizard? With my power being the prize you seek."

A frown furrowed his brow as he stared back at her.

"Do you believe I will control your magick, Marina? That is yours and yours alone. No Wizard can strip it from you."

"Not without my will." She bit at her lip, and Kai'el could not help the groan that tore from his chest at the sight. He would nibble there as well, if he could but convince her to play. "But we have proved already that I have little will where you are concerned."

"You have much will," he assured her, determined to test her boundaries, to show her the pleasure to be found in a darker, deeper touch. "Shall we put it to the test?"

That fiery little brow arched. Kai'el near chuckled at the sight. This one had a bit of arrogance, a bit of reckless daring that she hid most carefully.

"And how would we do this?" Her fingers moved in small motions against his chest, like a little cat flexing its claws, as she stared back at him in confusion.

"Allow me to bind you," he suggested, knowing the husky pitch of his voice and unable to cover it. He wanted her his way, just once, while she watched him, awake, aware of every touch. "It will hold back your magick, and allow only the pleasure. No alignment, no Joining, but I can bring you release, Marina. I can make you find the depths of pleasure you could never know in any other fashion outside the Joining."

Her lips parted as a shadow of fear flickered in her gaze.

"Are you going to play, baby?" He grinned back at her, daring her, knowing his expression gave reason for her to believe that he knew she would not. "I will, of course, understand if you do not wish to."

He could feel Caise then, his mind reaching closer, his magick joining his in the play he was attempting.

"You believe I cannot?" He could see the vein at the side of her neck pounding, in fear, in arousal. The fear was an aphrodisiac in some cases, he knew. The fear of losing control, or letting another have complete power, for whatever length of time, could be a frightening prospect for a woman of her strength. "How do I know you will respect the bounds of any game? What are the rules of this magick binding?"

"Should you wish to stop, you have only to say so, to think it so," he promised. "I vow to you, that should you do this, you will be released. Upon my magick oath as a Wizard, I will not hold you should you no longer wish it."

There was no vow deeper. It went beyond words, to the heart of magick itself. No matter how he might wish it otherwise, whenever she called their play to an end, his power would release her.

He watched her struggle for breath, for composure. Her thighs tensed over his as the short, sharp little nails pierced his chest.

"So be it," she finally whispered, lifting her hands free and spreading them out to her sides. "For now, I am yours."

Ritual words. They tore through his soul as she gave him leave to do what he had so longed for.

Instantly, fragile threads of pale blue and molten gold magick materialized around her wrists, drawing them behind her as she watched him, vulnerability reflecting within the depths of her eyes as he bound her hands at the small of her back.

"The magick will bind your powers as well." He kept his voice soft, comforting. "No alignment will occur in this, Marina. Only pleasure." He made certain the magick binding her held the complete spell. He couldn't risk even the smallest portion of her power slipping free to meet with theirs during this.

She nodded sharply, her legs tightening on his, the heat of her pussy licking at his cock even through the layers of material separating them.

"We will just play," he promised her once again, lowering his gaze to the metal clasps of her over-jacket, watching as they pulled free at his silent command, while keeping his hands at her hips.

"Captives are naked before their masters," he whispered then. "Will you be my captive, Marina?"

Shock widened her eyes, which did nothing to hide the darkening of their response. Her cheeks flushed a soft pink, her lips trembling beneath his gaze.

"I will say when I will have no more of your games," she told him fiercely. "I am not a child to have each move explained."

Of course she wasn't. She had known just such pleasure within the Valley of Dreams. Restrained, stretched out on the bed of flowers, her body a sensual offering to their feast.

"You are as willful as any new captive Consort," he breathed against her lips, stared into the midnight depths of her eyes. "Do you know what happens to such willful little girls?"

"They get their way." She tried to snap the words, but he could hear the tremor of fear and of longing in her voice.

"Nay," he replied, his hands moving to the metal clasps of her vest as he continued to hold her gaze. "Such Consorts are duly spanked by their Wizards, Marina. Will you take your punishment?"

He didn't give her a chance to reply, rather he sent his magick to deliver the erotic paddling he had decided upon.

His hands itched at the feel of her flesh, the power that struck the first blow between the saddle and the firm flesh of her buttocks returning to his hand the feel of her heated skin.

She flinched, a small O pursing her lips, and as her back arched the minute the bindings of her vest loosened enough to allow the rich inner curves freedom. He felt the shudder that raced through her, felt the heat between her thighs increasing.

"Many reluctant Consorts found their first taste of passion in just this way." He allowed another sharp slap to be delivered, feeling her response as it shook her body and he parted the vest further.

Another slap had her arching, her knees bending further to bring her flush against the hard wedge of his cock. Kai'el's teeth snapped together as her vest parted freely then, the swollen curves of her breasts with their hardened nipples lifting to him. Bedamned if he wouldn't have a taste of her.

He sent another slap to her ass, while Caise's magick delved into the silken cleft and raked the entrance to her anus with a delicate touch. Her head tipped back, her breasts arching as though in offering.

Kai'el could refuse temptation no longer. His head bent as he framed each globe in his hands, his lips opening to cover one perfect tip as a whimper of pleasure passed her lips.

He ached for her with a desperation he could but barely control. He felt the slaps to her ass, aware of Caise probing at the small entrance there, and closed his eyes as he immersed himself in the touch, the taste and the heat of her.

He could not push much further. He would have to end this soon, for Sentinels as his witness, he could not bear the torment much longer.

He suckled at her breast, gripping the nipple between his teeth to nip at it erotically as she cried out his name, then allowed his tongue to soothe the ache. The hard little tip was fiery-hot, the soft pink color now flushed a darker red from his mouth and her arousal.

"When the Wizard had shown his Consort her punishment, he then showed her the pleasure."

It was all he could do to breathe as he felt Caise probing at her ass and he sent his own magick to the liquid heat flowing from her pussy at the same moment his lips covered hers. Through the drenched slit he allowed it to slide as his tongue licked over the seam of her lips. He felt the silken spill of her juices as she gasped, her lips opening for him. He tasted her, his tongue easing into her mouth longing for the taste of her as the power covered her swollen clit and he imagined his tongue sinking into her pussy.

Her kiss was like fire as it tore through his brain, sending pleasure exploding through his system. Innocent, yet aware. Blistering hot and hungry. She opened to him, her tongue twining with his as she arched closer, writhing in need.

Now he knew why Caise had come so close to losing all control the night before. Sentinel's blood if she wouldn't destroy even the strongest Wizard's will as she rubbed and pressed against him, her body eagerly accepting each touch given it.

She was close, much closer than even she knew. He could feel the heat and hardness of the little bud peeking between the folds of satin flesh as his lips moved back, moved lower. It throbbed erratically, erotically, pulsing in time to the blood thundering through her veins.

His lips moved to her breast once again, his mouth sucking her nipple in as his magick moved in counterpoint at her clit. He licked and sucked at the hard bud, knowing what she felt there, she felt lower as well.

She writhed in his grip then, forcing him to clasp her hips to keep her seated in the saddle as Caise began to probe into the entrance of her rear. Her head was thrown back, mindless cries falling from her lips as he felt her, gods, he felt her explode.

She tightened in his arms, arching fiercely as the heat of her cunt dampened her breeches and seared his cock. He felt the flashing pleasure tear through her, exploding in her womb and sending hard, exquisite shafts of lightning-hot sensation to rip through her pussy, before detonating through every cell of her body.

The echo of it filled both himself and Caise. He jerked his head back from her breast, clenching his teeth as he fought back his own release. Sentinels, he could not allow his release. Should he do so, then the power holding her magick back would disintegrate, forcing a Joining as nothing else could.

The moment he felt the brilliant shards of pleasure easing within her he quickly, forcibly pulled his magick back, releasing her. He was fighting to breathe, panting as hard as she as a growl of sheer torment tore from his throat. Her hands moved to him, pushing at his shirt, tearing at the stays in an attempt to touch him. Her passions were roused, and the release, though exquisite, not near enough.

"Easy," he growled, his hands gripping hers, his lips pressing to her forehead. "Hold back, Princess, or we are both doomed."

Her head fell back, her eyes opening to stare back at him in hungry demand as he fought to rein in the magick building between them.

"I fear I am doomed anyway." Her hands clenched his shoulders, her fingers clenching in the fabric of his shirt as she leaned against him.

Marina could not believe what had just occurred. Even now, the pleasure tore through her in waves, demanding more despite the flight she had taken on rapture's wings moments before.

The need refused to abate. She would have no ease, no peace, she knew, unless the Joining occurred. And the time would soon come when her body and her magick would give her no choice. Once brought to life, it was said the pinnacle of magick would not sleep again, unless released; it would reach its peak, before withering away to nothing. She could not risk losing all her magick.

"You make it sound as a fate worse than death," he growled as he eased her around once again, holding her back to him, pressing her head to his shoulder. "What harm could befall you, Marina, in the Joining?"

What harm? Her lips curled in bitter awareness. When her Queen Mother returned from the Sentinel Temples, he would learn what harm could befall her. The Sorceress Brigade was now revealed, and soon she would have no choice but to acknowledge her place within it. As Guardian of the Lands, her power and her connection with the land allowed it to speak to the others, to whisper of evil, of deeds committed. Once her mother learned how she had used her power and the position given into her keeping, the eruption of fury would be heard far and wide. And she did not want to even consider how this venture into pleasure was going to affect what had once been a perfectly content life. Sweet Mercy, after such pleasure, she would never know contentment again without experiencing more.

"You could not even imagine," she whispered then. "You could not even..."

The words broke off as she blinked, a flaring sense of danger shooting through her mind as she sat up straighter. Her eyes narrowed, her gaze falling to the land below her.

Pleasure receded instantly as she felt the waves of fury and of pain, echoing from the forest below.

"Marina?" Kai'el questioned her sudden tenseness.

A scream grew within her mind, a call for help, not so much in words as in the danger flowing from the forest floor on invisible threads of magick. Her connection to the Sorceresses in the Brigade and the land itself created a bond, a connection easily accessed in times of danger for those she protected.

Clumsy, fighting to re-clasp her vest, her gaze turned to the green foliage as Kai'el's hands moved to quickly re-close the clasps that her trembling fingers could not work.

"There..." She pointed in the distance where the forest opened around a crystalline lake, a pure deep blue amid the brilliant foliage. "We need to get there quickly, to the southern tip."

She shook her head, fighting to dislodge the thick haze of desperation tormenting her pussy and to concentrate instead on the danger she could feel pulsing through the air.

"What's wrong?" His voice darkened dangerously but the great owl turned and dipped, tucking her feathers in marginally to gain speed.

"I'm not certain," she called back as the wind around them increased. "I only know several of the Sorceresses are calling out. They're in trouble."

"Sentinels bedamned," he cursed, shifting his body, the hard thighs alongside hers tensing a second before the owl pulled her wings in closer yet and picked up speed.

"There." She pointed to where two of the Sorceresses, Astra and Camry, were battling against two much larger, fiercer males.

Their magick surrounded them valiantly as sword met sword, but it was obvious the two women weren't strong enough to hold out much longer.

As she watched in shock, pale blue and golden bands of power streaked from Caise and Kai'el, moving to weaken the Seculars, to stay each blow aimed at the women as the owls pulled up abruptly, their great feather-covered legs lower as they came to a landing at a run.

Caise jumped from his saddle to tackle the first of the men as Marina caught sight of the battle waging in the trees. One of the great owls lay on her side just within the tree line, where four of the Sorceresses surrounded two fallen warriors against the six males facing them.

"Kai…" She pointed to them.

"Stay put," he yelled as he came out of the saddle, magick flying from him to sizzle around the men fighting to gain access to the two warriors.

Oh yes indeed, she would stay put, she thought with a roll of her eyes as she jumped from the owl, calling out to the land beneath them. Immediately, the trees began to sway, whipping around the fallen warriors and wounded owl, mixing with Caise and Kai'el's powers as they fought to provide a protective shield around the Sorceresses as they engaged the Secular soldiers.

"Camry, Astra, merge with me," she called out as the two women rushed to her side.

Their powers whipped together, as the four Sorceresses fighting against the Seculars had done. A rainbow of magick threads began to weave around the Seculars' legs, tripping them, binding them, allowing the power whipping from Kai'el and Caise to focus with greater efficiency.

One by one, they began to fall, bound by the Wizards as the Sorceresses' power aided in delaying their fight long enough for them to secure them.

It seemed the Wizards were not as all-powerful as they would have them believe, she thought with a snort. They could bind singularly, but against a group, they were hampered by that weakness. Which explained why Wizards fought in groups, just as the Sorceresses did.

"What happened here?" Marina rushed to the fallen warriors, drawing back as the Sorceresses parted to reveal two of the healers working desperately to use their powers to keep them alive.

"We cannot aid the owl, Princess," Selectra, their strongest healer called out weakly as the fiery glow of her magick infused the warrior she knelt beside. "Your Wizards must call for help."

"They're on their way." Caise came to kneel beside the fallen warrior, watching as the Sorceress moved her hand slowly around the wounds on the unconscious male's chest. They were near fatal. His brother lay sprawled several feet from him, blood congealing at his temple as Solara's brilliant emerald magick flowed over him.

"The wounds are grave," Selectra whispered as Astra came behind her, kneeling behind her to brace her weakened form. "They must hurry."

"Seconds, Sorceress, they are only seconds away," Kai'el promised somberly. "Where is the other owl? These warriors did not share their ride."

"The other we could not save," Samara, Selectra's younger sister answered then. "The owl went into the lake on the first shot from the Secular's crossbow. This one," she nodded to the fallen owl, "caught the brother in its great talon, but the next arrow brought it down as well. I do not know if she can be saved."

113

Marina was aware of the two owls Caise and Kai'el had flown moving around their fallen sister.

"Caise, The Veressi's warriors arrive," Kai'el called out from where he stood vigilance over the Seculars.

Marina looked into the sky, seeing the convergence of owls as they began to move into the area. They did not land — as they neared the ground, their warriors dropped gracefully from their backs while their owls ascended once again to the tops of the large trees overhead, which strengthened and welcomed their weight.

Four of the broad, dangerous warriors moved to those who had fallen, gently nudging the Sorceresses aside before laying their hands over the warriors' wounds. The magick that poured from them was shades of deep burgundy and maroon, the greatest of the healing magicks.

Several others moved to the owl that still lay at the tree line watched over by Caise and Kai'el's great birds.

As Marina watched, she was impressed greatly by how well the warriors worked with the Wizards who had landed with them. Power merged and shared, creating a secure force about the area as well as lending strength to the wounded warriors.

"What happened?" One of the most fearsome warriors, one of those sent by The Veressi, moved toward Marina, his striking midnight-blue eyes narrowed, the wealth of black lashes shielding them making him appear forbidding rather than handsome. His features were arrogant, striking planes and angles of chilling strength.

If this was a Veressi warrior, then Marina feared to see The Veressi themselves.

"Your warriors are too arrogant, Veressi." Selectra rose slowly to her feet, drawing the fierce warrior's gaze. "If this is an example of your keen minds and fighting skills, then I say we were doing much better before your arrival. At least then we had only ourselves to protect, instead of males too confident and certain of themselves to prepare for threats they cannot see."

The warrior braced his fists on his lean hips, turning to stare at the brunette Sorceress as she faced him, weak but undaunted.

"I am not Veressi," he informed her, his voice dark. "I am Talgaria."

"Is there a difference?" Selectra mocked his cool reply as Marina fought to hide her smile. If the warrior thought to use his glare to force that Sorceress to back down, then he had another thought coming.

"There is much difference," he grunted. "But my question has not been answered. Those are warriors of The Veressi clan, they would not have been so easily taken unawares, nor would their owls have flown them into such danger. I would know how this happened."

"When you figure it out, then you may inform us as well," Selectra snapped, her green-blue eyes flaring with anger.

"We heard the owl's screams from farther within the forest and saw the first fall. As we rushed to the area, the other had taken an arrow as well and the warriors lay on the ground, the Seculars rushing for them. We sent out a call for aid and the rest is as you see it now." She waved her hands to the Sorceresses gathering around her. "We can tell you no more than that."

He stared back at them, eyes narrowed, cold, icy fury filling his expression.

"Wizards, The Veressi will wish to question these," he gestured to the bound Seculars, "when they arrive."

"It is not the decision of the Sashtains, Talgaria." Marina stepped forward then, keeping her voice calm, her demeanor firm. "This is for the House of Sellane to decide, and I'm certain my sister will wish for our own Justices to question them. They are as effective as your Veressi."

115

The Talgaria warrior turned to her slowly.

"Rhydan, do not overstep your bounds," Kai'el warned him, a throb of power, of demand echoing in his voice as Marina stared back at the warrior, her brow arching mockingly.

"Aye, Rhydan Talgaria, remember whose land you occupy at this moment. This is not Veressi ground, nor Wizard lands. These lands are under Sellane rule and protection."

His lip lifted in a snarl as he turned from her. If she were not very much mistaken she could have sworn he muttered, "not for long". Marina's head lifted in determination. He would learn differently.

"Prepare to move out." She flashed Kai'el a hard glare as she spoke, anger surging inside her at yet another sign that the Wizards thought they could overtake Covenan by strength alone. It no more than proved her and Serena's suspicions. They would learn the women of these lands were not as weak as they wished to believe.

She stood back, her Sorceresses gathering around her as owls landed and the wounded were eased into the saddles, each with a healer behind him. The Seculars were finally bound with rope rather than magick and stood in the clearing for the great owls to then swoop down and grip them in huge talons before flying them toward the Covenan castle.

"Princess Marina, Tamaree awaits." Kai'el moved to her, his expression set, determined.

"Selectra, bring the Sorceresses in, we'll meet at nightfall," she muttered to the warrioress as she stared back at the Wizard.

"We'll be there, Princess. Good luck in peeling your shadows from your back, though." She nodded toward Kai'el. "Should you need help, call us. We'll manage somehow."

Marina feared that might be harder than any of them anticipated.

Chapter Ten

ဢ

"It would appear the Wizards have yet again roused your ire."

Marina turned in startled surprise as Garron's voice rumbled behind her. Her hands smacked to the table before her, rattling the goblets and bottle of wine that accompanied the platter of food laid out for her in her room.

"Dragon, I would appreciate notice before you materialize behind me," she snapped as she jerked her overcoat from her shoulders and flung it to the chair beside her.

Stalking across the room, she ignored the food and wine, running one hand over her hair as she propped the other on her hip.

"I have grown weary this day of dealing with the supposed superior male intellect. I would appreciate some peace," she informed him, glaring at the dragon over her shoulder.

He stood arrogantly in the center of his room, his forearms folded over his scaly chest, his brow lowered over his black eyes. He seemed less than pleased. The knowledge that she may have somehow disappointed him bothered her, though she couldn't be certain why.

"Peace is found in little enough supply, Princess," he sighed, his tone weary. "The warriors wounded in the forests are recovering. I checked in on them before coming here. Their injuries are serious, but recoverable."

She nodded, a short, sharp movement as she faced him, crossing her arms over her chest and awaiting whatever it was he had to say. It was certain to irk her to no end, but she knew

117

she had no choice but to hear him out. Garron wasn't easily ordered from any area of the castle. Even her Queen Mother had trouble convincing the dragon to obey her commands.

"Strange, that they were caught unawares," he murmured. "Cauldaran Warriors are normally quite diligent."

Her eyes narrowed.

"So the Talgaria informed us," she answered, keeping her anger at bay. "I can only assume there is a reason I am being told this yet again."

"You are the Keeper of the Lands, Princess," he said, his voice soft, without inflection. "Would you not sense unnatural magick upon your ground?"

She paused, her gaze sharpening as she watched him. Yes, she had felt a difference by the lake after the attack. A subtle, shadowy magick that she had attributed to so many temperamental males in one place. But the more she had thought about it, the more it had bothered her. And it bothered her even more now, at Garron's suggestion of unnatural magick. Dark, malevolent magick.

"There is much unnatural magick within Covenan, with the appearance of so many Wizards and warriors," she replied in frustration, tilting her head as she watched the dragon more closely now. "It would take time to sift through the differences to detect the darker powers."

He nodded. "I have sensed a difference this day in the magick weaving about the land, though I cannot place from where it comes, nor where it is directed. As Keeper of the Lands, Princess, you may have greater insight. Something is afoot with the strength the Seculars are gaining. They should have never been able to take those Wizards from the skies."

Marina breathed in roughly. It was no more than she had suspected herself. She had felt the hidden vibrations of magick each time she had confronted the Secular soldiers herself, though it was so similar to Wizard magick that she had been unable to separate the two and make sense of it.

"Do you suspect one of the Wizard Twins of being in league with the Seculars?" she asked, keeping her voice low. "They have grown stronger only since the Twins have invaded Covenan."

"If I knew this, I would combat it myself," he grunted. "Whoever or whatever aids the Seculars is well hidden, Princess. We can only attempt to separate the different magicks as we confront them, until we can learn the truth of it. Remember, each Sorceress, warrior and Wizard has a different feel, a different depth of power. Become familiar with them as you sense each."

"It seems to me that would be a job better suited to a dragon of magick," she replied with an arch of her brow at the suggestion.

"So it would be, if the dragon in question were not highly suspect as far as the Wizards are concerned," he informed her, sarcasm filling his voice as his forearms spread before him. "It seems they believe any dragon in league with the Sorceresses for so many years must certainly be weak in both magick and senses."

His expression was so droll, so filled with wicked amusement that Marina could do no more than chuckle at the sight.

"What do they know." She waved her hand negligently as she moved back to the table, pouring a goblet of wine as she considered the thought that another of magick would be working against them.

"Have there been Wizard Twins to turn against their own before?" She had heard the Cauldaran were amazingly loyal, adhering to a strict code of honor.

"I have not heard of such," he revealed. "But I associate with Sorceresses rather than Wizards," he reminded her. "The view is much better." He waggled his brows suggestively.

"I can see why Mother curses you so heartily, Dragon," she laughed at the sight. "I would wager you say such to her often."

"Of course." He shrugged at the suggestion. "Your mother is much fairer game in a war of words. Such intelligence to be so easily provoked." He clucked in mocking despair. "She strengthens by the year, though."

"Dealing with you, I would not doubt it." She sighed deeply before bringing the wine to her lips and fortifying herself with a strong drink.

Warmth spread through her insides as the delicate drink worked its effects through her system. The sexual effects of Caise's touch the night before, and Kai'el's earlier in the day still moved through her. She could feel it building in her womb with each confrontation, refusing to settle, or to abate despite the so-called release she had found this day. It had done nothing but force her to crave even more. She feared the apex of her power was building as well. Were that true, Sentinels help her, there would be no refusing the Joining when the peak was reached.

Her chest ached at the thought, and deep within, her heart clenched. If only she could trust her Wizards. To know they would understand her love of the land and not demand her removal from it. But she feared such would not be the case.

"You fight a losing battle, Princess," the dragon remarked then. "Even I can feel the power building within you. Soon, the decision must be made."

Rather than speaking, she drank further at the wine, hoping that in relaxing the surging anger flaring inside her that she could still the arousal. She feared such would not be the case.

"Such decisions must be delayed," she informed him, her voice sharp. "I must meet with Serena and the others for now. The Talgaria are fighting the questioning of the prisoners by our Justices and already demanding their immediate removal to Cauldaran. This concerns me greatly, Garron. Why would they not wish us to question those who strike in Covenan land? And why would they believe we would allow such a thing? Their warriors guard the cells now, and they appear immovable. Without our Queen Mother, there is little we can do except keep them here. But I fear they will eventually weaken the magick our Priestess has weaved about the cells. It is building to a confrontation."

"I have requested an audience with Queen Amoria at the Temple," he told her, nodding in agreement at her words. "I have not yet received a reply. Do I not hear from her soon, then other measures will be taken."

It was not unusual that her Queen Mother be out of contact while at the Temples. Especially to a male, even a dragon. But at such a time as now, it was highly inconvenient.

"I wish you luck," she sighed, finishing her wine before replacing the goblet to the table. "I must bathe and dress before this meeting, if you do not mind to leave."

She could not escape Kai'el's scent. As though it had sunk into her pores, tempting her, reminding her of his touch, his kiss. The heated bathing pools beneath the castle were her only hope. She needed to immerse herself into the cleansing waters, to find some peace, to wash the scent of those males away from her.

"Good luck, Princess. And should you need me, remember..." Black eyes stared back at her with piercing awareness.

"I need only to call." Aye, she remembered well. It gave her confidence, reminded her daily that no matter the threat, Garron would hear her call, just as he had once before.

"You need only call, child." The hard, leathery lips quirked with an affection she had grown to depend on throughout her life. He had filled the place left vacant by her father many, many years before. For her as well as for her sisters. Their instructor, protector, and even at times, their coconspirator in their immature pranks.

"And call I shall," she promised, holding back a sudden spurt of tears threatening to spill to her eyes. "Now, leave me be. I must bathe the scent of Wizard Twins from my body and prepare to meet with my sister. I would guess her rage will rival that of the Queen Mother's before this night is over. Already, she is threatening to throw the Wizards from the castle and their warriors into the pits. I am inclined to agree with her."

He chuckled, the sound raspy, rough. "And so shall I aid you should you have need. I go now to find my rest. I will be watching, though."

He blinked from sight, going wherever he went when he was not tormenting the castle with his mockery and male ways. Marina stared at the area where he had stood, her brow furrowing in worry. If, as he suggested, the Seculars were backed by magick, then trouble was definitely brewing. Perhaps more trouble than they could combat alone, as Sorceresses. And it was possible, just possible that the Wizards knew this. Which meant it was also possible that they were behind it.

* * * * *

Kai'el stood at the window of the receiving room of their suite, staring up at the rings of magick circling the moons overhead. There was a subtle thickening in one ring, it appeared not as misty as it had been before the Joining of Brianna Sellane and the Veraga Twins. The Wizard kings had taken their Consort back to Cauldaran, hoping to infuse the power within that land as he and Caise moved to secure their Consort. The Veressi would be arriving soon, intent on demanding the Rite of Reception from the Princess Serena. That joining would combine two of the greatest powers on the planet if the magick aligned. It would also open the way for the Wizards to begin settling within Covenan with selected

Sorceresses as others joined with their Wizards in Cauldaran. The separation of the Magicks would then cease once the two greatest powers of the land were aligned. The alignment of Princess Serena with the powerful Keepers of Cauldaran would effectively end the hesitation of the other Sorceresses in accepting the Wizards and Warrior Twins.

It was a deception that did not always sit well with Caise and Kai'el. It was one he greatly suspected the Princess Marina was already onto. Her distrust of them didn't help matters. And now, after the day's events, Kai'el was beginning to wonder at the plan himself.

"The magick was subtle," Caise informed him from the other side of the room. "Impossible to track or to follow, but near."

Kai'el grimaced at this news.

"Have the Seculars been questioned yet?" He gripped the rock frame of the window ledge, his eyes narrowing as he stared into the star-studded sky.

"The Sorceress Justices have enclosed the cells against the Wizards. We have several working to unravel the spells, but it does not sit well with them. Such deception is not one of honor, Kai'el, no matter what The Veressi believe. The Talgaria warriors are pushing for stronger measures against the Sorceresses' magick, but I've given the order to refrain for now. The antagonism it will engender will do more to hurt our cause than to see it furthered."

The Sorceress Justices had no idea the darkness moving around them, and until the Wizards could pinpoint the threat, there was no need in causing panic. The subtle shifts of magick were unmistakable, though. There was no doubt magick was strengthening the Seculars.

"We must find the Keeper of the Lands," he sighed then. "She would be one of the Sorceress Brigade, we know this. Which one is the strongest in magick?"

"Impossible to tell," Caise replied. "I've searched among the ladies myself, feeling for their magick, and cannot sense anything powerful enough for a Keeper. They have potential, each of them. Together, they are a force to be reckoned with, but still not as powerful as one Wizard set. The Keeper should be easier to detect."

"What of the Princess Serena?" Kai'el mused. "She holds herself carefully aloof, staying beyond most Wizards."

"Possible, but doubtful." Caise's response reflected his own suspicions. "She leads the Brigade, we saw that with Consort Brianna's abduction. She would be the strongest, as their leader."

"The Veressi would not be pleased to learn this," Kai'el grunted.

Nay, they would not be. The Veressi were Keepers of Cauldaran, they could not be separated from the lands they guarded. Just as the Keeper of Covenan could not be separated from her lands. To do so would be to tempt the very heart of the magick they possessed as well as that of the lands.

"I do not believe, though, that the Keeper is the Princess Serena," Caise finally sighed. "The others have been carefully courting the ladies we now know are part of the Brigade, they agree that none of those Sorceresses seem to have such power. So whichever one holds it, guards the secret carefully."

"Just as Consort Brianna does," Kai'el growled, pushing himself from the window. "Until we identify the Keeper and align her with Wizard or Warrior Twins, we will not have the answers we need. This problem grows more difficult by the day. When humans can pick our warriors from the air because of the magick shielding them, we are too vulnerable. And the power it would take to do such a thing and leave such a small trace concerns me greatly, Caise."

"The Talgaria are certain these Seculars would have the information they need if we could question them soon enough.

The Princess Serena refuses them at every turn, though. At the moment, we are at standoff."

"This deception will be the death of us all," Kai'el snarled as he faced his brother.

"We have no choice if we are to keep the secret of this knowledge." Caise shook his head at the problem facing them all. "By revealing ourselves and our suspicions, we would be warning the one behind it. It is obvious, if Wizards are behind this, that they have somehow managed to incorporate a spy within the Brigade. We cannot risk alerting that spy."

"What of the dragon, Garron?" Kai'el paced to the bar where a small cask of Wizards' Elixir awaited him. Sentinels, how he had missed that brew.

"Your guess is as good as mine where the dragon is concerned." Caise lifted his goblet and sipped from his own drink as Kai'el poured one. "The Sentinel Priests are not revealing anything, if they know much of him, and claim the dragon is loyal to the House of Sellane, which could mean anything."

Kai'el snorted in disgust. The Sentinel Priests were as helpful as wood slugs at this time. They supposedly knew nothing except that the alignment of powers within the heart of Sentmar magick was now in danger. Without the merging of Wizards and Sorceress once again, then all of Sentmar could be doomed by the Secular movement.

Their own problems with the Princess Marina were not helping matters. The alignment of magick was imminent, but getting there was threatening their sanity. The woman was the most stubborn he had ever heard tell of. Gaining her trust was not an easy matter. Suspicious, yet so sensual, so tempting that holding back their hungers was becoming near impossible. The burning needs and building magick were becoming impossible to control, especially with her experimental little touches and blistering kisses. Kai'el feared that much more would break their determination to allow her the time to accept the Joining on her own.

"There is no way to allow the time our Consort is taking, Kai," Caise sighed then, speaking the thoughts tormenting his own mind. "She may not be the Keeper, but she is our Consort. She will strengthen the overall alignments, if nothing else. We must move soon."

Aye. But in doing so, they would gain, rather than her love, her resentment. Taking her from Covenan would not please her. She loved her people, and her home, just as they loved theirs.

"The Talgaria will find the Keeper soon enough, I pray," Kai'el reflected. "The Veressi is willing enough to allow them to disassociate with their lands and to Consort with these instead. Though losing them will not go unnoticed in Cauldaran. They are strong warriors."

"They will do well here." Caise shrugged, though Kai'el knew he held the same concerns. That the Keeper would not be easily found, and when she was, convincing her to Consort with those of her magick counterparts may well prove harder than taking a Princess to Consort. Which was not easy at all.

Chapter Eleven

ফ

Marina sat at her sister's side in the receiving hall the next morning, taking Serena's place on the throne dais as Serena took their Queen Mother's throne to hear the objections of the Talgaria warriors in the case of the Secular prisoners.

The Sorceress Justices sat along the side of the room to the right, on Serena's side. To Marina's side sat the Wizard Twins acting as Justices for the warriors. Ranged about the room were the witnesses to each side, observing the proceedings with interest. Marina was growing irritated with the incessant arguing and she was certain the warriors were as well. The Talgaria were becoming more impatient as the morning wore on.

"Princess Serena, we greatly understand your position of authority in this matter," Rhydan Talgaria stated between clenched teeth. "We ask only that our Wizards or warriors be given a chance to question the prisoners as well. Two of our greatest warriors were nearly killed in the attack, and their rights to just answers and cause should be heeded as well."

"Warrior Talgaria, we do not in any way belittle the Wizards' just cause," Serena answered as calmly now as she had for the past hours. "I agree their wounds were grave and the attack committed on Covenani lands, but our laws, as I have stated, are our own, and not under Wizard nor warrior jurisdiction. Our laws state that only our Sorceress Justices have such rights where questioning or final judgment is concerned. It is not in my place to disregard those laws."

"The Ruling head of Covenan has the right to displace any such laws," he argued once again. "Even your Justices agree to this."

"But I am not the Ruling head," she pointed out, her features composed, her lavender eyes as cool as the glaciers in Winter Mountain. "I am only acting in my Queen Mother's stead until her return. I do not have these powers. I have requested that the Justices allow you your time with them — that request has been denied. There is naught else that I can do."

Marina sensed then, the stress in her sister's voice. She knew Serena had argued vehemently for the Wizards to be allowed to question the Seculars, but the wizened women had held firm in their denials.

Rhydan propped his hands on his hips, his eyes narrowing upon the throne with lethal fury.

"This is unacceptable, Princess Serena. I demand audience with your Queen Mother immediately."

Serena's laughter was light, her smile cool as she spread her hands outward in helpless denial.

"My dear Warrior, even I cannot gain audience with her at this time. As you know, she is currently in the Sentinel Temples conferring with the Priests and Priestess at this time. None can reach her. Even I."

Tension escalated within the room as the warriors muttered to themselves and turned to their Wizard commanders in whispered debate. Marina watched suspiciously as several moved to Caise and Kai'el, speaking to them in low tones as the Twins shook their heads, their gazes reflecting their building anger.

Something was afoot here, and clearly the Wizards were torn in regards to whatever The Veressi head warriors had to say.

Long minutes later, Rhydan returned before them, glaring furiously at Serena.

"Princess Serena, as you have stated, your Ruling head is unavoidably absent, leaving Covenan in a state of chaos amid these attacks. You are neither powerful enough, nor strong enough to defend yourselves..."

"I would cease this line of attack were I you," Serena snapped, her voice sharp, disapproving as she overrode the warriors. "These lands have been adequately protected, as you saw for yourself. Were it not for my Sorceress Brigade your warriors would be dead. Do not dig for yourself a hole you cannot climb from, Warrior."

The warning fell on deaf ears.

"By the mandates of our own bylaws, in such cases, the acting head may be challenged, and if defeated, replaced until the Ruling head once again returns."

Marina moved slowly from her chair, standing before the warriors and sorceresses now, aware of the Wizards looking on in interest as Serena shot to her feet as well.

"You would not dare to challenge me," Serena snapped. "You have no place here, Warrior. Neither you nor your Wizard commanders. And you have no rights within this castle. Do not test my patience in such a way."

"Or what, Princess?" he drawled, his voice assured, confident. "I challenge you to the right to Rule until your Queen Mother returns and can then take her rightful place. It is obvious you have neither the control nor influence over even your own Justices or Sorceresses. Your rule is weakened and therefore will your country be weakened."

A gasp could be heard by the Sorceresses who stood behind them, not so much in shock from his words, but by the fact that they were quickly relieved of their swords by the warriors flanking them.

Marina's gaze flew to Caise and Kai'el, fury mounting inside her as they stayed silent, their expressions brooding as they watched the proceedings. Marina could not believe that warriors, rather than Wizards, were attempting such an outlandish display.

"Do you think my Sorceresses are the only security this land possesses?" Serena's voice was one of forced calm now. "Do you believe this you are gravely mistaken, Warrior. You will have a war on your hands that even the Seculars could not match should you attempt to take this throne. Now cease your demands, return my Sorceresses' weapons and leave this hall immediately."

"Release your throne, Princess," Rhydan growled as though she were of no consequence. "Do you wish your weak-magicked males to be harmed, then so be it. But we will not stand by while Seculars take advantage of your weakness and overtake this land."

Marina's fists clenched at the warrior's demands, and the evidence that once again Cauldaran males would attempt to rule them where they had no cause. Their arrogance and superior attitudes were fuel to the flames of anger twisting inside her. Magick that lurked just beneath the surface began to build. Control which weeks before had been firmly held, now threatened to break free of the bonds she had placed on it.

This was her land. This hall was her sister's rule, not for warriors to challenge for and take as though their rights were somehow held in higher regard than their female counterparts.

The hall shook. Shock staggered the faces of Wizards and warriors alike as dust rained from the ceiling, and the floor beneath them tipped and swayed in response to his words.

"Think you that this land will allow you to overtake it, Wizard?" Serena asked carefully as Marina fought to control her fury. The ground beneath them shuddered at her protest, willing to quake and tremble at her slightest command.

"Think you that we will allow such theatrics to sway us, Princess?" He smirked then. "Even now The Veressi fly for this valley and the Rite of Reception they have claimed. Once the Joining commences, what choices will you have?"

Marina turned slowly to Caise and Kai'el.

"Stop this immediately," she ordered them, the fury rising within her nearly breaking her control.

"They do not command The Veressi, Princess," Rhydan growled.

"And you do not command the Covenani, warrior," Serena snarled. "Think you that you can walk in here and demand anything? At any time? Think you that I would allow such arrogance to overtake the Sorceresses as your ancestors thought they could overtake their will a millennium ago? You have not learned from the past, but by the blood of the Sentinels you will learn by the present."

A wave of magick suffused the room, heralding no great violence or shifting of the ground. Rather it heralded one irate, by all means disapproving dragon breathing steam from nostrils flared with fury.

Garron stood before the throne, his scales flared, glowing a wicked ruby-red as his eyes flared demon-bright and yellow.

"Do you dare to threaten women, Warrior?" His voice thundered through the room as a ring of fire began to burn before the warriors, forcing them back as they stared at the dragon in shock.

His head turned slowly, his yellow eyes glaring at the Wizards who had risen slowly to their feet, their magick whipping in threads about them.

A smile, cold and ruthless, shaped his leathery lips.

"We can do this the easy way." His voice seemed to echo from the very pits. "I can tell you simply that no Wizard will take by force so much as an inch of what the Sorceresses claim as their own. Rather land, castle, body or soul. Or, my dear Wizards, I can do this…" Magick flew from his fingertips. A rainbow of dark hues, swirling in thick threads about his body, hissing and growling as though demons spurred them as they strained toward the males filling the room.

"We learned our lessons a thousand years before, Warrior Talgaria," Serena snarled then, her voice echoing her fury.

"Never has the House of Sellane been without the protection the Sentinels swore it would always possess. You do not rule here. Not you, nor your Veressi Twins. And in this attempt you have made…" Her smile was cold, filled with triumph. "In the name of your Veressi, you have made a grave error. Until the Queen Mother returns, no other Wizard Twin or warrior of magick shall cross the boundaries of this castle…" Garron's magick whipped about the room before flashing through the walls to surround the castle grounds. "Until my Queen Mother returns, there will be no Rite of Reception, there will be no Demand for Courtship, and there will be no Joining with yet another betraying, controlling Wizard Twin by this Princess or any other Sorceress who wishes to refuse such. I will be damned before you will stalk into my hall, and face me with such blatant disregard. Think this over, Warrior Talgaria, while you await your masters' arrival and their response to your actions."

With that, she turned and swept quickly from the dais to disappear through the exit behind the thrones. Marina turned to Caise and Kai'el, anger churning inside her, betrayal whipping through her.

"Did you agree with this travesty?" she questioned them, dreading the answer, fearing the worst.

"Fortunately not." Kai'el's lips curved in dry amusement. "It would seem we chose the winning side for once, wouldn't you say, Caise?" he questioned his brother. Caise cursed, staring back at Garron in brooding anger.

"Bedamned if we didn't warn them about the dragon," he growled, shaking his head. "No, Princess, we did not agree to this, nor would we have upheld it. But…" His gaze darkened. "It does not change the problem as it stands. Your Justices will not find the answers because their magick is no match for a Wizard, and this you and your sister know well. As do your Justices. Perhaps you should consider this before the final decision to force their hand is made."

"We do not obey males." The oldest of the Justices rose to her feet furiously. "Our power to divine the truth is as strong as any Wizard's. Just as our power to see through the attempts to overtake us once again is clear."

"Garron, we will take our leave for now." Caise bowed mockingly to the dragon before turning to Marina. "And before this day is finished, we do request an audience, Princess." His tone was mocking, angry. "If you do not mind."

As one, they stalked from the Hall, the heels of their boots clapping loudly across the stone floors as Marina hid her wince. No doubt, they were as furious as Serena herself.

"Dragon, I request an audience in the Queen's parlor," Marina asked of Garron as she ignored the Wizards and their fury.

"In all haste, Princess." He inclined his head with mocking respect. "Please, do lead the way."

Magick slammed into the Talgaria warrior, throwing him to the ground as furious bands of pale blue and molten gold power sizzled around him, spearing through the dark shadow of the shield he had thrown up the moment the Sashtain Wizards had reach the clearing.

"You dare to threaten those women," Caise snarled furiously, holding out his hand as a burst of magick exploded into the ground at the warrior's head. "By whose order did you believe you could so disregard the rules of courtesy to a Sovereign?"

He was enraged. More furious than he could remember being, just as Kai'el was. The anger bled from his brother, increasing his, feeding one to the other until it burned into the very pits of their soul.

All he could see was the betrayal in Marina's eyes, the disappointment and hurt at the thought that they would allow the warriors to make such a threat. Her pain had pierced at him, sending him into a fury he had never imagined he could feel. Control was but a thread from snapping, and true violence lay just beneath the surface, waiting to unleash against the hapless warrior.

"Her rule is weak, Wizard." Rhydan showed no remorse, only cold, hard determination despite the threat now facing him. Caise would have been impressed were he not so bedamned enraged.

"She did not appear so weak to me," Kai'el snapped from Caise's side. "I do believe, warrior, that that Sentinel Dragon protecting her could have easily sucked the power from your very mind and left you as powerless as a human babe. This is not weakness, you fool."

Rhydan pulled himself carefully to his feet, cautious of the Wizard magick still whipping at his feet.

"Were it not for that bedamned dragon, the Keeper would have shown herself, and we would have had the answers we needed…"

"But that bedamned dragon was there," Caise snarled. "As we warned you he would be. Those women are not fools, warrior, as we warned The Veressi they were not. They have survived separation from Cauldaran and built an empire to inspire nothing but pride despite our ancestors' attempts to bring them to heel. Think you that you can do what they could not?"

"I did not wish to bring them to heel, Wizard," Rhydan growled. "But I will question those Seculars, Justice or no."

"You will question no one, fool." Caise could not believe the warriors had made such a grave error. As he had watched the proceedings earlier, he had felt nothing but a cold slide of foreboding inching up his spine. "If you have not noticed, you have now angered not just the Ruling head of this land, but whoever the bedamned Keeper of the Lands is as well as the Justices. You have done nothing, warrior…" His hand sliced through the air. "Nothing to further our investigation into this mess."

The further events proceeded, the more Caise was inclined to believe that such subterfuge was only harming their cause. The House of Sellane needed the truth before they would ever accept the Wizards help or their strength.

"The Keeper will be found." Rhydan crossed his arms over his chest, his arrogance grating on Caise's nerves, as the other man's confidence raked at his patience.

"The Keeper is no fool, you young whelp," he snapped. "I cannot believe The Veressi would countenance such an act."

Or perhaps he could. Those Wizards were more arrogant than most, as were their warriors.

"The Veressi will bring that Princess to heel soon enough," Rhydan grunted, his dark eyes flashing with anger. "Once the alignment is completed…"

"Silence." Caise was tempted to show the impertinent warrior exactly what he thought of such forced tactics. He highly disapproved of the demand of the Rite of Reception and was more pleased than most that the Sorceress Princess had found a way to deny the Wizards until her Queen Mother's return. "I will hear no more of this insanity."

"Will you hear that I managed to trace a small bit of the Keeper's powers?" the warrior asked then, snagging Caise's instant attention with the anger that sharpened Rhydan's expression.

"Her anger was her downfall," Rhydan continued. "She was not as careful as she has been in the past, Wizard. I believe I know who she may be."

Caise stilled, watching him carefully. The warrior wasn't just angry, he was furious at whatever knowledge he had gained.

"Go on," Caise ordered, fighting to control the violence rising within him.

"We were sent here to find the Keeper and take her to Consort." He indicated his twin who stood silently beside him, his expression closed, emotionless.

"Agreed." Caise nodded sharply.

"Your Princess Marina is the Keeper, Wizard," he growled then. "Will you relinquish her to the Rite of Reception as is our right? Or will you desert your own lands and your people for her?"

Caise stared back at the warrior as magick began to whip around him. The golden threads flowed around him like furious waves of malevolent fury that strained to strike the warrior who dared to make such demands.

At his side he could feel Kai'el, his own magick surging through him, reaching out, demanding that they forever eliminate any threat to the Joining they had been working toward. Everything inside Caise's soul screamed out a denial that any other male, especially one of magick, should dare to place such a demand.

"The Rite of Reception is no longer possible," he snarled. "The alignments are already occurring, warrior. Courtship is much more effective than force any day. And what decision we should make in regards to our lands is ours alone. You no longer have rights, should the Princess Marina prove to be the Keeper."

"It was agreed," Rhydan, protested, his voice dark, filled with anger.

"Aye, at a time when none knew who the Keeper would be," Caise snapped. "Just as it was agreed that we would Court the Princess Marina. Our claim was staked, warrior, and well you know it. Inform your Wizards upon their arrival of your mistaken display of power. And should they protest my decisions then they can contact us directly. But you, warrior, no longer have say within this land."

Caise motioned to his warriors, fourteen twins whose power and control rivaled that of the Talgaria any day.

"Madden, you will fortify this castle's defenses as directed and ensure the Princess Serena's wishes are carried out. Should any Wizard or warrior protest your orders, they may request audience with us to discuss this. There will be no forced alignments, and the Sorceresses of this land will be bothered no longer. Is this well understood?"

"Aye, Wizard, well understood." Madden nodded sharply, his light green eyes flickering to the Talgaria.

Caise turned back to Rhydan, one hand gripping the hilt of his sword as he lifted his brow, mockery twisting his features.

"Do you wish to argue this further, warrior?"

"Nay, Wizard," he growled. "But I am certain The Veressi shall."

"So be it." Caise turned on his heel, stalking from the clearing before entering the line of trees that sheltered the castle grounds.

Rage thundered through his blood, mixing with the arousal and his magick's reaction to the apex of power Marina was coming into. They had sensed the surging response in her the night before, the invisible fingers of her power caressing over their bodies long into the night as her dreams moved naturally toward them. The alignment had gone too far, there was no turning back, no matter who or what she was.

Were she indeed the Keeper of the Lands, then the ramifications of that could change all their lives forever. The Keeper was tied to the lands she protected, heart and soul, to take her from it would be to see her wither painfully in her magick. But what place was there here, in this land of Sorceresses, for Wizards who knew only control, only leadership?

There was none.

* * * * *

The alignments of magick were said to be mercurial, but once roused until after Joining, a torment shared between Wizards and Sorceresses alike if heart, body and soul as well as magick, were aligning.

This was the reason why, centuries before, the Sorceresses had left Cauldaran, because the Wizards had begun forcing the alignments of magick rather than depending on courtship and rousing the inner fires of a natural attraction and caring disposition to further the alignment. Pleasure became pain for the females, for the Sentinels had decreed that magick alone would not create the unions needed to further balance the power of the Sentmarian world. But balancing power had not been the end goal in those days. The gathering of power, prestige and riches had fueled those earlier Wizards to the point that in the years after the Sorceresses' desertion, their lands had gone to waste, their livestock had near starved and their cities and estates had fallen into ruin.

Caise could not countenance that his brethren had not learned their lessons in the centuries past. That there were those Wizards who would still force the Rite of Reception, or demand Courtship, rather than using their naturally given charms to ease their way into the hearts of the women who were their natural counterparts.

And yet, at this moment, as he and Kai'el stalked back to the castle, intent on confronting one deceptive little warrior Sorceress, he could well understand the sheer frustration that must have driven his ancestors. He knew this little Sorceress was well on her way to destroying the last shred of their control in the face of her secrets and her sexual wariness.

If she did not trust, then she would not hunger. And hunger that woman did, even in her sleep she came to them now, her magick whispering over them, tempting their control. The apex of her power was building, they could feel it, and knew she must be aware of it as well. They would force the Joining rather than see the peak of her power passed and the magick she possessed forever weakened by her own stubbornness. And they would learn if she was indeed the Keeper of the Lands.

The thought of bringing her into her power, only to lose her to the land filled Caise with an aching emptiness. They could not take the Keeper from the lands her soul was connected to.

"I can feel her even here," Kai'el muttered at his side, his voice dark, rough from the hunger that tormented them both.

Aye, Caise could as well. The driving heat licking at their flesh like a ghostly caress was nearly more than either of them could bear.

"I would have truth from her before we go further." Caise clenched his fists as they moved into the castle courtyard. "If she is indeed the Keeper, then the alignment and the Joining could well bring us not just an ease to this torment, but answers as well. And I tell you now, Kai'el, I grow tired of this deceit our Sentinel Priests have pressed upon us. They give us no clues as to their own suspicions but merely bid our silence. Marina will find no trust in us if we do not give her ours as well."

It was a point that pricked at them both often. There should be no secrets between Wizards and Consort. Once the powers joined, they were bonded for all time, body and soul, feeling as the other felt, sensing the other's pain or upset. Betrayal could not be allowed, for it blocked the power needed to sustain the bonds created.

"Perhaps it is time for such honesty," Kai'el snapped as they began to ascend the wide stone steps leading to the doors of the castle. "The time of Joining grows too near to allow this deception to go further," he agreed. "And I will have no more of her excuses or careful shifts from the conversation at hand. I would have the truth as well."

Kai'el's body was humming. His cock pressed hard and tight against his breeches, his muscles were taut, filled with a tension that he knew would not relax until he filled the deceptive little witch with every drop of seed building in his balls. His hands ached to be filled with the sweet, firm flesh of her breasts, his mouth watered to taste the hard little nipples crowning them. To eat at her as the addictive sweet she was becoming. To bury his head between her thighs and plunge his tongue deep inside the syrupy heat of her pussy and drown himself in her hunger.

Hell, he cared not if she was Keeper or peasant. He cared only that he see her soft mouth opening, her eyes dazed, face flushed as she sucked his cock inside the blistering depths of her mouth and suckled him with the same hunger he intend to lap at her sweet juices.

He was on the edge of insanity, the hunger was driving so hard within him. He could feel the magick building inside her by the day, reaching out to him, drawing him to her and knew she was not nearly as uninvolved as she pretended to be.

"She is in her rooms." Caise moved instinctively for the curving staircase that led to the upper wings of the castle.

Like threads of mesmerism, they could feel her, her magick pulsing, her arousal hot and tempting. It had been so since the first moment they had laid eyes on her, even before the Veraga Twins had made their journey to Covenan to demand Reception of the Princess Brianna. During the visit she had made with her mother to Cauldaran lands to discuss the reunion of Wizards and Sorceress magick, they had known she was their destined Consort.

Never had a woman triggered such instant, total arousal as the Princess Marina had. Never had their dreams converged on one female, their lusts pouring into the sleep-filled images until they awoke, drenched in sweat, aching for release. A release, not just of the physical, but of the magickal.

"She knows we are coming." Kai'el had been amazed in the past days, the bond they were creating with her, though they had yet to complete the Joining. He could feel her, sense her, knew when she was troubled, when she ached. Just as he knew that her ache was only building.

They stepped to the landing, moving with deliberate haste toward the wing the Princess occupied. As they took the rounded curve leading to her room, they slowed to a stop.

A frown creased Kai'el's brow as the dragon Garron, stood, leaning with deceptive human laziness, against the wall several yards from the Princess' door.

"Bedamned dragon," he muttered, knowing whatever plans they had would be, at the least, delayed.

"Wizards." The great scaly head nodded as leathery lips curved into a cold smile that revealed wickedly sharp teeth. "I would speak to you if I may." One powerful forearm extended to a room across the hall as a door swung open magickally.

As though it would do any good to deny him, Kai'el thought in resignation. He moved to the room, followed closely by his brother as they forcefully tamped down the irritation at the delay. They could feel Marina's arousal, her tempestuous anger, and the need to ease both. The pain they had seen in her earlier had affected them both greatly. Kai'el was amazed at how it had smarted, her distrust, her fear that they had betrayed her. If she did not care, then it would not matter to her if she could or could not trust them. Just as they knew they cared for her. Cared for her far more than they had ever intended to.

"Dragon, you are becoming an irritant." Caise scowled as he turned to the creature, hooking his thumbs into the wide sword belt strapped across his hips. "What could be so imperative that has not already been addressed?"

"Dark Wizards? Joinings?"

The reply had Caise and Kai'el stilling as the tempered violence rose within them once again. Dark Wizards they would not accept. The Joining was no business of dragons, magickal or otherwise.

"There is no such thing as a Dark Wizard," Caise snapped. "Our Sentinel Priests and Priestess would know of such a being and would warn us accordingly."

The dragon grunted, a look of such mockery crossing his face. The impression of Wizard form came so strongly to mind that it could not be ignored.

"Your Sentinel Priests and Priestess do not always know those things that they should, and often they keep their secrets well beyond a time when they should be known. But their knowledge of such evil is neither here nor there. You know it is true, just as I know you have sensed the magick protecting the Seculars as well as I."

"Sensing and scrying the secret of its identity are different things," Kai'el informed him, aware of the harshness of his voice. He could not countenance that a Wizard could fall to such evil. There were other explanations that could explain the magick that shielded the humans. "And I cannot believe a Wizard or Wizard Twins would sink to such levels. It is unheard of, even among Wizards who have lost a twin. There must be another answer."

"Such as?" The dragon's head tilted, his black eyes watching him curiously.

"There is always the chance that a human has somehow gained the ability to reach into the magick of the land." Caise shrugged. "Such has happened before, Dragon. A dark Sorcerer, perhaps of a union between Sorcerer and human. Such beings still possess great power."

"But never one of such strength," Garron pointed out. "But we will argue that point at a later time. You go to the Princess Marina now, thinking to complete the Joining rising from the alignments of magick. Am I correct?"

The dragon seemed intent on broaching the subject.

"This is no business of yours, Garron," Kai'el warned him, the magick rising within him darkening his voice, making it sound harsher than ever.

"It is much my business, Wizard," he snapped, his black eyes glowing with yellow sparks of fury as he glared back at him. "I have raised these Sorceresses. I have protected them when no other male stood to defend them. I have guarded this castle and its women far longer than you could ever know. Do not tell me what is business of mine and what is not. Now I say to you, do you go to her to complete the Joining, without the truth before you, hers as well as your own, you will damage the very bond you wish to create."

"What bond do you speak of?" Caise snarled, the conflicts raging inside him suddenly bursting free. "The one we will create with a Keeper? A Sorceress who cannot leave her lands, cannot survive within ours? Aye, Dragon, 'tis a fine bond the Sentinels blessed us with. Our Consort. A Consort who will cleave not to us, but the land she accepted as her own."

He turned from the dragon, raking his hand roughly over his face as he fought down his anger. Lust and fury combined inside him, twisting his guts into knots as he thought of never having her as he should. Sheltered between himself and Kai'el each night, her body warm and receptive to their touch, her magick filling them as they filled her.

Once Wizards took a true Consort, there was no adultery. The magick and the pleasure could not be found elsewhere, just as Caise knew that no other woman's touch save Marina's would ever satisfy him again.

Humans called it love, but for the magick realms, it was much more than any one word could describe.

"You are not Keepers of Cauldaran," the dragon pointed out, his rough voice rasping through the air and setting Caise's nerves on edge.

"We are not Keepers, but Wizards bound to the land they hold rights to," Kai'el reminded him forcibly. "You know this, Dragon, if you know anything of Wizards."

The dragon snorted. "I know Wizards are by their very nature prone to theatrics." Sarcasm dripped from his voice. "Are you men or babes? Simply because it is yours does not mean it cannot belong to another as well."

Kai'el stared back at him in horror. Give up their lands? Their people? What sort of abominations did this dragon believe they were? No Wizard abandoned his estate or the people depending on him.

Garron shook his head. "If she is the Keeper, as you said, she cannot be taken from this land, Wizard. She is also your Consort. What I wonder, will her feelings be on the abandonment coming? And how this affects her acceptance of any Joining?"

The dragon's head tilted as the eyes once again turned that deep shade of the darkest black and filled with mockery. As Kai'el watched him, his eyes narrowed, a leaping response of magick twisting his insides.

"Marina has left her room," he said, his voice soft, dangerous. "Where does she head to, Dragon?"

If she thought she was leaving the castle now, while the magick was gathering so deep inside them, she had another thought coming.

"She goes to her ladies, where she will be prepared in case a Joining occurs," he sighed, his expression turning somber. "I have spoken to her this night, explained to her the risks of refusing you as she does. But..." he snarled as Caise and Kai'el tensed in anticipation, "this does not mean your Joining is assured, my Wizards. Merely that she understands the need to be prepared. This is no simpering little maid you go to, but a woman, one of strength and courage. Betray her, and no magick in the land will aid you in her hatred of you. Fulfill her, and you will require no greater power to aid you. Remember that. For it may ease your way later."

With no further words, and definitely no explanations, he was gone. As though he had been no more than a figment of their imaginations blinked away, silence now occupied the space he had held.

"She prepares for the Joining." Kai'el felt as though he were strangling with his own lusts now.

She would be massaged, relaxed, the curls shielding her silken pussy removed, and then sent to the heated pools beneath the castle to reflect upon the coming night, if there was anything to reflect upon. Ofttimes, it was then that a

Sorceress had decided if the Joining was right for her. At least, this was how it had been before the separation of the magickal sexes.

Caise inhaled deeply. Sweet Sentinels. His hands clenched into fists as he fought to keep from going after her then and there. To hold back the hunger firing through his body, engorging his cock further, if that were possible, and sending the blood thundering through his body.

"You know, Caise," Kai'el sighed, the sound rough, filled with vexation, "between that dragon and our Sorceress, I may well not survive this venture outside Cauldaran."

"You best." Caise frowned heavily at the thought. "Bedamned if I'll even attempt to weather that Sorceress storm alone, Brother. So do not even think to attempt escape. I may well have to expire myself out of sheer desperation, and torment you within the Pits for the shadowhell you will cause. There is no force on this planet that would convince me to take on that woman alone. Keeper or no."

They both sighed in morose acceptance of the fact that one small, delicate, recklessly courageous woman was turning their lives upside down. Inside out. Ripping it apart at the seams… And they decided, at the same second nonetheless, that no other woman would do.

Chapter Twelve

ℬ

The heated pools beneath the castle were rich with magick, alive with a power that sank into the very pores and eased the spirit. They weren't as powerful as the pools of silver magick that could heal even the gravest injury and restore power lost during grueling battle. But those pools were not soothing, nor filled with comfort. They were tempestuous, increasing magick, and strength.

Silken water splashed now against the rock-lined walls, creating a haunting, delicate rhythm of peace. The precious gems embedded in the walls and ceiling sent prisms of light dancing over the water, like magick itself, creating a rainbow mystery within the shallow depths that stroked over her naked body.

Between her thighs, the undefended flesh of her newly shorn pussy ached with sensitivity, with the memory of magick suckling at the hard little bud that ached with increasing demand. Now, as she lay back on the smooth slanted stone just beneath the waters edge and stared up at the colorful explosion of light from the gems above, she began to have grave misgivings about the step she had just taken.

Once your mound is shorn, your flesh undefended from the magick of the castle, denying the Wizards' power and the Joining will soon become impossible, Keeper, the priestess had warned her. *Your curls defend you, provide the only measure of protection allowed to a Sorceress against Wizards. Their touch will be temptation itself.*

Remove it. She had been determined.

Why had she had been so determined? Had she taken leave of her senses?

No, those bedamned Wizards had stolen her senses with their touch. They had ripped through her defenses, her fears, and become so much a part of her that she did not know if she could survive without the Joining. Sweet Mother Sentinel, she ached. She was on fire for their touch, their magick. Every part of her soul reached out to them, despite the knowledge that she had made a grave error.

She, Keeper of the Land of Covenan, had given her heart, and was now ready to give her soul to Wizards she could never hold, to men who could never accept what she was, and what she needed to survive.

She was a warrioress, her magick, her heart, tied to the land in a way so elemental that the bonds could never be broken. And they were Wizards, men who commanded an army of warriors whose lives were in another land. A land so far removed from hers that there was no chance of bridging the chasm.

She should have gone to them when this strange courtship first began, she now knew. She should have told them the truth of herself, rather than hiding the knowledge as she had been advised to do.

In times past, before the separation, Sorceress Keepers were the most sought after, the most courted in all the lands. Great riches were offered merely for the chance to court, and later, in the search for power and greatness, they were forced to hide, to shield their powers for fear of kidnapping. The story Kai'el had told her of reluctant consorts was no lie. It was a part of their history, and the reason why Sorceress Keepers had always hidden their knowledge and their connection to the land. They were now secretive, always aware of the risks of revealing who and what they were.

Gods, what had she done?

She pulled her knees up, raising her upper body until she could wrap her arms around her legs and huddle into a ball of misery. She should have put a stop to this weeks ago. She should have accepted suit from one of the Covenan humans and given up on the ideal of love and true passion. Had she done so, she would not be in this mess.

Had she done so she would not have known pleasure as she had while flying on Kai'el's owl.

Merciful Sentinels, she was doomed. She had doomed not just herself but Caise and Kai'el as well. They had lands in Cauldaran, warriors and landholders who depended upon them for their welfare. They could not leave. And she would never survive outside her own lands. And now, she didn't know if she could survive without those bedamned Wizards. They had made a mockery of her vow to resist them, her belief that she could control her magick as well as her heart. When in actuality, she had controlled nothing at all.

And here she sat, as she had as a child, railing at fate and the Sentinels when she knew it would do little good. Things were as they were, and there was naught else she could do but make the best of it and pray for a resolution that would at least benefit the land. She was the Keeper of the land, and once her full magick was attained, would be Keeper of the secrets of the land, a position she had never thought would fill the lands of Covenan. For no Sorceress gained full power without her Wizards. For a millennium the land had not known a Keeper of its secrets, only a Keeper of the land itself. A protector.

She should be happy, yet it was bitterness filling her. For her heart, a part of her very soul would be sacrificed in the attainment of that dream.

"Ah, Keeper, what sadness flows around you. I have heard it said the land itself fills the Keeper with her joy. Where then is yours?"

Her head snapped up, shock flashing through her mind, deadening her reflexes as she stared back at the two Wizards now watching her from the moss-cushioned stone on the other side of the pool.

Magick swirled around them, pale blue, molten gold, mixing with the colors of the gems above to create a halo of power that cast a brooding aura over both men. Both were blond, their shoulder-length hair framing faces of hard planes and angles, one identical to the other, yet as separate as night from day.

Keeper. She felt her heart speed up in her chest. Sentinels, they knew. How had they learned her secret? Had others?

"'Twas a grave mistake you made this day, Keeper." Kai'el sighed as he lowered himself to one knee, staring back at her implacably. "When you called upon the land to protect your sister against the foolishness of that warrior, rather than trusting the Wizards pledged to you, you betrayed yourself."

Gods. She had prayed the slight lapse had been undetectable.

"You would not tell…" she gasped.

"But we were not the ones to trace the power." His eyes gleamed with secrets, knowledge and hunger. "'Twas the Talgaria warriors, Keeper. The very ones sent by The Veressi to find the Keeper and force an alignment with her. Remember the tale I whispered to you as we flew above the land? The tale of the reluctant consorts stolen from their lands, their magick forced into alignment with warriors and Wizards they had not chosen?"

Merciful Sentinels, what had she had done?

"Aye. I remember." Her voice was hoarse, weakness flooding her limbs, as she guessed at the direction of this moral.

"You have placed yourself at grave risk, Keeper," he growled. "We are not willing to allow such a thing to happen. Even the risk of such a thing is more than we can tolerate."

Arrogance and male determination filled his voice, his gaze. Caise was no better. His arms crossed over his chest, his eyelids lowered with brooding intensity as he observed her with heated lust.

"More than you can tolerate? And what have you to do with what should be tolerable? It would seem to me it is now my life, and my power in jeopardy." She fought back her tears. Dear Sentinels, how was she to let them go when the time came that she had no other choice? Surely it would have been kinder to have allowed her magick to align with those sour-faced warriors than with Wizards who would steal her heart?

"Neither your life nor your magick is in jeopardy, Keeper," Caise growled. "Think you that we would ever allow another to touch you? That we would at any time risk another forcing an unnatural alignment with what is ours and ours alone?"

The magick coalescing around them began to crackle with energy as it slid slowly from their forms to the water at their feet. Marina could only watch, mesmerized, as it made its way across the pool, heading unerringly for her.

Marina trembled, her arms tightening about her legs as the swirls of power moved slowly closer, sending frissons of electric energy through the small waves of water that rippled about her body. She stared back at the Wizards, misery settling deep within her heart. An ache that flooded her soul tormenting her emotions.

"I cannot leave the land," she whispered, her voice husky, tears clogging her throat. "I cannot be the Consort you would have me be."

Caise's gaze flickered in regret, the flesh along his cheekbones tightening at her words.

"You are the Consort destined for us," he growled. "We can only live the lives we are given, Marina, and accept the cost of each path we take. We will not regret this path, no matter the obstacles before us. There are always ways to find happiness, we must only search for the paths that take us there."

Their magick reach her then, wrapping about her body like tendrils of exquisite, pure pleasure. Undiluted. Uncontained, the sensations flickering over her flesh took her breath and left her gasping for air as weakness flooded her being. The deep violet threads of her own power began to pulse low within her stomach, tightening her womb as the misty aura began to surround her, awaiting direction, sensing the Joining to come.

"Come, Keeper." Kai'el held his hand out to her, the brooding intensity of his gaze sending nervous impulses of trepidation to skate through her body as their magick tugged at her, wrapping about her to tease her senses with their hungry touch.

Water cascaded from her hair, her limbs as she rose slowly to her feet, following the wide ledge which led to the other side of the ever-deepening pools. With each step, she could feel her nervousness deepening, trepidation washing through her. When the Joining had been no more than a thought, a distant event that would come, it had not held the power to remind her of the past.

Now, shadows formed within her mind, twisting remembrances of brutal hands, teeth biting at her tender flesh as pain resounded through her soul. Could she truly do this? Her fists clenched at her side, knowing that ultimately, she had no choice. The apex of power was now churning inside her, the mystical forces of the land, of her very being aligning with the Wizards before her. Running was no longer an option, but Sweet Mercy, her legs ached to do just that.

As she neared them, Kai'el rose to his full height, staring down at her with eyes slowly darkening as magick glittered within them. His arm lifted then, his fingers reaching out to push the sodden curls behind her shoulder, to reveal the swollen, engorged flesh of her breasts.

"We could ease your fears," he whispered, staring deep into her eyes. "We could transform our rooms to Nirvana, our touch to the petals of flowers as you find confidence in our touch."

Her eyes widened. "You..." She swallowed, a tight, shocked motion as she shook her head in confusion. "Wizards cannot control the Valley of Dreams, how could you dare?"

His fingers trailed over her collarbone as Caise moved closer, his arms dropping to his sides as his head lowered, his lips caressing the opposite shoulder.

Sentinels. Flames erupted in her pussy, burning her with the savagery of her need as her magick began to course through her very blood.

"We would dare very many things to bring you pleasure, Marina," Kai'el growled as he cupped the hardened curve of her breast, his thumb flickering over the distended nipple. "Many, many things."

Dazed, her mind rippling with power and remnants of fear, she watched as his shoulders dipped, his head lowering as his lips parted over the flushed peak a second before his mouth enveloped it.

Ah gods. She lost her strength even as the magick began to build inside her, her legs threatened to collapse. His mouth tugged at her, sending darting fingers of fiery sensation to pierce her womb, her cunt, as her juices began to dampen the unprotected folds between her thighs while magick began to flicker there. She now knew what the priestess meant by leaving her flesh vulnerable to the magick. It whispered over her, heated her, licked at her with a ghostly touch even as it probed with sensual delight at the soft cleft of her rear.

The Wizards did not leave her pleasure to their magick alone. As she watched Kai'el's cheeks draw at the sensitive peak of her nipple, a wicked flay of heat seared the opposite breast as Caise too began to suck at her. Heated nips, moist licks, suckling heat. Their hands refused to be still as well. They roved over her, spreading her legs, smoothing down her thighs, never touching the parts of her blazing for their caress, but teasing her, taunting her with their magick and their mouths at her breasts instead.

She could have never imagined such delight, such erotic, exotic intensity as this. Each pull of their lips at her breasts tugged at her womb, at the very depths of her pussy until she was twisting against them, cries falling from her lips as the shadows of fear disintegrated beneath the blazing heat of their touch.

"How pretty you are," Caise muttered as he lifted his head, his gaze going first to where Kai'el still yet tortured her sensitive flesh, then to her gaze as she fought to focus on his features. "Your pretty breasts are flushed, Marina, taut and heated from your pleasure."

His thumb raked over the distended tip as his head lowered, his lips smoothing over hers as she whimpered into the small kiss.

"What you do to me," she cried out, arching to her toes as Kai'el's hand came close to the burning center of her being. "I cannot bear such pleasure, Caise."

"Poor little Princess," he crooned, his hand moving to the small of her back, fingers trailing to the curve of her buttocks. "And here I had such plans in my hunger for your sweet little body. To move behind you, just so…" He stepped behind her, one hand curved around her jaw to draw her head back to his shoulder. "I would hold you against me, Marina, as Kai finds other ways to pleasure you as well."

Her hands were buried in Kai'el's hair, clenching tightly as his lips left the painfully sensitive nipple, and began stringing kisses down her torso.

"There, little love," he murmured as he held her to him by anchoring one hand at her hip, the other at the curve of her ass. "There are so many adventures we can take. Are you certain you cannot bear just a bit more pleasure?"

"Gods. Sweet Mercy. Kai'el…" She screamed his name as he knelt before her, his tongue probing at the shallow indention of her navel as Caise tugged at the flesh he held, parting the cleft of her ass, sending shooting darts of dark fire into the tiny entrance there as she felt magick rippling over the area.

"He is firstborn," Caise growled at her ear. "He has demanded first taste of your newly revealed flesh. Come, Princess, surely you can bear just a taste."

Hard, calloused fingers moved between her thighs, parting the folds a second before Kai'el's head dipped lower and his tongue swiped a burning path through her sensitized, dew-laden slit before circling her clit in a rasping caress that had a blaze of color exploding before her eyes.

She would not survive this pleasure. She could not.

She arched as Caise's arm wrapped around her front, his broad palm cupping the weight of a breast as his brother continued to taste. Taste? Gods have mercy on her, this was not a taste, but rather a devouring. She jerked in their grip, struggling, she knew not for what, as Kai'el parted her further, one strong hand lifting her thigh until her foot rested against his shoulder, allowing him greater access to her secret flesh.

"Gods. Mercy," she screamed as his tongue plunged quickly inside the gripping depths of her cunt, only to retreat and the licking of the drenched folds continued.

"Mercy, Princess?" Caise growled at her ear, his fingers dipping between her thighs to spread the moisture easing from her cunt along the cleft of her rear as she writhed against them. "What form of mercy would you prefer? Should we halt? Or should we bring you ease?"

He spoke as though she had senses left to respond to such questions. She was out of her mind with the pleasure, shaking between them as she waited in suspended anticipation for the touch he continued to tease her anus with. All the while, Kai'el tortured her, fucking his tongue into her pussy with a quick, hard stroke before retreating to suck at her clit, lick at her folds, lap at the syrupy juices easing from her pussy.

Her foot dug into Kai's shoulder as she lifted herself to him, tilting her hips to allow for the deliberately brief thrusts, for the tormenting feel of his tongue licking into her, only to retreat, circle her clit and consume the juices easing rapidly from her body.

And Caise was no voyeur to the play. His arm held her firm to his chest, his hand cupping the weight of her breast as his fingers tormented the nipple. And behind, he had slowly lubricated her ass, his finger beginning to ease into the relaxing entrance.

Sensations, pleasure, the bite of fire, flooded her senses as she felt the magick building within her. If she did not find relief soon...

"Speak to me, Marina," Caise growled in her ear then. "Do you not feel our touch? The heat of our magick licking over you? Come, sweet little love, tell me what you desire."

He could not be serious. She cried out harshly at the order, barely able to form thoughts, let alone words. Words required effort, thought. If she dared to think now she would be horrified at what she was allowing.

"Should we stop now?" He licked at her ear before his teeth caught the lobe, tugging at it with a sharp little nip that was pleasure and pain combined. "Come sweetheart, tell us what you need."

"More." One word, she could handle this. A demand for completion. Bedamned Wizards were driving her insane.

"More of what?" he crooned at her ear. "More of this?" The tip of his finger entered the small opening to her anus as Kai'el's tongue thrust inside her pussy once again. The next second, both retreated to merely tease at her flesh again.

"Yes," she gasped, her hands pulling at Kai'el's hair as mewling cries left her lips. How she ached. She was stretched upon such a rack of pleasure that she felt she would lose her mind did they not complete her.

"Or more of this?" Magick teased her then. Marina froze as she felt a slender band of power ease inside her ass, barely parting the tissue, warming her, caressing forbidden tissue as it sent a sensation of soothing moist warmth in its wake.

Kai'el's lips and tongue were at her clit, devouring her as his magick began to push into her pussy, slow, such a slow, easy glide of heat that she felt shudders of a warning release spasming through her body.

"Gods. Yes. Yes, more."

"More of which, Princess?" he questioned her then. "Which do you need more of?"

She ground her teeth together in frustration. She would not speak of this. It was bad enough that they were turning her body into a sensual creature of lust-filled hunger, but they would not turn her mind. She would not tempt them with the language they sought. Sentinels, she would be mortified when the pleasure had dissolved and reality returned.

"Should we stop?" The magick eased from her entrances despite her growling protest, the needy arch of her body.

They were playing with her, she knew they were. Gentle persuasion to attain their ends while withholding the most indescribable pleasure. 'Twas unfair. She would not allow such blackmail. She was not a plaything to be so toyed with.

She waited, panting, gathering her strength as Kai'el began to ease up her body, kissing, nipping, torturing her in reality. 'Twas extreme torture. Such pleasure should be outlawed before all Sorceresses were defeated by their own weaknesses.

She would consider the merits of this later, but first, she would show her Wizards a thing or two about a warrioress. She was no doll to lay in their arms and whisper the words they wanted to hear. Nor was she so weak-minded as to be this easily blackmailed. She would show them the mettle of a true Sorceress of the land.

But she must time her own caresses exactly. Move too quickly and she would lose their attention beneath their own drive to control and dictate the speed of their Joining. They were, after all, Wizard males, and not exactly easily controlled.

But the wait... She moaned as Kai'el's lips moved over her stomach, his teeth nipping at her as his fingers eased between her thighs. Behind her, Caise growled at her ear, clearly not pleased that she had not given in to their demands.

Just a bit more. She writhed against them, rubbing her body against the material of their clothing, desperate to feel naked, bronzed flesh against her.

As Kai'el stood fully before her, she moved. It wasn't an attack, it was as simple as forcing her hands from his hair, smoothing them over his shoulders and allowing her lips to press against the bare flesh showing between the opening of his shirt.

She licked at his skin, aware of his startled stillness as her magick flowed from her fingertips, making quick work of the clasps that held the material together. They were too dressed, she thought frantically. She needed them bare.

"Princess," Kai'el groaned as she pushed the material aside, her lips moving down his chest as she began to lower herself before him. His hands clasped her upper arms, but he made no other objections as she sent the small spirals of violet energy to begin opening his breeches as well.

"This is not the situation to attempt a bluff, Marina," he growled as her lips moved lower, her body sinking before him. "You are going to get more than you may be bargaining for."

"Shut up, Kai," Caise snapped as her power began to enfold him, the sensations of each touch upon Kai'el's flesh, given to him in turn as her tongue flicked out to lick at the small beads of perspiration gathering on Kai'el's abdomen. Following others lower, moving to the thick stalk of his cock rising from between his thighs.

Kai'el was in a state of disbelief as he threaded his fingers through Marina's hair, watching in complete fascinated ecstasy as one small hand cupped the taut sac below and the other attempted to wrap about the thick base. If this were not torturous enough, the little vixen opened her lips, her pink tongue flickering out to swipe over the small pearl of moisture gathering at the tip.

He cursed, the sound rough, guttural as she lifted her lashes, staring up at him as her lips opened further, and the flushed, mushroomed crest disappeared into the heated velvet of her mouth.

Bedamned. Where was the timid, frightened Sorceress he had believed her to be? This woman would not know timid if it stalked to her and smacked her on her decidedly curvy little rump. Not that experience filled each touch, she was exploring, hesitant, but each movement was more erotic, more sexually intense than any other woman he had ever known.

The blistering heat of her mouth overwhelmed him, causing his hips to thrust, to spear more of the needy shaft inside the suckling riches it had found within her mouth. She moaned, the sound vibrating on his cock as her soft little fingers caressed his balls and sent his senses spinning.

And her magick. Gods have mercy on them both, her magick had loosened Caise's breeches as well, wrapped around his cock and drawn him to the same painful pinnacle of pleasure that Kai'el was now poised upon.

The little witch. She had turned the tables on them, and Sentinels only knew if he had enough strength to draw from her and get her safely to their rooms before completing the joining.

Calling upon every shred of magick he still had the mind to direct, he ignored her desperate, protesting cry as it looped it around her wrists, drawing her back from him as he retreated from the sweet prison of her mouth. He didn't stop until she was kneeling before him, glaring up at him as the magick bound her wrists behind her back.

"Naughty little witch." He shook his finger at her before forcing his breeches closed over the straining length of his cock, aware of Caise doing the same as he stared down at her in amazement.

"Release me, Kai." Her voice was husky, thick with need. "I was not yet finished."

Kai'el swallowed his laughter. Any more finished and he could well damage that peak of magick she was ascending to. The first release could be attained at only one point. Together. The three of them, their magick blending, pouring into each other as their releases poured from them. Once the magick began aligning through sexual play, there was no other way to attain satisfaction without losing a considerable amount of the magick that would then bond them together. And Caise and Kai'el were damned tired of waiting to find their pleasure.

"No, little witch, you are not yet finished," he agreed, smiling down at her with wicked pleasure. "But I promise you, before this night is over, you shall be."

Chapter Thirteen

ॐ

She was bound by bands of Wizard strength, powerless in all but her own magick. She did not take to being physically helpless without a fight. As they wrapped her in a thick drying sheet, her magick curled around their thighs, slipping between the metal clasps of their breeches to stroke the hard length of their cocks. As they struggled to keep the bonds in place as well as blocking her erotic caresses, she allowed the magick to drift beneath their shirts, to tickle over their abdomens, their sensitive ribs.

"Woman, still your magick before you are molested within the halls of your own castle." Kai'el's voice was thick, hoarse with his lust as she managed to direct the seeking warmth of her power to curl around his buttocks, slipping between his thighs to cup his balls over the taut leather of his breeches. They were tight and firm, drawn high against the base of his cock as the double doors leading to their suite were flung open as though by an invisible hand.

"She needs to be spanked, Kai'el. We must teach her the value of obeying her Consorts." The erotic threat had her heart rate picking up further, the blood thundering through her veins in excitement.

She should have been furious, outraged, terrified. Instead, she was determined to make the most of the time she would have with these Wizards who were stealing her heart, immersing themselves into her very soul. All too soon they would be forced from her, and she would be alone.

For now, she would revel in their touch, in what pleasure they could bring to each other.

"A spanking is definitely in order," Caise growled moments later as Kai'el threw her to the bed before flipping her to her stomach.

She struggled, fighting the bands of magick as she heard them moving behind her, undressing, she hoped. She could feel the power building inside her, her magick rioting at the arousal and the need to touch. She was near insane with the need, certain there could be no force greater than this on the entire planet than the lust arising within her, the sheer depth of hunger, the need searing it, all built into a conflagration she wondered if any of them would survive.

"So pretty," Caise whispered behind her as his hand smoothed over the rounded curves of her buttocks. "Do you remember your dream, beloved, deep within Nirvana? The phermona spanking these delicate curves? 'Twas my hand striking the blow, 'twas my fingers working inside your sweet little opening as Kai'el tasted of the passion of your sweet pussy. The flowers of the valley loved you, Marina, with our lips, our hands."

The gentleness of his voice belied the coming action. She expected a caress, perhaps a kiss, she did not expect the small, stinging little slap to the curve of her buttock at the same time the binding force of their power lifted her hips, forcing her to bend her knees beneath her.

"Bedamned Wizards!" She struggled against the bonds, panting, not from fear, but from excitement, arousal. She was so hot she expected to see flames pouring forth from her body at any moment.

She was kneeling before them, her pussy creaming, her flesh warming beneath the next small slap as her eyes rounded in shocked pleasure. Should something which should have been degrading, be filled with such pleasure?

The next touch was a tender kiss to the warmed flesh, the stroke of an agile, teasing tongue.

Oh aye, yes. There should be much pleasure in this, she thought, as a whimper tore from her lips. Much pleasure indeed.

"Ah, Princess, before this night is through, you will be screaming for your pleasure," Caise warned her, his voice dark a second before his hand landed again. An aggressive, fiery warmth filled her buttocks at the slap, then another to the opposite cheek, causing her to jerk, to moan in pitiful hunger.

Such depravity should be reviled, she thought with distant amazement. Instead, she was pushing back, attempting to raise her buttocks higher to his slaps rather than struggling away from them.

As she writhed beneath the alternating smacks, gentle kisses and soothing licks along her derriere, she was only distantly aware of Kai'el moving to the bed, kneeling before her as the bands of magick began to lift her shoulders.

"Now, little witch," he growled, "you can play all you wish."

He lifted her head, one hand cupped her cheek, while the fingers of the other gripped the base of his cock, pressing it to her gasping lips. And she opened for him, opened and consumed the heated crest, tasting the salty male flavor of his essence as she felt heat radiate higher along her buttocks from another carefully placed slap.

Her hands were still bound behind her back, all that held her in place was the magick wrapped around her torso. She was helpless before them, vulnerable to any touch, any desire they would have. And she reveled in it. Never had she known such excitement, such exhilaration. Such freedom.

There was no need to worry what she should do, how she should act or if she should accept the pleasure being meted out in such large quantity. They were Wizards. They were her Wizards. And the pleasure was irresistible.

She closed her lips around the thickly flared crest of Kai'el's cock, sucking it to the back of her throat as her tongue flickered beneath it in rapid little strokes. She could feel the throb of arousal, of excitement just beneath the silk-enclosed erection. Behind her, Caise was kissing the rounded curves of her ass, slowly parting her thighs further as his fingers cupped the bare folds of her pussy and his tongue probed at the snug pucker of her ass. Decadent. Depraved. Or so she thought. Until that lazy moist extension wiggled at the entrance a second before spearing it with a heated thrust that had her crying out in need.

"Here, baby..." Kai'el was awaiting just such a move. His cock slid past her lips, his teeth clenching on a ragged moan as she enclosed it, slurping eagerly on the thickness as Caise continued to invade her little rear.

Caise's fingers parted her, stroked her, Kai'el glanced from the sight of his dick spearing between her lips long enough to watch the devouring of her sweet ass. And how his brother was enjoying his play. His tongue fucked past the tight little hole, stretching her but marginally as her moans echoed around the thick flesh filling her mouth.

He pulled his gaze back to that sight, his hands clenching in her hair, teaching her the movements he preferred.

"Aye, witch," Kai'el growled. "Suck it harder. How pretty you are, your lips stretched about my cock, your eyes dazed with your hunger."

He fucked her lips slowly, watching with mindless pleasure as her reddened lips stretched around his erection, tightened and suckled him with hungry intensity. Her sweet, hot little tongue licked the underside, probing beneath the crest as he felt his balls tighten, felt fire lash at the base of his brain as pleasure seared his nerve endings.

"Your sweet little mouth tempts me to fill it," he groaned, knowing he could not find his release, not yet. "I would watch you struggle to take each drop of my come, but not yet. Not yet, precious."

He ignored her mewling protest as he slid free of her, releasing the bands of magick that held her arms behind her back as he did so. Giving her no time to find the strength to use her magick against them, to caress them as he knew she craved to, he quickly aided Caise in turning her to her back, pressing her shoulders to the bed as his brother moved between her thighs. His head lowered and as Kai'el pressed his cock once again past her lips, he watched as Caise buried his tongue in her greedy little cunt.

She nursed on his erection with noisy abandon, her eyes dazed, staring up at him, her arms stretched above her head as Caise lifted her legs, pressing them back as he spread her wide. She was open, receptive, so very, very ready for them.

"Suck my dick, baby," he growled, watching as Caise fucked her pussy with his tongue. "Show me how much you enjoy his tongue pressing into you, lapping all that sweet nectar from your little pussy. Show me how much you need a hard, hot cock filling your sweet cunt."

His explicit words sent a flush blooming across her cheeks, though it fed her hunger, quickened the eager lips sucking his cock.

Marina's senses had no idea where to concentrate and on which pleasure. Kai'el's cock fucked her lips with shallow, fierce thrusts, sinking to her throat as his large hand, broad and calloused, cupped her breast, his fingers capturing the hard tip of her nipple to torment it with almost painful pleasure. Or between her thighs, where Caise ate her with decadent greed. Lips, teeth, tongue, suckling at her clit, licking through the drenched slit, flickering over the aching entrance to her pussy as his fingers smoothed over her thighs, forcing her to arch closer, silently demanding more.

She was awash in sensual flames, shuddering beneath their touch as she felt her magick tearing through her body to blend with theirs. The pleasure was indescribable, unlike anything she had heard of, known of. Gentleness and dominance all at once.

"Sweet Sentinels, you burn a man alive with only the touch of you." Kai'el pulled back, his hands gripping her hair, tangling in the curls as he lifted her, his cock plunging past her lips.

She struggled to focus on him, seeing the darkening of his pale eyes, the way his magick whipped through the air, sizzled over her body.

"You are destroying me." Her breath hitched as she sucked him deeper, taking him nearly to her throat as Caise's tongue plunged into her pussy, flickered, retreated as Kai'el pulled from her mouth, ignoring her desperate cry, her need to taste the explosion she knew he was only seconds away from.

Ignoring her cries, Kai'el's lips went to work on her breasts, the needy tips flaming beneath the moist touch as she began to writhe in desperation beneath their touch. It was surely too much to bear. A pleasure unimagined sensitized her body, each stroke, each breath of a caress against her flesh had her crying out her hunger for these Wizards. Surely they had somehow bespelled her. How else could they have controlled her lusts so easily?

"There, little witch," Kai'el whispered as his magick held her wrists to the bed despite her struggles. "Watch me. Look at me, Marina. Let our magick prepare you beloved."

Her eyes widened as she began to feel that cursed, bedamned magick. It whispered between the bed and her buttocks, stroking through the cleft of her ass as Caise continued to feed with greedy abandon at her desperate pussy. She couldn't help arching to him, pressing herself closer even as she gave the threads of molten gold and soft blue magick room to torment and torture her further.

"There, little one," Kai'el crooned, his voice soft as she felt the first tentative swipe of the power across her anus.

Lust convulsed her womb with a brutal blow, taking her breath as her head tossed upon the mattress, her body eagerly seeking more of the wicked temptation as Kai'el's strong, hard body lay beside hers.

"Feel it, Marina…" Aye she felt it, probing at the little entrance even as Caise's lips and tongue licked and sucked at the folds of her cunt. "It will prepare you, ease you for the Joining. Do you feel your own magick building? It whispers over my flesh like a ghostly kiss, pleading for release, begging to join with ours."

Marina whimpered as he continued to speak. Aye, she felt her magick touching him where she could not. She licked her lips, imagining those fragile threads of power wrapping around his cock, suckling at him as she would with her mouth were she free.

His heavy groan assured her he was feeling at least near what she had intended. But in the next second, there were no thoughts. Her hips lifted from the bed, a strangled cry leaving her throat as velvet power pierced her ass. A heady warmth began to fill her there, stoking the need for more, it delved deep into her anus. It flooded her with sensation, stroking nerves which had never known such a touch, expanding, filling her, until she was screaming with the sensations.

Fiery pleasure whipped through her, a searing warmth and building pressure as she felt his magick prepare her for what was to come. Moist heat eased the way as the power of Kai'el's magick lubricated the tender entrance even as it stroked, caressed and enflamed her further.

"Kai…" She gasped his name. How could one endure sensations of such strength, those which transcended the lines of pleasure and pain, and hovered somewhere between the two? "Kai, I beg of you…" She screamed again as a quick little slap was delivered to her arched buttocks.

Caise's hand. Not his magick. But the vibration of it pierced her clit even as it sang through her ass.

"There, love," Kai'el soothed her, his lips and hands easing over her upper body as she shuddered mindlessly. "You are ours, forever from this day. Feel the pleasure, Marina, the heat of all we are, given unto you, beloved. Feel us..."

Another slap to her opposite cheek sent her pussy spasming as release hovered just beyond her reach.

Caise's tongue flickered over her pussy again, licking at her folds, circling her swollen clit as Kai's mouth began to devour the nipple closest to him, suckling, nibbling, tugging at the little point with his teeth until Marina thought she would expire beneath the extreme sensations racing through her. Heat blossomed not just from their touch, but inside, rippling through her stomach, her womb, building in her chest until she was panting for breath, writhing beneath the Wizards as her hands strained at the bonds holding her to the bed.

"Release me," she screamed, as she bucked beneath them, desperate to get closer to their touch.

Perspiration dampened her flesh as she fought the hold their magick on her, fought against her inability to fight for the release building inside her. They were deliberately teasing her. Torturing her. She could not bear such sensations much longer.

"Caise, damn you, fuck me now!" she cried out as his head lifted, his hand reaching out to cup her cheek as his lips whispered over hers.

She stared back at him, hazily aware of the threads of color blooming around them, of his strained features, the arousal which had darkened his golden eyes.

"Aye, nearly there, beloved." Kai'el's voice was a harsh growl as he levered himself up beside her, turning to stare at Caise as the hungry caresses between her thighs eased.

The magick still probed at her anus, licked over her swollen pussy, but as Marina followed Kai'el's gaze, her eyes widened.

Caise knelt between her legs, the thick length of his cock gripped in the fingers of one hand as he stared back at her. The flared crest was darkly flushed, the thick veins beneath the flesh throbbing erratically as she felt her hips being lifted to him.

"Bedamned Wizard magick," she sobbed, fighting to touch him, to make her mark on them the same as they had made on her. "Release me."

Breathing was next to impossible as she watched her body line with the hard erection aimed for her. Her breath caught in her chest as the thick crest nudged against her sensitive pussy. She could only watch, eroticism wrapping around her as she felt the first touch of his cock moving against the sensitive entrance to her vagina.

Weeping, writhing, Marina fought for the first thrust, the torturous heat burning through her vagina driving her mad beneath them as she felt the blunt tip press against her. Magick held her to him as he spread her thighs further, his face a mask of building hunger as she felt him stretch her entrance.

"Kai." She raised beseeching eyes to the Wizard slowly coming to his knees beside her. "I cannot bear…"

Her breath was stolen as Caise pressed forward, the flared head working itself into her snug entrance as she tried to arch closer. Sweet Mercy, fire tingled over her body as she felt her magick swirling through her bloodstream, heating her further. It was ecstasy, it was agony. Her head tossed upon the bed as she felt his hips move, felt him slowly, agonizingly work the thick erection inside her tight pussy.

Keening moans echoed around her as she felt each slow, digging little thrust. Nerve endings never before stretched in such a manner began to scream to blazing life as she felt her juices slicken and ease his entrance.

Her bound hands clenched into fists, her lips opening on a soundless scream as she felt each smooth, inward caress stretch her further until finally he met the resistance of her maiden's shield.

Marina felt Caise pause then, his hands gripping her thighs as she forced her eyes open to meet the gold of his gaze. He stared back at her, brooding, fierce.

"Just do it," she cried, her voice ragged. "Sweet Mercy, Caise, fuck me before I die."

His features twisted into a grimace as a hungry growl left his throat. Retreating, he worked in again, pressed into the shield, retreated, then plunged deep.

Kai'el's arms wrapped around her as she bucked violently, holding her close, his lips slamming over hers as a scream tore from her throat. Not from pain, nay, if only it were pain attacking her flesh then, she could have borne what mild sensation as that would have been. When compared to this pleasure, the fullness of him stretching the tender sheath of her pussy, burning nerve endings never before caressed, sending her senses reeling, pain would have been a welcome relief.

Caise had known great pleasure in his life, but never pleasure such as this. Buried balls-deep inside the tender, virginal pussy that gripped and milked his cock like a hot little mouth was unlike any ecstasy he had known previously.

This was rapture. He gritted his teeth, feeling the satiny tissue flex around him as Marina's cries of pleasure filled the air. His hand clenched her thighs, his eyes closing tight as he fought to hold back, to hang onto his control despite the need to lunge inside her, to fuck her with all the hungry abandon filling his soul.

"Kai, I can wait no longer," Caise snarled as he thrust involuntarily against her, shuddering with the need to lose himself in her. "We must finish it. Now."

"Stay still, Marina," Caise groaned as she bucked against him, driving him deeper. There were only precious minutes to finish this.

He watched as Kai'el lifted her to him, catching her in his arms as he settled his cock inside her deeper. Turning, he moved carefully to his back, ignoring the frantic thrust of her hips, holding her tighter as Kai'el moved behind her.

Kai'el parted her buttocks, his fingers smoothing through the cleft, caressing the entrance his magick had prepared. She was slick there, the nether-hole clenching in response to his touch, gleaming with the lubricant that had been administered by the magick that impaled her earlier.

"Easy, my love," he crooned gently as he shifted, pressing the head of his cock against the little hold, feeling the heat, the pleasure to come. "'Twill be naught but pleasure. Pleasure and magick and...Sweet Sentinel of Mercy..." A groan tore from his lips as he began to press inside her.

He felt the entrance part, the untouched muscles clenching, easing, rippling around his cock as he invaded her. The sight of her, her tiny ass parting further, further, accepting the width of his cock as it speared inside her, was nearly enough to trigger his own release in that moment. But, if he came, it would be over. The pleasure would subside. He could not bear the thought of it.

Heat whorled and whipped, ripped and tore through his system as he fed every hard inch of his erection inside the protesting entrance. She was screaming beneath him, but not in pain, in a mix of agonizing pleasure as he finally filled her fully.

"There beloved." Kai'el's voice was tormented, thick with pleasure he felt her flexing along the shaft buried inside her ass. "Now, sweet baby, we will love you fully," he swore as he began to move.

Beneath her, Caise began moving in counterthrusts, filling her as Kai'el retreated, retreating as Kai'el's cock filled her ass. Both of them fucking her, possessing her. The primal urges swirling inside Kai'el were destructive. His hands gripped her hips as he began to rock, to plunge, to hammer inside the delicate entrance with quick, blinding strokes that sent pleasure ripping through his brain.

Marina was lost in a haze of erotic, primitive lust. Twin cocks fucked inside her, desperate male groans echoed around her as her flesh began to tingle and she felt her womb tightening. Each concentrated, thick impalement pushed her higher, threw her further into the riptide of sensations overtaking her. Her eyes opened, dazed, uncomprehending as she watched the mix of magick before her eyes. No longer threads, but now a thick, overlaying mist of violet, blue and rich gold mixing together, swirling ever deeper, ever darker as the tension tightened within her.

She couldn't last. She couldn't survive. She tightened on the surging cocks, feeling her release gathering, pulsing within her, building in heat, in strength, until she jerked in their hold, screaming as it overtook her.

She exploded, fracturing as the detonation overtook her and sent her careening into a world of light, magick and fearless pleasure as she felt the Wizards, beneath and behind her, finding their pleasure as well.

Thick, fiery jets of semen began to pulse inside as a catatonic quake of magick erupted in her chest. She flew, mindless, her senses scattered as rapture overtook her.

Caise and Kai'el were in little better shape. Never had pleasure surrounded them in such a way, took them over and flung them through space as this was doing. And before their eyes, they watched the magick merge into a kaleidoscope of color and heat that exploded, and amazingly, flowed into them all.

It was more than they had ever imagined. The bond they had been missing as twins throughout their lives merged. Kai'el knew Caise's pleasure, his love for Marina, his need, just as Caise felt his. And from the depths of the woman they held between them, they felt the fear, the regret and the pain of loss, of losing them, mixed with a pleasure and a love they knew held the potential to destroy them all.

Chapter Fourteen

ഇ

Morning arrived, overcast, filling Marina with a lethargy she could feel clear to her soul. She lay in the bed between her Wizards, and stared up at the ceiling as weak sunlight fought to battle the clouds to cast a ray of light through the colored glass panels along the top of the window.

Spears of blues, golds, deepening reds and violets filled her room. Never before had she paid much attention to the cut glass panels or the array of light they produced, but now she found much to dread within them.

The reds worried her most of all, since there were no reddened panels to produce the color. The omen of death and deceit pricked at her, causing her to worry her lower lip with her teeth as she sought an answer for it. She could feel no emanations from the land, no warnings of danger that normally heralded an attack. But neither did she feel calm.

She blamed the restlessness on the Wizards lying close beside her, though. Caise had wrapped his hand around her breast, even in sleep, often caressing her sensually, while Kai'el's hand lay at her thigh, his fingers barely brushing the sensitive outer flesh of her cunt.

It was disconcerting to awaken in such a way, warmed from head to toe by hard male flesh, trapped within her own bed by the oversized male forms she had given herself to.

She was now a Consort. She breathed in deeply, not certain how she felt about that. Not certain of the changes it would make within her life now. Shaking her head, she carefully disengaged herself, crawled to the bottom of the bed and extricated herself from the blankets.

Caise rolled restlessly to the opposite side of the bed, tugging at the sheet and tearing it from Kai'el's body. A small corner dragged across Kai'el's already hardening cock as he grunted irritably, his hand fumbling for the blankets. Catching hold of the quilt, he pulled it over his lean frame before twisting to his side as well, a small snore leaving his lips as he settled back against his pillow.

Marina smiled. She could do naught else but allow the warmth burgeoning inside her free. They almost looked innocent. Were it not for the scowl twisting Caise's expression as he tugged at the quilt, and Kai'el's sleepy snarl, they may have, for a few seconds at least, convinced her that a shadow of youthful innocence remained.

Shaking her head, she shrugged on her robe, waved her hand toward the fireplace to restart the small blaze which would quickly warm the early morn then slipped carefully through the small entrance that led to the private heated pools below. Caise and Kai'el had been aware of the small corridor that led to the pools beneath the castle. Magick normally hid the entryways from unknowing eyes, but she guessed when they awakened it would be easily found.

She wasn't unaware of what had happened the night before. The mix of the magick, the feel of their power sinking into her and the bond it had created between the three of them. Keeping her secrets to herself would also be much harder now that the Joining had been completed. She could already feel the connection to them building within her mind, reaching out to them.

Would it warm her during the cold nights to come without them?

Marina shook the morose thought away as she stepped into the steamy warmth of the private bathing pools. There was much to do today. She had to get to the griffon lair, check on the babies as well as the nearly mature adults who were now in training to carry the Sorceresses. Years of preparation had gone into the griffons, searching out the scattered few left, convincing them that the Sorceresses could protect them, train them once again to protect themselves and the land. For some reason, after the separation of Wizards and Sorceresses a thousand years before, the griffons had been left untended, forced to fend for themselves within the mountains. Centuries of human hunting had dwindled their numbers severely, leaving only a few dozen to be found.

Marina's grandmother, the creator of the Sorceress Brigade, had found the griffons and brought them back to the sheltered valley they now lived in, and set about training the immature winged lions. Playful, fierce, protective, as adults they would have little problem defending themselves with the addition of the magick safeguards the Sorceresses would lend them. But alone, without magick, they had nearly perished beneath the humans' cruel blows.

Shrugging the robe from her shoulders, she descended into the warmth of the water, nearly groaning aloud as its healing properties immediately began to work at her stiffened muscles and oversensitive flesh. Surely the Wizards had not known sexual relief in ages, if their play the night before was anything to go by. Satisfaction had not eased their stiffened cocks until well into the night. And lusty? They had surpassed lusty with their first taking of her, the deeds otherwise performed did not bear thinking of. They brought a raging flush to her flesh and a heat building inside her pussy that she had no time to consider taming.

She dipped her hair beneath the water before straightening and moving to the small shelf along the side and scooping a small palm of cleanser from the wooden bowl holding it. Rich, scented lather built in the tresses as she massaged it through her hair, tingling along her scalp, lifting away the feel of dried perspiration from the night before and leaving it soft, silky as she bent back to rinse it.

The steps leading into the pools held small dry shelves which contained folded cloths for cleaning the body, and richly scented soaps that cleaned and purified the flesh. The rich lather dispensed quickly within the steamy water, leaving her clean, her body well scrubbed. Had she wanted to erase the memory of the Wizards' touch from her body, though, she was doomed to failure. There was no cleaning it from her, either from her flesh, which still tingled with sensitive pleasure, nor from her mind which insisted on replaying some of the more extreme events and leaving her breathless with the memories of them.

Shaking her head, she quickly dried before wrapping her long hair in one of the towels and donning the thick robe about her body once again.

"Your Wizards are neglecting you it would seem."

She turned in surprise, facing the somber-faced dragon who had materialized behind her.

"Garron, you really must learn how to warn a body you are arriving." She breathed in deeply, stilling the hammering of her heart as she gazed up at him. "What brings you here this morn?"

"Veressi Twins." His voice rumbled with menace. "They have arrived outside the shield I placed around the castle. They are not pleased by their reception, it would seem. I expect them to send a very loud, very imperative message soon to the Keeper of the Lands to aid them in passing through."

Marina snorted at the idea. "I believe they will gain nothing but their own disappointment," she assured him.

"The Sashtain Wizards know of your secret now, Princess. Even I felt the bond of magick within my lair at the Joining. It was strong, a vibrant merging of strength and awareness." A brilliant flush suffused her face at the thought of all those connected to the magick knowing of the Joining. Of course, it was true, she had felt it at her sister's Joining. But it did not mean she must like it. In truth, she hated the thought of it.

"What is your point? So they know I am the Keeper. As my Consorts, they are honor bound to hold my secret, and I do believe they know that which is the definition of honor," she argued fiercely.

"Aye, they know honor well." He inclined his head in agreement. "But they are also Wizards, tied to their land, and therefore tied to the Keepers. Just as those who tend the lands and estates of Covenan are tied to you as well, Sorceress. They will attempt to convince you of their reasoning to intercede on the behalf of The Veressi."

Marina crossed her arms over her chest as she stared back at the dragon who had raised her for most of her days.

"Garron, the Joining has not weakened my mind, I would have you know. I would not betray my sister for a hundred Wizard Twins."

"Would it be betrayal?"

The question had her stiffening in surprise.

"What? Would what be betrayal? To intercede or use my powers to aid the Wizards?" she questioned him harshly. "What else would it be?"

"The survival of Covenan perhaps." His voice was silky-smooth, rasping through his leathery lips as his black eyes stared into hers in silent demand.

This was not Garron. She stepped back, suddenly certain that the creature standing before her was not the caring, often mocking dragon who had come to her most of her life.

A sudden smile lifted his lips as she sent out a strong, silent, strident call throughout the castle.

"Marina, for shame. Do you believe I would harm you?" He tilted his head in question as she swallowed tightly.

He moved like Garron, spoke as he did, yet, she knew, to very depths of her magick that this was not the dragon who had trained her in the past years. The one who had guarded her and her sisters. Never would he suggest lying to or betraying her sister, even for the sake of the land.

"Who are you?" She was aware of the strange tension filling the cavern, almost anger, as thick as the steam which poured from the pools. "You are not Garron."

A rough growl of irritation passed his throat. "Of course I am Garron." He lifted his lips in a slight sneer. "Do you know of another dragon senseless enough to align himself with Sorceresses?"

"I am certain I could find several, if they made themselves known to me." False sweetness filled her voice as another strident call was sent.

Why was none responding? Where were her Sorceresses, her sister? Where were the guards who should have heard her mental call? Unless he was blocking her. Sweet Mercy, she refused to be undefended, Garron had taught her to fight, to reason, she would not allow this dragon to defeat her.

She was the Keeper of the Lands. Nothing or no one could block a call from the Keeper. She redirected the call, sending the magick not outward to the castle, but into the very stone and the land beneath her feet. It responded immediately.

The castle walls trembled as Garron's head lifted in a short, jerky movement, his eyes narrowing.

"Very, very good, Keeper." Black eyes narrowed on her then. "You are learning well."

"I should be. Garron is an adept teacher." She lifted her brow mockingly as the heated waters began to surge and lift within the rock pool holding them.

The water shaped into a wall, wavering at her side as she backed farther from the dragon. Dust sprinkled from the ceiling as the land trembled beneath their feet once again.

"Little bitch," he suddenly snarled at the sound of running feet echoing from the private corridor Marina had used earlier.

With a flash of power, he was gone. The magick he had used to enclose hers wavered as she focused on it, the deep red of blood and betrayal shimmered within the air, mixed with iridescent hues of burgundy, maroon and scarlet. The colors of rage, blood and betrayal.

As the magick disintegrated, Caise and Kai'el rushed into the room, followed by Serena from the main entrance, several of the Sorceress Brigade and several castle guards.

"Marina?" Serena slid to a stop, staring at the wall of water twisting overhead, moving to place itself between the new occupants and its Keeper.

Marina waved her hand, sending the force to tumble gently back to the pool as she stared at the small waves thoughtfully. Garron was suddenly not truly Garron, Wizards were ruling her heart, and magick she hadn't known herself capable of moved through her now as though she had trained to control it for years.

"Marina?" Her Wizards stepped near, dressed only in their leather breeches and boots, their impressive chests bare as they sheathed their swords slowly, watching her in confusion.

"How many magick dragons exist on Sentmar?' She waved her hand toward the water, forming a fisted hand, then cupping the watery fingers to a cradle. As surely as she watched it form, she knew it would shelter her within its grasp.

"We know only of Garron," Serena answered.

Marina raised her eyes to Caise and Kai'el. "It is my Wizards I ask this question of." She kept her tone soft, gentle, despite the rage tearing through her. "How many magick dragons still exist on Sentmar?"

Caise's eyes narrowed. "To our knowledge, there are no true magick dragons." His answer was more shocking than she expected. "There never have been. True dragons are small, affectionate pets to Sentinel Priests and Priestesses. Only ones of great magick can take the larger forms of your Garron. I thought you knew this? Garron must be a Wizard Twin."

No, they had not known it. At least she hadn't, and if Serena's expression was anything to go by, she hadn't either.

"Garron's magick is that of purity and strength. White, shadowed to the edges, and filled with the healing sparks of emerald and true blue. The Garron I faced moments before is not the Garron we know. His colors of magick were those of blood and betrayal."

She turned to her sister, knowing that whatever deceit was building against them had suddenly changed the course of whatever decisions would be made.

"Garron has an imposter."

"This is not possible," Serena whispered, her hand gripping the hilt of her own sword now, her eyes scanning the room as though searching for the truth. "Garron's magick protects us, the same as Mother's. No imposter could breach it, not for reasons of harm, nor deceit."

"Mother's magick no longer surrounds us, Serena," she whispered, the knowledge of the magicks now moving throughout the land slowly filtering through her soul. "Mother is no longer able to protect us, and Garron is missing. I fear we are now on our own until he sets right whatever has gone wrong." She had complete faith in her Garron. He was the Queen's protector above all things. He would not leave her mother's side if she still lived, and did she not, then he would be by Serena's. It was not possible that either of them no longer lived—all births and all deaths were revealed to the Keeper. There was no way to hide it. And the death of one so close to her heart as her mother would have been like a blow to her inner self.

"Marina, your mother's magick still shields this castle," Kai'el growled then. "Even Caise and I feel its power. It is not gone."

"The castle, aye," she answered with a bitter smile. "And so it shall until a new Queen sets her own spells about the land. But her magick does not shield us, myself and Serena, as it did before, Kai. Our Queen Mother as well as our dragon is no longer here to defend us and wherever they are, their magick is blocked as well. We are now on our own."

She turned to her sister, staring into her pale features, her enraged gaze. Serena was no Consort, her true power still lay trapped within her, unable to defend the castle or the people of the land. Marina's powers extended only to the land itself, not to the people.

"Marina, you are not undefended." Caise stepped to her, his hands lying heavily on her shoulders as Kai'el moved to her side. "We will pledge ourselves here, to this castle, until the truth can unfold. You are not without resources or strength now. The Wizards of Cauldaran will see to this."

She turned to them slowly.

"Only Wizards of great strength can take the form of a dragon and wield the magick of the ancients," she reminded them, feeling fear build inside her, grief pitching through her stomach. "It is Wizards betraying us, my Consorts. And now you ask us to trust their brethren? Possibly even trust the very ones portraying the dragon we hold in highest trust? By law, any Wizard set may now claim the throne. How do we trust?"

Kai'el scowled at her words but it was Caise who held her attention. Sudden anger burned within him, turning his gaze to molten gold as he turned to his brother. Whatever passed between the brothers, she wasn't certain. Until they turned as one and went to one knee before Serena.

"As Consorts to the Keeper of Covenan, we lend you our magick as is our right by law, both Covenan and Cauldaran, Princess Serena," Kai'el, as oldest of the two spoke the ritual words. "From our hearts to our Consort, and into your hands."

Magick flared, true, bright, a blend of blue, gold and violet whipping through the air to merge with the surprising flare of lavender which whipped about Serena.

Marina stared at her sister in shock, sensing her surprise in the move as well as the surprise of those gathering about them. It was unheard of, even in times before the separation, for a Wizard set to ever, at any time, lend their magick, even to those of their brethren, for even a brief amount of time.

Marina turned back to the Twins as her sister nodded slowly, her hands lifting, accepting the magick lent to her.

"Why?" She knew it did not weaken them, nor take from their strength. But Wizard Twins were not exactly the sharing sort outside their own units. "Why would you do this? You weaken your own ties to Cauldaran in placing your magick here in such a way."

Kai'el lifted his head, his eyes reflecting the same rage lingering within Caise's.

"None will threaten our Consort, nor what she holds as her own," he snapped, fury darkening his voice as they came slowly to their feet. "As Keeper of the Lands, you are bound here, your magick, aye, even a part of your soul. And by the gods I will not see even an inch of what belongs rightfully to you and to your house stolen. No more than we would see our own lands taken from us. It is true, we weaken our bonds to our land, but land is nothing, Consort. It is but dirt and shrub, an illusion of power. There are some things much more important than such illusions."

Nothing could have been more surprising, more shocking. Or so she thought until Kai'el gripped her arm and began dragging her from the bathing chamber and back through the private corridor.

"What are you doing?" She struggled, not as fiercely as she could have against their grip, but enough that she hoped they well understood her displeasure in it.

"Returning to your room," Caise growled behind her. "Sentinel's blood, I knew Consorting with a Sorceress was going to detrimental to my temper. You can't stay out of trouble, can you, Princess? Even with our magick guarding you, you manage to find it. As Sentinels are my witness, my heart will expire before the Joining ceremony can even commence."

"There will be no Joining ceremony until the Queen Mother returns," she reminded them, frowning at her own disappointment. She admitted, in a small corner of her heart, that the ceremony, filled with such beauty and pageantry, would not be delayed for long.

"Aye, remind me of something more to tempt my temper," Kai'el injected as they reentered her room, magick slamming into the entrance as they passed, protecting them from any ears which would listen or eyes that would see.

"Tempting your temper was not my aim, Wizard," she bit out in reply, turning to face them as Kai'el released her, her hands going to her hips as she clenched her fists to stay her own irritation. "But I am certain it does not concern me overmuch."

Kai'el grimaced as Caise snarled. Neither man looked in any way pleased at the moment.

"Sweet Sentinels," Caise fumed as he turned from her, his hand rising until his thumb and forefinger pinched at the bridge of his nose as though warding off a headache of monumental proportions. "I cannot fathom it. You find trouble faster than the griffons that once flew about Cauldaran. Always into something, forever scratching at things that are better left alone, and spitting and sputtering no matter the trouble caused. No wonder the beasts disappeared when your magick left the lands. They had no partners in their crimes."

Marina tightened her lips at that comment. That one, she would not touch, not at this moment. No matter the complete untruth of their claim. Griffons were merely playful creatures, nothing more. There was no need to so insult them. And it was more than obvious that the beautiful, intelligent creatures had nearly become extinct from a sheer lack of love within the Wizards' lands. Damned men. Well, they were now found, and well-loved. Soon, very soon, they would fight among the magick of Sorceresses once again.

183

"She is not speaking," Kai'el pointed out as though the thought brought him no end of worry. "Nor is she arguing. She's plotting."

They turned to her, their expressions accusing, suspicious.

Marina's eyes widened.

"How dare you say so?" she sputtered, fighting back the flush which would have stained her cheeks. "I was merely allowing you your say, no matter the complete injustice of it. Mother has always said that men must expend their natural irritability as it arises or it festers inside them like an ugly growth. I would not wish an ugly growth upon you."

She blinked back in all innocence as their frowns grew heavier.

"This is what you have sentenced us to, brother," Caise suddenly snarled back at Kai'el as he held his hand out to Marina as though in example. "Look at her, all innocence and sweet warmth. Have you ever, at any time in these past months, to know so much as a moment, even a thought of innocence to pass her expression? I would swear she has arranged these matters to bind us here, to her side. No matter it is what we would have chosen eventually, still she would do so."

Caise knew the moment he said the words that he had known, even from the beginning there would be no returning to Cauldaran. The moment he learned her destiny, her power as the Keeper of Covenan, he as well as Kai'el had unconsciously accepted this fact.

"I was perfectly innocent until your lecherous magick trapped me within my own dreams and fouled my mind with your wickedness," she informed them both as she lifted her chin in defiance. "How dare you so slander me, Caise? And I, your Consort, claimed by you both, ruined for any other's touch by your magick? I do believe these insults are going to result in a cold bed for you, my dear Wizard."

Oh ho, already she thought to use their bed as a bargaining chip. They would not have it. No, by the gods, she and the Sentinels had somehow conspired to tie them to this land and to this woman. Well, by their blood she could now accept it as her due.

"A cold bed? You dare to threaten me with such a thing?" Caise turned to her, his eyes narrowing intently as he stared back at her furiously. "You, Consort, have stripped us down to naught but hunger and would make such a threat?"

Indecision flashed in her eyes for but a second.

"I would." She crossed her arms over her breasts then, glaring back at him. "You stand there and rail as though Joining with a Sorceress were a fate worse than death or a loss of magick. How am I to feel, when it was myself you have Joined with?"

"You should feel guilt," he snarled then. "This morning we should have awakened to the warmth of our Consort and her gentle body. Instead, we awoke to the bedamned walls shuddering around us and your cry echoing in our heads as you faced a dragon who we cannot name nor find. Aye, Princess Consort, feel guilt, for you are to blame."

She snorted at the accusation, which only enraged him further. They had made no plans to stay in this land, not until they felt the danger she faced and knew that such separation could never be tolerated. This was one woman that Wizards would have to watch daily. Otherwise, only the gods knew what manner of trouble she would seek out.

"I warned you weeks ago we would not suit." She lifted her shoulder negligently, causing their cocks to clench with a fierce, overriding hunger. Oh, she was pushing. Soon she would push them past all control. "You have made your beds, now you must lie in them as you see fit. You are as trapped within this Consortship as I myself am. I will not accept blame when I warned you accordingly."

"My lady Consort." Kai'el's voice rumbled with danger, and echoed Caise's lust and need to submit to this woman's passions.

Marina turned to him, staring back at him hesitantly as his eyes sparkled with a darker, more intense magick than ever before. The removal of their clothing was done with haste. The bodies hungered, the need to touch her, to taste her, to submit her desires, became paramount.

"I would advise you to heed a fair bit of caution in your words at this moment." The dark rasp had shivers chasing up her spine as he stepped closer, his dark blond hair tangled around his sensual face, his eyes brooding, intent. "And I will also remind you, that it is your bed we call our own for now. Should any caution be required, or any made in lying within it, then it would be on your part. For you are but one." His hands gripped her upper arms as he jerked her closer, his head lowering, his eyes staring into hers. "And we are two."

Kai'el knew, had always known that this association with Sorceresses would make them both mad. He and Caise, they had spent their lives separate, without the bonds many other twins shared, independent of one another. Until now. Until this woman and this magick. She made a mockery of their control, of his control. The taste of her, the touch of her satin flesh, the sound of her laughter or the sight of her anger, they aroused him as nothing or no one else ever had. Affected him as nothing, even his magick, had ever had the power to affect him.

His hands clenched in her hair, long spiraling curls that wrapped around his hands in tendrils of silken fire, just as her magick wrapped around his body, through his soul. He could feel it building around him now, licking over his flesh as her tongue licked back at his, her kiss just as greedy, as tempestuous and hot as the lust flowing around them.

For Caise it was no less intense. Kai'el could feel the bond with his brother, the connection forged in her magick, and building as the heat of their lusts built. And emotion. As his lips devoured her kiss he removed her robe before his hands roamed over her naked body, emotion slid in, wrapping through him, around him, weakening him with his need for this one woman.

He was aware of Caise behind her, his own pleasure in touching her body, his emotion swelling inside him as well. How did one small stubborn Sorceress weaken them so? They had a job to do while here, not just the Joining to this Princess, but to learn where the emanations of dark magick were coming from.

There was no dark magick here, though, in this room.

A strangled groan left his throat as he felt her hands moving down his abdomen. Hands of the softest silk, hands that wielded a sword, that fought for her land, yet their softness was unlike anything he had ever known.

He could not get enough of her. Not her taste, not her touch. The need whipped through them both like bolts of fiery magick, destroying any defenses set in place to protect their hearts. She was their heart.

Her hands, soft as the petals of a flower, as warm as the sun, wrapped around his erection, drawing a harsh groan from his lips as he tore them back from her, moving along her jaw, her neck, licking, tasting her flesh as Caise tilted her head back to his shoulder and gave her his kiss instead.

Which left her body open to Kai'el. And despite the pleasure he found in her hands upon his raging cock, there were much greater, much sweeter pleasures to be found upon her body.

Kai'el lowered his hands to hers, disengaging her fingers as a grimace of need contorted his face at her moaning protest. His eyes opened to see Caise's lips consuming her, drawing the sweetness of her response from her lips as one hand cupped her jaw, the other held her hip, keeping her securely within his grasp.

Her long, slender neck was arched, her sweet breasts lifted, the cherry-ripe nipples hard and elongated, stiffening into tempting points that drew his lips. He bent to her as he brought her hands carefully above his waist, holding them firmly as his tongue licked over the erotic fruit beckoning him.

Her strangled cries urged him further. Her response to him sending shards of desperate need pulsing in his balls. The spheres had drawn tight beneath the base of his cock, aching, burning with the need for release. But even greater than that need to release was the need to taste her. To fill his mouth with her sweet essence and feel her climax rippling through her pussy.

As he left her breasts, moving ever closer to the bare folds of her cunt, he was aware of Caise's hands covering her breasts, his fingers plucking at the hard points. He could feel the echo of her pleasure racing through him, the magick and the touch of their hands lifting her to greater heights of sensation.

And this was how they wanted their Consort. Liquid with her need, accepting, giving unto them.

His teeth scraped over her slender abdomen as he felt it ripple beneath him, her womb convulsing as his hands smoothed down her thighs. He placed small kisses along the flat plane then licked at the sweetness of her perspiring flesh. She was damp from head to toe, the heat and the pleasure making her body slick, not just between her thighs, but along the creamy sweet flesh.

Parting her thighs, he groaned at the scent of female need wafting from her heated pussy. The scent of the newly awakened land, clean, clear, a promise of the sun's heat building within it. His mouth watered, a groan tearing from his lips as he nipped at her abdomen.

"I can smell your need, Marina," he growled. "Like the sweetest nectar, drawing my lips, filling my senses."

She bucked in response to his words, her cries muted by Caise's lips as he drank from the willing passion of her kiss.

Her thighs parted, the folds hiding the swollen bud of her clit parting to reveal the tempting fruit. Laying his hands along her upper thighs, he used his thumbs to part the glistening flesh, to gaze upon the flushed, blushing richness of untold pleasure.

"Like the most delicate sweet," he crooned, blowing gently against the ultrasensitive bud, feeling her magick intensify within him, around him, as her pleasure built higher. "I could lose myself within this richness, Marina."

Kneeling before her, he leaned closer, lifting one slender thigh and placing her foot upon his upraised knee, opening her further, revealing the sweet juices of her ever-growing need. Small dewy drops of her syrup built upon the delicate folds, cream and syrup mixed, mesmerizing him with the lush promise of passion.

He could hear Caise's groans now. A tight smile crossed his face as he became aware that in releasing her hands, she had found flesh to torment. The hard length of Caise's cock was currently receiving her exploratory caresses. His brother's control would soon break, as Kai'el knew, his would as well.

He lowered his head, using his tongue to catch the small drops of sweet juice from the swollen lips of her cunt. She jerked in his grip, a hoarse scream shattering the heated atmosphere as her thighs tightened.

"Mm. Such heat and sweetness." He leaned back for but a second, glancing up to see Caise's hands pulling at her nipples as his teeth, lips and tongue tormented her neck. She stared down at him, the heavy skein of riotous curls falling over one shoulder, her violet eyes near black now, all thoughts of tormenting Caise forgotten as her hands wove through his own hair.

"More," she whispered, her lips swollen, pouty with hunger.

"More?" he teased gently. "More what, Princess? What do you seek?"

She bit at her lip, a beseeching moan vibrating in her throat as he leaned forward, lapped once at the saturated flesh and drew back.

"Please, please..." Her words were cries now as she pushed her hips closer.

"Tell me what you wish, my love," he urged, the need to hear the words pounding in his head. "Tell me what you what."

"Kai..." Her eyes fluttered closed for a second, heat further mounting in her sensual face before they opened once again. "Lick me again. Lick me deeper."

His teeth clenched together with the violent storm of need suddenly racing through him. He did as she bid, lowering his head once again as he nudged firmly against the folds. In one, slow lick he parted the narrow slit and sent a shuddering cry tearing from her throat as he licked around her pulsing little clit.

"Do not stop." Her voice was hoarse, beseeching, her hands pulling at his hair in an attempt to bring him nearer as he leaned back, licking the essence of her from his lips, his senses exploding with the riot of flavors that her sweet flesh held.

His cock was pounding in furious demand, his balls aching like the deepest wound as he stared back at her.

"What more do you wish?" He demanded the answer.

"I wish you to fuck me," she snarled, the need now greater than her hesitancy. "I want you to shove your tongue so deep inside my pussy I—" She screamed again.

Kai'el did as she commanded. His tongue drove inside her, licked, lapped, fucked into the tight slick pussy, milking it with desperate hunger as he began to eat at her. He was possessed, addicted, caught within a storm he could not control as she exploded against his lips.

Her cunt wept with her joy, ecstasy flowing into him, magick and sweet cream intoxicating him as his control broke. There was no control within this woman's arms. Pushing himself quickly to his feet he moved as Caise followed, pushing her over the arm of the nearby chair as Caise moved before him, Kai'el slid behind her.

His hand landed on the taut flesh of her ass, a growl leaving his lips as the colorful weave of their magick began to surround them all within a heated, sensation-rich bubble that only heightened the pleasure.

As her lips parted to cry out at the erotic excess, Caise moved to claim the sweet territory with his bulging cock. His brother was near mindless with his own needs now, and Kai'el knew he was quickly losing his own sanity. He smacked her ass again, watching her buck, her thighs part further as he moved to claim the dark, hot confines of her pussy.

Lifting her hips higher, he watched his cock, its width nudging against the fragile entrance to her pussy, watching as pink flesh surrounded it, milking it in with each hard contraction attacking the inner flesh as his hand landed once again on her well-rounded rear.

"So hot, so tight," he growled, unable to steal his eyes from the sight of her taking him, opening for him as he worked his erection slowly within her. His eyes were blurring with the pleasure, his balls drawing so tight against the base of his cock that he knew he was only seconds from exploding within her.

His head fell back, his eyes closing as he gripped her hips and slid forcibly into the gripping depths of her pussy. She surrounded him with fire, with magick, with a pleasure he could not deny, nor could he bear for long. Already sizzling fingers of sensation were building at the base of his spine, warning him that release was nearing. Control was but a thing of the past, a hazy memory of little consequence.

He could hear her sucking Caise's cock, her moans rising in crescendo as Caise's voice worked her deeper within the spell of lust weaving about them all.

Kai'el urged himself to take care, the thought distant within his brain as he began fucking her, bucking against her, feeling the heat and liquid fire encasing his cock, rippling over it as he began to pound into her suckling cunt. His teeth clenched as he fought to hold back, feeling her release building in the tremors racing through her pussy. She was near. So near.

He held to her, sending his magick below her to entrap her clit, to suckle it with the same heat and loving grip his mouth would have used.

"Fuck yes," he snarled as he felt her tighten. "Come for me, beloved...tight, soft, fuck, yes!"

The violent contractions seized her as he lost his own control. Slamming inside her, once, twice, he felt the tearing, searing explosion of his semen jetting from the head of his cock and spilling inside her even as Caise began to fill her mouth.

Never-ending, a pleasure that tore through the heart, filled the soul and once again made them three parts of a whole, merging them, magick and mind in a kaleidoscope of color and emotion, sensation and pleasure until it flung them brutally into ecstasy.

When reality returned, it was to watch in satisfaction as threads of gold and blue followed the violet magick as it eased back inside her, settling over her body, their bodies, like a mist, before evaporating, returning to that inner space inside them where all magick dwelled.

And for a moment, for the briefest time, he sensed her as he never had before. Fear, pain, regret, and a love that shook him to the very core of his being. For there would never be another to complete them as she did. Just as she would never find such pleasure with another male. They were bonded. And it was for life.

Chapter Fifteen

೫ာ

The griffons were safe and sound within their sheltered lair, the new babes were curled against their mothers, suckling hungrily, the two fully mature males were testing their strength against each other, battling with care within the clearing. Their great wings were unfurled, slapping and smacking with powerful gusts as sheathed claws slammed into powerful necks, or sharp teeth bit into tough hide.

There were a dozen in all. Several immature males were mimicking their fathers, beginning to learn early the way of griffons by slapping and pawing at each other. Even the females were joining in, learning that they too had strength and the ability to fight.

Griffons lived for centuries, and maturity took decades to be reached. It was the reason the Seculars had found them so easy to hunt and to destroy. They had poisoned them with contaminated meats, shot the babes from the air, and without the shield of their Sorceresses' powers, the creatures had been unable to defend against such strikes.

Here, within the Emerald Valley, by combining their powers and setting the strongest spells Garron had taught the Sorceresses in the past, the immature orphans gathered nearly a century ago were finally coming into their strength. Soon, once they reached the age where they could bond with the magick of the land, and the warrioresses who cared for them, they would be marginally safer. As they multiplied, their strength would become enduring.

For these griffons would not be protected solely by the magick of the females who commanded them. Marina was slowly building an awareness within the adults of the magick they possessed as well. The intuitive bond to the land that all creatures held, but had been wiped from the griffons by Wizards of the past, to tie them forever to the Sorceresses they had been assigned to watch over. That had been a millennium ago, and Marina had learned the great, gentle creatures had been abandoned for that reason alone. All ties to the Wizards had been broken. Even these.

As she stepped silently into the clearing, the two adult males broke from their play and bounded toward her. Their wings folded at their backs, their lion's manes flowing in the wind as they ran across the clearing. Braking quickly, they came to a stop just feet before her, amber eyes staring back at her in adoration as she moved to them.

"What beauties you are," she laughed in delight as her fingers raked through their well-brushed manes. Tawny fur rippled over their bodies as muscular legs quivered in anticipation of her touch.

She took her time petting each of them, watching as the Sorceresses assigned to their care moved back into the clearing to gather the immature creatures together to lead them back to the lairs.

Malose and Mustafa purred beneath her touch, though, feline arrogance apparent in their fully developed heads and wide features. They butted at her for attention, clearly demanding permission to hunt.

"Go." She swept her arm toward the protected forests that sheltered them before standing back and watching them turn before breaking into a run and lifting their great wings. Within four strides they were taking to the air and winging their way along the magick-enclosed boundaries set aside for them.

"They are learning quickly now, Marina." Solara moved toward her, several of the frisky cubs following at her knees. "With the maturity of the two males, the babes are progressing much quicker also. They are learning things our grandmothers had no hopes of teaching them without the adults' participation."

She waved at the cubs, sending them loping back into the clearing to chase the magick rabbits that materialized within the thick grass that filled the area.

Aye, they were all learning quickly now. Learning once again to hunt for themselves rather than depending on the Sorceresses to feed them, as well as learning to protect themselves.

Marina gathered the Sorceresses together often to send parties of magickally created Seculars to hunt for the creatures as several other Sorceresses worked with the griffons to teach them to defend themselves. They were learning to work as a unit, to use their great strength and the magick inside them to discern friend from foe. Soon, perhaps when her grandchildren walked this land, they would finally be ready to roam freely within Covenan once again.

"I knew you would be here soon," Solara sighed as they linked arms to walk to the lairs where the mother and babes waited within the shade. "I could feel your worry for the griffons each time I've seen you."

It was the responsibility of the Keeper to oversee all phases of the griffons' new emergence. They were a part of her, dear to her.

"We will need them all soon." Marina breathed in deeply as she knelt beside the new mother, caressing her features gently as a rumbling purr began to vibrate through her body.

Easily twelve feet long and five feet standing, the griffon female was smaller than the males, but powerful and quick. She was the best hunter of the group when she had no babes to protect. She had taught the males to hunt once she reached maturity, applying all that the Sorceresses in the past had taught her as she matured.

"Well, my beauty," Marina whispered. "You have done well this year." She gazed at the four cubs suckling beside the griffon. "Three males and a single female. You will increase your pride immensely at this rate." The majority of the young were female, until this birthing. The three males would add strength to the pride.

She moved to run her fingers over the soft white down of the cubs' wings, marveling at how small they were. The size of a normal babe, within the first year their growth would increase daily. But for now, they were a mere armful, so defenseless, so helpless, they would be tragically easy to kill. As would their mother. Until the cubs were weaned she could not fly, could not defend herself, all her strength would go to strengthening her young.

"Can you stay long?" Solara asked as she leaned against the rock wall, her arms crossing over her leather vest as Marina glanced up at her.

The Sorceress' expression was closed but her eyes were filled with worry.

"For a bit." Marina moved to her feet, calling the other young to her to check them over, using her magick to discern any problems they may have.

In the first decades of life, the griffons were prone to many maladies that only the stronger magick of the Keeper could heal. Without her, many of them would die. It was but another spike driven into her soul. Another tie to Covenan which could never be broken.

"Your Wizards stay close." Solara pulled at the thick black braid lying over her shoulder, playing with the ends as worry darkened her eyes. "Will you still yet be able to work the males in their training?"

The others were not powerful enough, their magick too weak to control the huge beasts during these years of training while within the air. It was imperative that Marina work with them, that she lend the magick of the land as a safeguard while they learn to reach in for their own hidden magick to protect themselves. She dreamed of a day when the griffons roamed Covenan as the ancient legends told that they once roamed all of Sentmar.

"I will work the griffons," Marina answered as she ran her hands over the muscular wings of the young, checking for deformities or injuries from their rough play.

They batted at her hands, growled playfully and nipped at her fingers as she tickled them beneath their paws to check for sensitivity there. They were in perfect health, growing strong and fierce just as they should be.

"What of the Wizards, Marina? Especially The Veressi, they are due soon to arrive. How will we protect the griffons then?" Solara questioned her. She knew the legends as well, the stories of how the Keeper of the Cauldaran lands had dimmed the memories of the griffons, stealing their abilities to fend for themselves, to survive without the Sorceresses in retaliation for their desertion.

The Veressi, they had held the magick of the land for as long as there had been record of such things. Just as the house of Sellane had birthed the Keeper since they had claimed Covenan as their own. Their rage and petty deceptions had been the cause of countless Sorceress deaths in those first years after the separation between the two magicks.

"They will be protected." She shrugged, as though the thought did not worry her. "My Consorts have given Serena unquestioned access to their powers through our Joining until our Queen Mother arrives. With the land's help, we shall prevail, just as we always have."

"Marina, what of the rest of us?" she asked then. "The Veressi warriors will not be stopped any more than their masters will be. Rhydan stalks Selectra even now, convinced their powers will align. She hides to ensure he and his brother cannot force the alignment. We need her fighting with us, not hiding from bedamned warriors."

"I will speak to Caise and Kai'el." Marina straightened from the young and stared into the sky where the two adult males were diving to the ground, pulling up only spare feet from crashing to lift gracefully back into the air.

They were growing in strength, in endurance. Already they were learning how to place their magick shields, and how to connect with the land for signs of trouble. Not that they could ever be powerful enough to defend against all things, but while in the air, they would be effective in preventing attacks from below.

She could feel Solara behind her, her worry bringing an excessive amount of frustration at Marina's short answers. What could she say at this time? Too many things were yet hidden from her, the deceit shadowing them was staying well hidden. The knowledge that there was another dragon, one able to mimic Garron almost perfectly, was cause for great alarm. He was their final defense. Their ultimate protection against any threat.

"Marina, we fear," Solara said softly then, her voice quivering at the admission. "We cannot fight the alignment if the warriors force it. Our control and our choice will be taken from us and these warriors seem well able to call it forth against our will."

"Caise and Kai'el have forbidden it, Solara. They are Wizards, the warriors must obey them." Marina's fists clenched as her own frustration began to grow.

"But Marina, The Veressi are the Keepers of Cauldaran, just as you are the Keeper of Covenan. They rule, even ahead of the Kings of Cauldaran. Your Wizards are not greater than they."

And this was what she feared most of all. That The Veressi would enforce Caise and Kai'el's vows to Cauldaran to always protect the land and The Keepers. Just as her Sorceresses made their own vows upon coming of age. Each was honor bound to do whatever she dictated was best for the lands she protected.

"They would not have pledged their protection could they not enforce it." She finally breathed in deeply, convinced of this. Aye, her Wizards hid much from her, and this she knew. But they would not voice a lie, they would only hide the truth. "I must return to the castle, Serena needs me at her side for now. Have Selectra and Samara stay here with you for the next few risings. Together, the three of you can lay in added protections against The Veressi detecting the griffons. I will return in a few days to see if the males are yet ready to begin their training over the forests. We cannot begin their lessons until the magick has gained enough strength within them to combat any Wizard influence."

She feared it wasn't the Wizards at the castle, or their warriors that they had to fear. Whoever had taken Garron's form and now backed the Seculars was their greatest worry.

As she turned to make her way back to the underground caverns of the castle, Mustafa's enraged roar brought her to a surprised halt. At the same time, she felt an imperative summons, a soul-deep alerting of danger resonating within her.

Mustafa and Malose hovered at the very edges of the protected area, their wings beating at the magick, their demand for freedom echoing through the valley even as the call echoed through Marina's magick.

She sent a strident command to the griffons to land and cease. Left untended they could harm themselves in their rage.

"One of the farms is being attacked," she yelled back to Solara. "Prepare to ride…"

She broke off as Malose and Mustafa both dived for the ground, kicking up great clods of dirt and grass as their claws dug into it, their wings sending a force of air that nearly took Marina from her feet.

Malose's eyes glowed with fury as he roared back at her, clearly demanding to be given his freedom.

"Selectra must be in danger," Solara cried out as she ran to her. "Malose is most protective of her. Nearly as much as Mustafa is with you."

"Go!" She commanded the huge beasts, pointing imperatively to the lairs. "You are not ready."

At that moment power glowed about their underbellies and the heavily muscled legs. Magick resonated along the areas they were weakest within the air. Mustafa roared, but Malose, for once, was louder, fiercer.

"Bedamned, we have no time for this. They are untrained." She could not leave them, yet they refused to stand down or accept her assurances of the Sorceress' safety. And the calls for aid were growing more strident.

"Solara, you will ride Malose." She made the decision quickly. "Stay connected with me and I will lend you the strength to control him and aid his shields. We can wait no longer."

At that moment, with no gesture to allow them to mount, both griffons went to their bellies as the Sorceresses jumped to their backs, holding tight to the thick harnesses they wore when at play to accustom them to the weight and to prepare them for the saddles.

The griffons did not await the order to fly. Within seconds of the sorceresses securing their feet within the wide stirrups, the creatures lifted their wings, took one hard lunge and were lifting into the air.

Malose roared in rage as Marina opened an exit in the barrier of magick for them to pass through. As she did, she felt a sudden shift in her power, a merging, an increase in strength she had not expected.

We will be in the air within seconds. Kai'el's thoughts suddenly poured into her mind, his magick wrapping around her and the griffons protectively. *We will follow your power and be behind you before you know it.*

Dark magick flows. She could feel it, twisting the purity of the magick which usually flowed along the land. *They attack the farms on the eastern edge of the borders. Selectra's sorceresses are pinned down. They will not last long.*

She sent a burst of power to the land, commanding the strength to center around her warrioresses. She could feel it

201

flowing, building in the magick currents below as it sped toward the other women.

Malose roared, gaining speed as they caught the currents of air, catching the hidden magick buried within it and adding it to the shield at his underbelly as they sped through the sky.

Marina marveled at the griffon's abilities in the past months, the magick they were gaining and their abilities to tap into it. As they flew for the outlaying farms, she was aware of the snow owls suddenly appearing at her side, the warriors leaning close to the owls as they sped through the air.

Following suit, Marina gripped Mustafa's mane tighter, leaned closer and felt the small increase in speed as they hit a thermal current leading toward the battle.

We have warriors closer, Caise's thoughts mingled with her fear. *They are heading there now.*

Marina nodded fiercely, concentrating her magick on the creatures she and Solara flew with, enforcing their shields, aware of Caise and Kai'el doing the same with their owls. She monitored their strength, the stamina, and watched carefully for any sign of weakness. They had never been in battle other than play, and had never faced the true enemy. She could feel her heart racing in her chest, fear chilling her backbone that one of them would weaken, or she would somehow fail them. They couldn't afford to lose even one of the adult males. Without them, they would be several more centuries rebuilding the griffons' strength.

As they neared the battle, she felt a sudden shaft of pain slicing through her chest, felt fear and pain override her as the sudden image of Serena falling to the ground, blood blooming across her abdomen spurned a scream of horrified rejection.

The griffons streaked to the ground as she sent a pulse of magick, enraged, furious magick that buckled the ground, sent trees swaying, branches breaking to collapse on the attacking Seculars as the winds began swirl in mini-cyclones, picking the humans from their feet only to slam them back to the ground below.

She was flying from Mustafa's back as the griffon landed, reaching her fallen sister as Garron suddenly materialized, her mother at his side.

Chaos filled the forest as the fury of Keeper magick, strengthened by Wizard power, ripped through the small Secular force. Selectra, Samara and Solara moved around Serena's fallen form, their magick enveloping her as Marina stepped before Garron, Keeper magick halting his rush to her side.

"Marina, you will stand aside." Amoria stared at her in startled surprise as the blast of magick held her and Garron in place.

"Marina, what is the meaning of this?" the dragon growled, his black eyes flashing with yellow sparks as he indicated the magick holding him.

"I see a dragon, form and bearing, size and strength of the great Garron," she whispered the chant to the land and the magick heeding her call. "Reveal to me light or should he be dark, magick true and magick deep, friend shall linger, foe shall sleep."

The land, the magick, the power of her Consorts' strength blazed into a cauldron of deepening power, swirling around Garron to blaze in a fiery splendor before slowly receding.

"You will explain yourself later," Garron snarled as he brushed past her, lifting Serena into his arms as a rainbow hue of velvet magick enveloped them both. Just as quickly, they disappeared.

"Marina, what is in your mind?" Amoria burst out as Wizard Twins and warriors began to round up the few Seculars still living to enclose them within bonds of magick.

"What is in your mind, Mother?" Tears dampened her eyes as she faced her Queen, her mother, her soul rocking with Serena's wounds, with the treachery which must have surely happened. "Look around you. See what began here. See what endangered your daughter's life to your orders that she receive these warriors as well as their Wizards." She pointed to the two dead. Wizard warriors had fallen among the Seculars as the land revealed the truth to her. "We took in The Veressi warriors, Mother, and two of them have betrayed us."

"Marina, this is not possible." Kai'el stood at her side, his hands suddenly gripping her arms as Caise stared at her broodingly from behind her mother.

"They are Veressi warriors." She jerked from their grip. "Their forefathers betrayed the Covenan a thousand years ago and now they betray us once again." Turning to him, she felt his anger, his rejection that such a thing should have occurred.

"Ask your Talgaria warriors," she sneered, pointing to Rhydan and Torrian Talgaria standing stoically beside the fallen warriors. "Ask them, for it was their magick that destroyed them as they sent the killing blow to my sister. What else, my Consort," she snarled the title, "could have ever broken through the magick you gave her to wield? What but Wizard magick could have them the strength. Veressi magick."

Knowledge came slowly to Kai'el's eyes. He released her, staring back at his brother furiously.

"I gave no order," Amoria suddenly snapped. "What say you that I would demand such a thing in my absence? Garron came to you to shield the castle against their demands when you sent the call to the land, but no other contact has been made since I left for the Temples. I would have never asked such a thing from either of you."

The riotous magick filling the area slowly calmed as Marina stared back at her mother, uncomprehending as Mustafa moved closer, protectively to her back. She blinked, taking in the rage transforming her mother's features as she faced her.

"Your messenger arrived with your personal seal and your command that Serena allow the Rite of Reception to The

Veressi. Only their Talgaria warriors' arrogant demand for the throne until your return allowed her to deny that command."

Amoria stepped back, paling, her bright emerald eyes widening in shock.

"I would do no such thing," she snarled, her lips tightening as she turned to stare at those now gathered within the site of the battle.

Wizards and warriors stood well back from the Sorceress and the Sashtain Twins. Their heads were bowed, their expressions enraged. They liked this no more than Caise and Kai'el it would seem.

For now, they were silent, but Marina could feel their building fury.

"Dark magick is at work here, Mother," Marina told her, her voice hoarse from the tears she held back. "A dragon we believed to be Garron has been within the castle several times, meeting with Serena, attempting to convince us to allow The Veressi within the castle, to convince our sorceresses to allow alignment and Joining. Commands came with your seal, and our warrioresses have been attacked twice in as many weeks. We are at war, and The Veressi are somehow involved."

"We will discuss this later." Amoria drew herself erect, regal. "Gather your warrioresses together and get those griffons back to their valley. There is no way to hide their presence now, so I will add additional magick to strengthen that which your Wizards have in place." She nodded to Caise and Kai'el. "Garron is calling me to your sister's side, Marina." Grief twisted her features as her lips trembled. "Hurry home."

As quickly as the words left her lips, she was gone.

"Serena." Marina felt her legs weaken, felt the tears that filled her eyes at the thought of what her mother's words meant.

"Come. We shadow-walk," Caise growled. "Give your commands to your warrioresses now, Consort." His body was stiffly alert as was Kai'el's, their thoughts now shielded, but the rage that poured from them had their eyes glowing, their expressions a terrifying sight to behold.

Only the strongest of Wizards could shadow-walk, learning that hers had the ability did not surprise her overmuch. She gave her commands quickly, reinforcing to Mustafa and Malose to return to the valley to protect the Pride before turning back to her Wizards.

Each gripped an arm, and in a dizzying surge of power, swept through space and time to the hall outside Serena's suite.

"We will leave you here. Should you need us..." Kai'el's fingers touched her cheek as Caise's lips pressed into her hair. For a moment, such incredible warmth surrounded her. Protection. Security. Her breath hitched at the sensations.

"Should you need us, we are but a thought away," Caise finished as his hands ran down her arm and Kai'el leaned lower to kiss her trembling lips as he whispered. "Beloved."

Then they were striding from her, their tall muscular bodies tense, prepared, as though heading to battle. And she feared, they just may well be.

Chapter Sixteen

ဣ

The castle of The Veressi rose in regal splendor on the outer edges of Cauldaran. Perched upon the mountain above the Raging Seas, shimmering with a pearlescent glow, it gleamed with the magick and the secrets of the land they held as Keepers. Below the castle, the waters of the Raging Seas tossed and buffeted themselves against the cliffs below, while shadowed forests and dark valleys protected it below on the other sides. It was a place of mystical power, of secrets long kept and chaotic magicks. It was here The Veressi guarded Cauldaran, and once Covenan as well. From here, at a point where it was said time and magick began, they oversaw all of Sentmar.

They did not rule, for those who protected the land were forbidden to rule its people. Above, the twin moons of Sentmar oversaw it as eyes of the Sentinels, peering endlessly into the fortress of the Keepers.

Caise and Kai'el landed their owls within the huge stone-enclosed courtyards, before dismounting with tense anger. The daylong flight to the sanctuary had done little to still their worry, and even less to calm their rage. The warriors in league with the Seculars had been, as Marina accused, warriors of The Veressi. They had been two of their most powerful, most trusted twins within The Veressi's ranks. It was impossible to believe that the Wizards had been unaware of the foolhardy actions of their warriors.

As they approached the tall pearl-encrusted double doors, they swung open on silent hinges, the magick flowing through the castle wrapping about them with a comforting embrace. It had always been so. Here the magick of the land was born, from here it flowed into the Raging Seas and the streams which led from it. It fed all of Sentmar through every direction. It fed the roots of the plants that in turn gave its bounty to the air. The animals of the land were nourished by it, as were the people. Except for the land of the Seculars. Magick had retreated from those lands long ago, refusing to stay where it knew no welcome. The humans vilified it, cursed it, denied it, until the magick deserted it.

"Sashtains, The Veressi welcome you." From the shadows of the great hall a young woman appeared. Midnight hair flowed to her hips as wide silver eyes gazed upon them from a face of perfect beauty.

Caise and Kai'el halted before her, frowning broodingly down at the High Sentinel Priestess. She was one of the most powerful of their land, among a select few whose powers were second only to the gods, the Sentinel Select, themselves.

"Priestess," Caise growled her title, bowing in respect as suspicion rose within him at her presence.

"Caise, it is my greatest pleasure to greet the Consort of the Covenan Keeper." Her smile was warm, a delicate curving of her ruby-red lips as her eyes twinkled with humor. "The alignment of such great powers pleases the Sentinel Select greatly."

Kai'el inclined his head politely.

"We are here to see The Veressi, Priestess." He kept his voice respectful, despite the fury surging through him.

"Yes. I know this." She clasped her hands at her waist, her calm demeanor doing little to still their anger. "The Veressi are not available at this time." Her eyes darkened in sadness. "The learned the deception of the Delmari Twins as the battle began. They have gone to learn the cause of such deceit. They are deeply sorrowful and seek to learn why such powerful warriors would turn to the dark arts. They ask that I convey their regrets, and hope to see you within a few days' time when they arrive in Covenan."

She lies. The knowledge was surprising. Caise felt it, the same as he heard Kai'el's brooding thoughts within his mind.

Aye, she lied. How he knew he wasn't certain. She resonated beauty and life, magick in its purest form just as the other Priestesses to the Sentinel Select did. Only the purest, the strongest of the magick sects were accepted as Priests and Priestesses to the Sentinel Select. Their gods accepted nothing less.

This one, Nemesis, had never resonated with anything less than the purest magick, the sweetest demeanor, until now. But there was no challenging her. Not at this time.

"They have been forbidden to enter the Sellane Castle, even the Keeper herself has set the land to guard against them," Kai'el pointed out calmly. "They still yet plan to arrive?"

Nemesis smiled slowly. "They are the Keepers of magick, Sashtains. Not just the keepers of Cauldaran magick. The land will respond to them as is fitting. Even Covenan magick must bow before the highest Keepers."

She was not so certain of herself as she appeared. Caise was careful to keep his expression clear, his magick tightly contained and his secrets barred as he felt the minute echoes of her power probing at him. Little witch, to believe her magick was greater than Wizard sets. Who had dared to convince her of such foolishness?

"We thank you, Priestess, for meeting us with this news." Caise followed as Kai'el bowed, the words slipping easily from his brother's lips despite the anger brewing within him. "We will meet with The Veressi upon their arrival."

Nemesis inclined her head gently as they rose.

"And when will you be breaking the Keeper of Covenan from her lands?" she asked with studied casual concern. "I understand such a thing is wrenching for a Sorceress, but being Consort to Wizard Twins always requires adjustment."

"It is our understanding Keepers can not be separated from their lands, Priestess." Kai'el assumed interested concern, despite the brewing storm he felt within him.

Nemesis smiled with patient cheer. "Not at all. You must just force her to accept the demands you place upon her, Kai'el. Sorceresses are enduring, their strength comes from their Wizards, never from the land. She will at first protest it, as will her magick, but in time, she will accept it."

Upon her death perhaps, Caise raged with Kai'el's mind. *We leave now, brother. Suddenly, I fear we may have made a grave error in flying to this place.*

Aye. And alerted The Veressi to much more than our anger, Kai'el agreed, finding comfort now in his ability to reach out in such way to Caise. It was strengthening, sharing not just their thoughts, but their magick as well.

"We thank you once again, Priestess." Kai'el bowed. "We will take our leave now."

They turned as one, striding from the castle and making haste back to the owls who ruffled their feathers in nervous awareness of the strange emanations of power coming from the Keepers' castle. Caise and Kai'el both sensed the magick attempt to push past their defenses and probe into their deepest thoughts like a shadow lurking at the edges of a candlelit room.

Mounting the owls with an order to fly, they stayed silent, guarding themselves and their thoughts until they were well clear of the center of power.

Sentinel's blood, what goes on here? Caise's question blasted into Kai'el's consciousness. *Suddenly we can neither trust our Keepers nor the Priestesses of the Temples. The dragon isn't the true dragon and Wizard warriors are working with Seculars? I tell you, Kai'el, I do not like the deceptions I suddenly sense. Nor do I enjoy the suspicious arising by the day.*

The Veressi have access to great power, both the power of the land and the power of darkness. Just as our forefathers sought to restrict the Sorceresses and destroy their bid for freedom, so it would seem these Veressi also seek such a thing. But I cannot believe it without seeing it for my own eyes. If our Keepers have surrendered to the miniscule power of the underworld, then Sentmar itself will be lucky to survive the cataclysm coming. I cannot believe the Keepers, aye the land, would allow such a thing.

But he could not be certain. Nemesis was considered one of the most powerful Maiden Priestesses. She had taken neither Wizard nor Priest to Join with, and moved about the temples as an icon of serenity and strength. To believe she would deceive them... The ramifications did not bear thinking on. This was knowledge the others must know, the Wizards and warriors awaiting outside the castle for the news they would bring. But who could they trust and who would betray them?

* * * * *

Magick surrounded Serena, a magick unlike any Marina had ever seen. Garron stood at her bedside, his leathery claws hovering over Serena's wound as amber, green and shades of darker reds resonated over her. At his side, her mother paced, her face wet with tears, her emerald eyes dark with pain and rage as her hands clenched and unclenched at her side.

"Amoria, cease your pacing," Garron growled, his eyes still closed as he worked the magick over and through Serena. "Have I not sworn she would be well?"

He was the calm in the center of the storm, as he always had been. That was the one thing Marina had noticed with the imposter. There was no serenity, no calm with the other. Garron was mocking, sarcastic and rarely polite, but he was generally amused or irritated, but calm.

"Another of my daughters attacked, nearly murdered, and I was not even here to protect her." Amoria shook her head, her platinum-blonde hair falling from the crown atop her head to flow below her shoulders as the skirts of her gown swished at her feet. "I have bowed to the politics of the Justices and the Pre-Select long enough." The Pre-Select being the Priests and Priestesses who presided as the voice of the gods. The most powerful of the magickal bodies on Sentmar, and considered the most wise.

Amoria was a beautiful woman still yet, barely through the first blush of life. At two-score and five years, she appeared much younger, and had she been willing to risk the wrath of the Sentinel Priests and Priestesses would have still yet been leading her Brigade Sorceresses into battle. Marina feared her mother's attempts at diplomacy had now ended. Already the castle Justices were being summoned to meet with her, as were the Sorceresses gathered outside the hall to protect the rooms of the heiress to the throne.

"Amoria, calm yourself." Garron's voice was patient, though grumbling. "I have spent many years protecting this headstrong young woman, I will not allow death to take her so easily from you."

Marina tilted her head, watching the magick flowing from him, a frown creasing her brow as she committed it to memory. The aura and feel of magick was unique to each individual. Garron's was particularly strong, as well…familiar perhaps. She could not put her finger on it, or describe, even to herself the feel of it. She knew it was one of comfort, though, irritation sometimes, frustration often, but always a magick one could depend upon.

"Your imposter has had fun running amok within the castle during your absence," she finally commented as Serena began to breathe deeper, a small flush coloring her cheeks where before they had been white and wan.

She had been transported to the mercury pools first, the molten magick itself had sunk inside her, beginning the healing. As her mother had related, Garron had fought stubbornly for her life during those first crucial moments. Now, he fought just as hard, even giving of his own strength to heal her.

She watched the dragon's leathery features tighten as a silent snarl lifted his lips.

"Whoever that bedamned Wizard is, he will find his way blocked henceforth. I will find him, Keeper, you will have no doubt of that."

"I believe finding maybe be easier than you are letting on." Marina crossed her arms over her chest, glaring back at him. "Those were Veressi warriors, Garron. There is little doubt their Wizards are behind this."

A grimace contorted his features.

"Not now, Marina," he growled. "We will discuss this later, when your sister is healing and my strength is renewed. Find your Wizards to harass and leave me be."

"You would defend them?" She straightened slowly from the wall, staring back at him incredulously. "Surely, Garron, you would not dare?"

"I would dare to bar you from my presence until my work here is completed do you not obey me," he snapped, his voice harsh. "I know well how this attack appears and I will see to the matter myself, Keeper. You will return to your Wizards until I call you to me. Now."

It was a voice brooking no argument.

Marina pushed her fingers wearily through her tumbled curls and gazed at her still unconscious sister, her chest tightening in pain. How had those warriors managed to wound her so easily? She had Caise and Kai'el's magick at her fingertips, yet she had refused to use it. And Marina feared she knew why. Serena was determined to show her people that they did not need the Wizards any more now than they had needed them before. How foolish they had both been. The dark magick now working with the Seculars were forcing an alliance between Wizards and Sorceresses which could only lead to pain. If not betrayal.

"Marina, child." Garron sighed at her hesitancy. "You are near ready to collapse yourself. Do as I bid you and soon we will discuss this as is your wont. This I promise you."

His voice had gentled as she gazed back at him, torn between her need for the Wizards and her need to stand at her sister's side.

"Go, Marina." Suddenly, her mother's arms were around her, tight, comforting, as they had been throughout her life.

Her breath hitched in her throat as tears suddenly tightened her chest.

"I could not get to her in time," she whispered for her mother's ears only. "I did not know how to aid her."

It was her failure. She should have sensed the warriors' betrayal, should have known where to aim the magick of the land reaching out to her.

"'Twas not your fault, my little babe," Amoria soothed her, holding her in arms which tightened about her in love. "She will be well. I am certain of this, just as Garron has swore." Amoria leaned back then, smiling, the curve of her lips trembling as tears hovered upon her lashes. "Go now, do as Garron has bade you. I will send word when Serena has awakened."

She would go, but whether she did as anyone bade her was another thought entirely. She accepted her mother's kiss upon her cheek before turning and heading for the doors. As they locked behind her, she met the worried faces of the Sorceresses. All were here except the three guarding the Emerald Valley and the griffons gathered there.

"Electra." She turned to her second, the only other Sorceress in the land with the power to touch the land. The black-haired beauty stood to attention, her velvet blue eyes watching her in worry. "You and Astra are in charge until my return. No warriors or Wizards will pass these doors. Is that understood?"

"Understood, Keeper." Electra nodded as they moved into position to align the powers needed to form a protective shield of power about Serena.

"Keeper, will Her Highness recover?" Electra's voice trembled as she asked the question.

"Serena will recover, Garron has sworn she will. He would not make such a vow were it not possible. I have much to do now. Should you need me, call to me and I will come."

With one last commanding look to her Sorceresses, she turned and moved quickly to the end of the corridor, the stone door swinging open within the wall to admit her into the dark, long tunnel which led far below the castle.

The braziers on the wall lit with magick flames as the door behind her closed. Below the castle, far from the magick springs and the bathing pools was an area few knew of. A place where magick brewed thick and sultry, whispering from the spring that flowed directly from the center of all magick near the Raging Seas. There and only there would Marina have a hope of finding the answers she needed.

She wound her way through the stone passageway, taking several turns, moving deeper within the layers of rock and dirt the castle had been built upon. The ruling estate of the Covenani had been built here for a reason, directly over the underground spring which ran from the Raging Seas, a direct link into the most powerful magick contained within the land. The magick it was said The Veressi commanded.

Stepping into the thick swirling mists of purely physical magick, Marina inhaled at the ever-present shock of the magick settling around her, on her, like heavy dew in the early morning forests. She inhaled the magick. It sank through her pores.

Her head tipped back, her arms outstretched, and the magick became her own. No other Sorceress Keeper had been accepted by the magick in centuries. It flowed from others, evaded their questing pleas, and rebutted their advances. But it called to Marina.

The pleasure of its touch was comforting, heated. It filled her with a sense of security, of protection. And it whispered to her. Answers dwelled here, if one knew the questions to ask.

"Sentinels of Sentmar," she whispered the plea to the Sentinel Select, the gods who watched over them through the eyes of the twin moons. "I come to you humbled." She dropped to her knees, feeling the rough rock floor soften, accepting her weight with no discomfort. "I come to you, pure of heart, pure of mind." There was no hatred, no anger no rage. This was no place for such emotions.

She felt the magick moving through her, testing her words and still finding her worthy.

"I come to you, Sentinels, in fear and in pain. Prick me I shall bleed. A blow shall render me broken. I beseech unto you mercy as I come to you, begging your aid."

A chill wind blew through the cavern, following close upon its heels a heated breath of a breeze echoing with an eerie moan.

The magick tightened around her. She felt the constriction at her throat, about her abdomen, whipping at her wrists.

"They attack our land. They come to us, bringing only blood and death," she rasped against the pressure at her throat. "I beseech you…" She coughed, holding back her fear, believing implicitly in the mercy of her gods and the magick that comforted and protected.

The pressure eased, marginally.

Drawing in a deep breath, she lifted her eyes to the thickening mists above her head, the rainbow of color, every brilliant shade imaginable.

"I seek knowledge," she whispered, her voice rough. "I seek the power to protect…"

The magick wailed. There was no possibility of wind to reach this portion of the caverns. There was one entrance only, except for the underground stream of magick flowing through it. It screamed, screeched though in protest tugging at her hair, tightening about her neck as though in chastisement for what she sought.

And if she wasn't mistaken, she heard the names of her Wizards on the mystic winds, flowing through the cavern, whipping around her.

"I must know," she whispered hoarsely. "I must learn who backs our enemy. Whose magick threatens us..." She coughed again, then collapsed to the floor as the restraints suddenly lifted from her.

Tension thickened in the cavern, a faint feeling of surprise, of shock moving around her as she felt the magick building in her chest.

"Magick backs our enemy..."

"*Heed your Wizards!*" Marina jerked upright at the sorrowful, moaning wind that bore the words. "*When Wizards Rule, the Sorceress shall strengthen!*"

"I do not understand." She shook her head fiercely. "Wizards do not rule in Covenan."

There was no such chance. Caise and Kai'el were her Consorts, she could not heed them, would not place them upon the throne even if it were possible.

"*When Wizards rule, power flows, builds and burns. Enemies' ancient art revealed, power foretold art awakened. When Wizards rule. Heed your Wizards, Keeper!*"

The winds blew fierce and hot around her before just as quickly, they were gone. Marina lay upon her side, feeling the rough stone now as it should have been, biting into her skin as she stared at the magick easing around her once again.

Comforting. Gentle. If only it were understanding as well.

"Understanding comes in many ways, Keeper."

The dark voice had her jerking upright, the hard baritone, chillingly polite, dangerously warning came from the vision of dark power standing in the cavern across from her.

The Veressi.

They were identical. Dark. Eyes as black as the shadowpits, hair falling to their shoulders, gleaming with rich ebony, their sun-bronzed faces seeming cast from stone. Dressed in black leather pants, boots, and black riversilk of their shirts gleaming across their broad chests.

They were as dark as the magick she suspected they possessed.

"You have no rights here." She lifted her hands to gather the magick around her, satisfaction filling her as it whipped about the room before heeding her command.

Their lips quirked in a hard, cold smile, black eyes watching the merging colors with some emotion akin to amusement.

"Where there is magick, so can we be." One lifted his broad shoulders as the other leaned casually against the rock wall.

"Why then are you here?" She moved slowly to her feet, drawing the power deeper inside her as she faced the dark visions.

Their eyes narrowed, brooding anger flickering across their features before they were once again filled with ice.

"Order your Sorceresses to stand aside and that bedamned dragon to lift his wards," the lead Veressi growled then, his voice brooking no argument, sending a quiver of fear racing through her. "We have no desire to harm you or yours, Keeper. Give us leave to enter the castle above or we shall take it."

She felt Caise and Kai'el then. The power flowing through her connected them instantly to her as she picked up the fury raging through them.

"You would have taken it if you could," she snarled then, suddenly certain of that answer. "You have no rights here, Wizard! You stand on Covenani land. This is not a Cauldaran holding for you to dictate unto. These are Sorceress lands and your demands are as dust on the wind."

The Sentinel Select had sworn protection to those of Covenan a millennium before, they would not remove that protective embrace now.

She felt Caise and Kai'el inside her, pouring power into her, flying quickly to the castle.

"Keeper, you are honor bound to aid our cause." The Wizard waved his hand, but the magick about her refused to dissipate. He was attempting to force it from her, she could feel it.

"I am honor bound to protect this land and its people, just as you are honor bound to yours. No more," she snapped.

She could feel Caise and Kai'el drawing closer, felt their rage pounding in her head when suddenly, they were there. Marina gasped in surprise, stepping back as they moved in front of her, facing The Veressi now, their broad forms crackling with power.

"Shadow-walkers." The lead Veressi shook his head, his lips curving in dry amusement. "Strange, you did not inform me of this ability you had gained," he accused the Wizards coolly.

"You should have known." Caise's voice dripped with ice. "You are barred from this castle, Veressi, by the dragon, the Keeper of this land and the Queen who rules it by rights of her heir. What do you do here, confronting our Consort?"

Rage throbbed in Caise's dark voice, tightened his and Kai'el's muscular frames.

"You lent your magick to this castle." Veressi waved his hand once again, showing the masculine colors which now blended within the kaleidoscope of magick gleaming in the mists. "Even within Cauldaran you have never done such."

"Such was never needed." Caise's voice throbbed with his fury as Marina pushed herself between them, growing frustration with the view of their backs.

She didn't need their protection, she needed instead to sense the magick The Veressi contained, the feel of it as it moved through the cavern. She needed to identify it, to match it the dark strands of malevolence she had felt at the battles where magick had backed the Seculars.

"And now it is needed?" The Veressi leaning against the wall straightened then, his gaze settling on Marina, the pinpoints of power glowing ominously within them. "Since when, Sashtain Wizards, has anything of Sentmar needed protection from its Keepers?"

"Since the Keepers decided to force a Joining for power rather than for love," Marina snapped then. "You would command Serena to the Rite of Reception, using deception, threatening a rift between mother and daughter for your own ends?"

"We would do much to protect Sentmar, were it needed." He shrugged then, muscles rippling beneath the black riversilk as he moved to stand by his brother. "You will learn, little warrioress, there is nothing on this planet that magick cannot touch…"

"But there is much that the Keepers cannot," Caise snapped in reply. "Do not test this matter, Veressi. You have no rights in this castle, neither on our Consort, nor on the heir to the Sellane throne. Force was not agreed upon."

Magick blasted through the air, whipping from The Veressi toward them. Sentmar magick. Magick pure and undiluted, called from the very bowels of the Raging Seas to follow their commands.

Marina threw a shield before them the moment she felt it surging. She felt Caise and Kai'el, their strength merging with her as she called upon the land, felt it ripple in response before it caught the power and in a blink sent it hurling back to The Veressi.

Just as quickly, The Veressi were gone.

Marina blinked at the spot where they had stood, seeking through the mists of power for the source of their direction.

"Keeper, we will talk. Now." Caise gripped one arm, Kai'el the other. She felt her form moving, quick, light as air, through time and space until but a second later, she stood within her room rather than the cavern of magick.

Chapter Seventeen

෨

"I was not finished." Marina stepped away from her Wizards, ignoring the flaring sexual heat rising between them as well as the anger she could feel coming from them in waves. It seemed they were agitated beyond what the situation warranted at this time, at her. Now if they had been angry at The Veressi, then so be it, they more than deserved it. But she sensed their frustration was more directed her way.

"What more was there to do?" Caise growled as she turned to face them. "You drew those Wizards to you deliberately. For what reason, Marina? What made you believe you could face such power on your own?"

She resisted the urge to roll her eyes.

"Aye, I am but a weak little Sorceress," she replied, allowing a mocking smile to twist her lips. "Far be it for me to believe that what minute power I possess could ever allow me to face any danger upon my own."

Kai'el made a most distressing sound. Like an animal in pain.

She glanced back at him, seeing his head lowered, shaking slowly as his hands rested upon his hips.

"Is he ill?" She stared back at Caise in surprise.

"Aye, we are both ill," he snarled, his lips drawing back from his teeth with his anger. "You near gave us a stroke as we felt you facing The Veressi. Even now our owls are landing themselves, wondering why their Wizards would desert them so abruptly, in the air nonetheless. 'Tis too bad they do not know you as well as we, otherwise, perhaps they would understand our dilemma."

"Oh poor babes," she crooned, narrowing her eyes at the Wizard. Infernal males, as though she needed this superior attitude. "I was facing them quite well, I believe. This is my castle, my land, the magick which protects it would not have allowed them the power they believe they hold."

"She has lost her mind," Kai'el snapped. "You deal with her, perhaps you have the patience. I must meet with the Wizards awaiting us before The Veressi get to them first." He cast her a chilling glare. "While you are it, perhaps you could remind her of the dangers of warning suspected enemies of your strength. A lesson I would have thought the land would have aided her in learning by now."

He stomped to the door, jerking it open and slamming it behind him as he left the room.

Marina arched her brow as she turned back to Caise.

"Is he aware you're going to be fucking me before his return? Or have you agreed to this ahead of time?"

Fury nearly consumed her. Nearly. She felt her arousal spiking as well, her pussy throbbing as the magick echoed within her body, reaching out to the Wizard as her womb convulsed in lust.

It was, unfortunately, one of the side effects of using great magick, she had heard.

"I no longer have need to tell him any such thing," he snapped, his voice dark, furious. "You forget, *Consort*, the bond created with this Joining now connects us in many ways."

She arched her brow, certain that it wasn't wise to push him, considering whatever this strange mood which had overtaken the Wizards, appeared to push them to dangerous passions. She admitted, though, pushing them was a challenge she could not seem to refuse.

"I believe this Joining is no more than Wizards' excuses to practice their dominance against women they know to be just as strong, perhaps stronger," she suggested mockingly, "than they themselves are. What think you of that?"

A short, impatient wave of his hand and he was nude. Just like that. As surely naked as the day he was born, his cock thrusting out sure and strong, the ruddy head flared and throbbing before her slowly narrowing eyes.

Now how did he do that?

Marina propped her hand on her leather-clad hip, tilted her head and stared back at him with mocking patience.

"Impressive little trick," she drawled as she delved into the residue of magick to learn the secret he had used.

His eyes were like pinpoints of brilliant, molten gold. With a quick gesture toward her, her clothing was gone as well. And there she stood, naked, and of course her nipples were hard pleading points of hunger. Such traitors they were. The bare mound between her thighs glistened with her juices, she knew it did, she could feel the air cooling against it, a sharp contrast to the heat filling her pussy.

Bedamned Wizard.

She kept her hand on her now naked hip, tilted her hips and arched her brow with a slow, deliberate movement.

"As I have said once already. Impressive." She kept her expression cool, her voice sweetly sarcastic. "Now what, my horny Wizard Consort? Are you going to spank me again? What sexual exploits have we yet to experience?"

She couldn't imagine anything they had yet to show her. The Joining itself was a near orgy of sexual delights.

Marina watched as Caise's expression became darker, his eyes more brilliant in the sun-darkened expanse of his face.

"You, Keeper Consort, are a menace unto yourself," he growled as he approached her, his step slow and measured as he moved behind her, weaving a curl along his finger as he tugged at it. Gently. He displayed the utmost controlled gentleness. It had her shivering, almost in dread. She would have much preferred a display of dominance.

And traitorous bitch that her pussy was, it began to weep at the thought of such restrained lusts, for surely he would lose his control of them soon. It was a unique experience as well — thus far, she had been accosted by both Wizards, never by one. What differences would show themselves? she wondered.

Ah, her Wizards.

"A menace, am I?" A bittersweet smile tugged at her lips.

They were hers for now. She would not allow those painful thoughts to mar the time she could steal in this moment.

"Aye, a menace." His head lowered as his hand drew her hair back from her shoulder.

Marina shivered at the delightful caress of his lips upon her flesh. A second later a screech of outrage left her lips as his hand landed smartly on her rear.

"Bedamned Twin," she snarled, turning on him then. "'Twas no love pat you gave." She rubbed at the offended curve of her rear, staring back at him defiantly. "Such abuse is not warranted."

"What did you believe you were accomplishing? To face The Veressi in such a manner?" He was truly outraged. What she had believed was only mild anger, she now saw for true fury.

Marina stepped back from him, wary now, uncertain of this Wizard she faced.

"You have no right to so berate me," she argued back. "I am Keeper of these lands, it is my place to guard them, my place to find this dark magick invading our home. I will not stand silent while Covenan is torn apart by war with such evil."

"You will not fight alone. Never. Not ever again, Consort."

Before she could elude him, he was upon her. His hands bracketed hers, no magick restrained her, which was more frustrating than ever. She could excuse her inability to fight against such power, but becoming weak within his hold alone grated at her pride. Where was she to find an excuse for giving in to him so easily? She couldn't let him know she truly was a pushover for both his and Kai'el's sexual advances. It just wouldn't do.

"And you dare to order me in such a way?" she snapped back, glaring at him with the beginnings of her own anger. "I survived quite well before the arrival of the almighty Sashtain twins."

Who were they to say when she would or would not battle? They had no rights in placing such restrictions upon her.

"You are a stubborn woman, Keeper." His snarl was impressive when combined with the glitter of darker gold behind his narrowed eyes.

He backed her to the tapestry-covered wall, his larger, harder body holding her with no apparent effort as she struggled against him. Her arms were stretched above her head, held in place by one large, broad hand, his fingers firm and strong. He pressed against her, the hot length of his cock searing against her lower stomach and sending a chaotic response tingling through her body. Her pussy wept, there was no other word for the juices that slid enthusiastically between the swollen lips. Her breasts became flushed, tight, her nipples straining as they stabbed against the hard, muscular wall of his chest.

"Release me at once!" She strived to inject anger, forcefulness in her tone. She was horribly disappointed in its lack of strength. 'Twas a sad day indeed when she, a Keeper, a Sorceress of power, could not battle even her own arousal against such a male as the Sashtain Twins.

"Release you," he snorted, his voice rough, deepening with the mix of arousal and anger. "We will never release you, Consort. Ever."

His head lowered, his lips taking hers with fierce, untamed hunger. Her lips parted on a gasp, her hands forming fists as she strained upward. His tongue stroked over her lips, a hoarse groan leaving his throat as hers met it. It was a kiss of barely restrained savagery, one of tempestuous greed and overriding lust.

She met it with equal intensity, straining against him, lifting to her tiptoes to allow the base of his heavy erection to press into the damp mound of her pussy, to caress the swollen nub of her clit.

She nipped at his lips, grinning as a fierce male growl echoed from his throat and his hand threaded through her hair, holding her head back, holding her still for the ravishment of her mouth.

"Vixen," he growled as he pulled back, staring down at her with raging hunger. His expression triggered a surge of need inside her, deeper, hotter than before.

There was only Caise. Only one Wizard to contend with. Surely she could handle one overgrown sexual libido much better than two?

"Think I will let you off so easily, Consort?" He held her hands to the wall as the other hand moved from her hair to smooth down her side. His fingers cupped her hip, caressing it with calloused warmth as she stared up at him, breathing harshly.

Sweet Mercy but he was as dangerous alone as he was with Kai'el. No wonder her foremothers had left Cauldaran as they had. These Wizards were a hazard to any Sorceress' sanity.

"And why should I need such mercy?" She gasped as his hand shaped the curve of her ass. "I have done naught to deserve punishment, Caise, and will not accept it."

"You, my dear Consort, threaten a man's sanity by your very looks," he growled. "Add your reckless independence and you fair shake all his beliefs in his control."

Marina leaned forward, nipping at his chest before a husky laugh left her throat when he jerked back.

"What control?" she questioned him breathlessly. "Why should you have control, my Wizard, when you leave me none?" She leaned forward once more, her tongue laving over a hard male nipple.

He jerked against her, his cock pressing deeper into the heated mound of her cunt before he caught her hair once again, pulling her head back, staring at her in narrow-eyed intent.

"Consort, you would test any man's control," he groaned then. "Feel me. Feel how desperate you make me, how hard my cock throbs for you."

Aye, she could feel him well. She lifted to her tiptoes, desperate to force him closer as she moaned in weakening need.

"Will you torture me through the night?" She gasped as his lips moved to the shell of her ear, her neck. His teeth nipped at her. His tongue soothed her. And all the while her body pulsed and pleaded for him.

"I'm going to fuck you until you scream for mercy," he threatened at her ear then. "I will spread you before me, Consort, and watch as my cock stretches that pretty, hot little pussy. And when I have finished, Kai'el will have returned. And he will take you as well. Your screams for mercy, my love, will go unheeded. You will learn before this night is finished who is Wizard and who is Consort. Who rules, and who submits."

"Like shadowhell—" Her furious words were cut off as his hand landed with erotic promise on her rear.

"Restrain your language," he growled. "There will be time enough for your curses when you are pleading for your release."

He lifted her in his arms then, appearing less than impressed with her struggles before bearing her to the bed.

"You cocksure Wizard wannabe," she screeched, enraged now.

'Twas too bad her fury did nothing to alleviate her arousal.

"You will release me this moment." She bucked in his arms before a weak scream left her throat as she felt herself being tossed to the bed.

She bounced, fighting through the tangle of hair to find a defensive position in which to kick his Wizard balls to his throat for making such an asinine declaration. There came a time when a Sorceress, especially a Sorceress Consort, must forego the pleasure to show her Wizards they have surely stepped over the line.

Unfortunately, before she could find such a position, she found herself shackled to the bed, magick wrapping around her, spreading her arms, her legs, lifting her rear and cushioning it as her hips were elevated from the bed.

"Now there surely is a most wondrous sight," he crooned, his voice dark, entirely too sexy to be comfortable as he knelt between her spread legs. "You are wet, my Consort. Glistening with your hunger for me. Are you certain you do not wish me to continue in this regard?"

"I wish you to shadowhell," she snarled, though she truly wished he would just finish the torture he had begun and bring her release.

Bedamned Wizards.

"And yet, I am still safely within your room." He tsked with a tight grin. "Endurance, my love. It is time to test your endurance. Let us see your boundaries for pleasure. Begging and vows to heed our words will get you much in this case."

"Bedamned, egotistical Wizard," she spat. "I will beg you for nothing." She jerked at her arms, desperate now to break free of the magick holding her. And 'twas not just Caise's magick restraining her, but Kai'el's as well.

"We shall see, will we not, beloved?" he whispered as his hands smoothed down her thighs, causing the muscles to clench involuntarily at the touch. "Give me your vow to never again face such danger alone and we will proceed much differently, I promise you. We will bring you release time and time again rather delaying that much-needed completion you will plead for."

Sweet Mother Sentinel, she was in such trouble now.

"These are my lands, Caise," she fumed. "I will protect them as I must."

"You do not fight alone, Consort," he snarled furiously. "Whatever I must do to convince you of this, I shall. Until then, I will have the vow from your lips that you will heed my words. You do not battle such violence as the dark arts alone. Agree with me on this. Do it now."

"Go to shadowhell!"

His hand landed on the tilted curves of her cunt as her eyes widened and pleasure tore through every nerve ending she possessed.

She growled at the extreme pleasure, her eyes narrowing as he watched her response. Aye, he knew well her response, already her magick filled the space around her body, twining with theirs, intensifying the heat and the pleasure she felt.

"You play by a coward's rules," she snapped. "Release me and we will see who shall do what."

He chuckled at the challenge, obviously unaffected by the slur.

"My lady Consort." His hand smoothed over the flushed curves then. "I know well the power you hold. I would never tempt my own demise in such a way. Nay, I think you will stay bound just so, until the vow I seek pours from your lips in exchange for the release you will soon be ready for."

She bit her lip. She would not hold out for long, so why not make the vow and then heed only the letter of it. They were but Wizards, she was a Sorceress Keeper. There were many technicalities she could find, she was certain. And she would. Aye, she would do such, except she knew by all the Sentinels most loved, that they would only push for more once this vow had been made.

They were Wizards. They knew no other course.

"Or perhaps it shall be your pleas I hear," she dared him in exchange.

They had restrained her hands, but not her magick. And though she knew her efforts to still their dominance had failed before, she could only pray that in this instance, she would be successful. There were ways to restrain a male's release, she had heard. Often, the servants of the castle were a font of information when need be.

Now, she had only to keep her head 'til the time was right to apply what she had heard.

Chapter Eighteen

ஐ

"Ah, my pretty little Consort." Caise knelt before her as the magick lifted her, raising her until she sat, spread-legged in front of him, her breath gasping from between her lips as the eroticism of his dominance sparked a fire inside her that raged through her blood. "How very beautiful you are. Soft..." His fingertips smoothed over the rise and fall of her tummy. "So soft, you nearly tempt me beyond control."

Damn him. He made her hunger, made her want to accede to any wish he may have, if only she could.

"I will not give you what you wish, Wizard." She fought to inject strength into her voice rather than the overwhelming hunger. "I cannot. You know I cannot."

"Ah, but you will, my dear," he sighed, his lips curving into a slight smile as his hands reached up to frame the swollen curves of her breasts. "I know your pleasure and your need, and you will submit to me. There can be no other answer."

As vexing as it was to her, Marina realized in that moment, in that one tension-filled, angry moment, that she might very well love her Wizards. Not that now was an opportune time for such a revelation. Perhaps it was the sheer confidence, the arrogance that radiated from him with as much strength as the obvious emotion for her radiated in his eyes.

She wasn't the only one who cared. Her Wizards had been greatly concerned when they arrived at the cavern. Furious. Not because The Veressi had dared to face her there within the well of magick, but because she had risked herself to face the Cauldaran Keepers without them at her side.

They hadn't said the words any more than she had, but she could feel their love, as surely as she felt Caise's fingers plucking at her nipples. And that caress was most distracting.

She was doomed.

Her breath caught as his fingers tightened on the hard points of her breasts, tugging at them, massaging them with destructive results as her head fell back and her breathing became rough, ragged.

Mercy, it felt good. The moan that left her lips surprised her, a keening growl of lust that echoed around her and pleaded for more. As though Caise needed any such plea.

"There, my pretty," he whispered, leaning forward, his lips covering one tormented tip insistently.

The firm drawing motion of his lips sent shards of sensation striking brutally at her womb and echoing in her needy pussy. His tongue flickered over the peak, sensitizing it further as his teeth rasped it delicately.

His hands were never still, his lips refusing to end their tormenting. Marina's hands struggled against the magick that held her restrained as she fought the pleasure ripping through her. But how to fight her own desires was her problem now.

"Such delicate pretty breasts." His lips moved to the next, suckling firmly before he leaned back to observe the taut tip, his eyes dark, his face flushed with his own passion. "Sweet against my tongue, a delicate feast of silken flesh and desire."

"Tease," she gasped. "I will repay you for this, Caise. You may consider that a vow."

"I shall look forward to it, beloved." He smiled, the thought evidently doing little to cool his ardor. "Now, shall we get on with things here? You may surrender at any time, little Consort."

His teeth nipped at her nipple one last time before his lips began to travel down her belly. She couldn't draw in enough air, couldn't still her spinning senses.

He licked at her rounded tummy, his hands massaged her taut thighs. Marina felt herself being lowered slowly back to the bed as she watched him, watched his lips, his tongue paint a course leading steadily to the glistening curves of her cunt.

The raised position of her hips afforded her the perfect view as he moved farther between her splayed thighs. The swollen curves of her pussy parted for him as he blew a waft of heated breath over it, cooling the flesh before he made it burn.

Leaning forward, his lips covered her straining clit, suckling delicately as he watched her through narrowed eyes and she bucked against the restraints.

"Nectar," he murmured as his lips lifted. "A feast for the gods." His tongue licked through the juice-laden slit as she jerked, a strangled moan leaving her lips as she watched him lap delicately at the syrup building there.

She could see her own flushed folds hugging his tongue as he licked at her, drawing the thick juices to him, consuming her as she felt sensation after sensation exploding through her senses.

"You are wicked," she gasped, her head tossing upon the mattress as her fingers formed fists to hold back the pleas rising to her lips.

A second later a hoarse scream left her lips.

Caise's tongue circled the entrance to her vagina with diabolical heat before pressing forward, his hands separating the swollen folds of her pussy as he fucked her with hard, driving strokes, driving her closer…closer….

"No!" She screamed the denial as he pulled back, within seconds of her release.

"Make the vow," he growled then.

"Fuck yourself," she screeched in return. "Bedamned Wizard. I'll not do it."

He moved closer, his face flushed, matching the ruddy, reddened crest of his cock as he slid it through the saturated folds of her cunt.

"You will," he growled. "And will do so soon."

"Do not bet on it," she gasped, feeling the thick head nudge against the tender opening. "Do not do this, Caise. Do not turn what we have into a war between us."

"There will be no war. But you will give in." He began to press forward, sending fire and lightning streaking through her senses as pleasure erupted within her cunt.

She was panting with the excessive pleasure, trembling as his hands gripped her hips and watched as his cock parted the lips of her pussy and pressed inside. It was the most erotic sight she could imagine. She could feel the penetration clear to her soul, washing through her, filling her.

"So hot and tight," he crooned, staring down at her, his features taut with sensuality, his lips appearing swollen, his eyes nearly closed from the pleasure he was receiving as well. "Working inside your snug little cunt is an exercise in restraint. I want only to pound into you, to find my release, my pleasure, and yet, I would wish that it could last forever."

Marina gritted her teeth, fighting not to beg. She must remember her own objective, maintain enough focus to make this work, otherwise, she would be as lost as her ancestors were a thousand years ago.

Ah, but the pleasure. She whimpered, tried to arch closer, to force the steady impalement of his erection as she watched him grimace with hunger.

"Make the vow, Marina," he urged her then. "I do not relish the thought of finding my release without you, but this I will do. Over and over again until you do as you must."

As though she were so weak.

She licked her lips, fighting within herself before whispering, "Do your worst."

And that he did. His eyes narrowed, his muscles bunched and before she could finish inhaling the steadying breath she fought for, he forged inside her.

"Ah gods," she cried out, her body tightening, her pussy clenching on the invader that stretched her, filled her. "Bedamned Wizard."

Magick. Magick. She chanted the word to herself, fought to fill one small corner of herself with one thought, one command that his magick could not counter. As he began to move, thrusting hard and strong inside her, his cock swelling, his release pending, she sent the fragile thread of power to just the right portion of his anatomy. It wrapped about the very base of his cock, tightening, exerting pressure on one delicate spot as his release neared.

"Damn you!" he snarled, pausing, staring back at her in shocked surprise. "You would not."

"I would. I would." She shook her head, moaning in near rapture as her pussy contracted around him. "You will find no release, Wizard, until I gain mine. I will not allow it."

"Little witch," he growled furiously. "You will have no mind left to hold your magick. I will see to this."

His movements were powerful, slamming into her, fucking her with hard thrusts, with destructive rapture that always, always stopped within seconds of her fulfillment. He demanded, he cursed, until they were both dripping with perspiration. Her body was so sensitized, so extremely primed for release that she swore the next stroke would surely bring it.

Instead, it only drove her higher. She fought to twist in his grip, to meet each thrust to force him to give her ease, but he stayed one step ahead of her always.

His fingers plucked at her nipples. He bent to her, sucked them, nipped at them, laved them with rough flicks of his tongue as his hips drove his cock deeper inside her, only to pause, to still before beginning again.

"Give me your vow." His voice was a hungry growl of desperation.

"Give me ease." She fought back. "I will not give you what I cannot. Please, please, Caise…" She was on the verge of tears, her pussy convulsing in desperation as her womb tightened further.

"You can and you will make this vow." He thrust heavily inside her, paused, retreated, thrust again until she swore he filled not just her vagina but her soul as well before he eased from her once again, panting hard, heavy before returning with a slow, merciless penetration that had her screaming out her need.

"Poor Consort." She turned her head to Kai'el's voice as he closed the door behind him, nearing the bed, removing his clothing as he neared them. "How much more, I wonder, can you bear?"

They would kill her. She could not bear more. She shook her head, shuddering, dying for breath as Caise continued to move inside her, each stroke slow and sure keeping her poised but on the edge of ecstasy.

She would not falter.

As Kai'el lay on the bed, she could feel their magick preparing her, lubricating her anus, slickening it as she was turned to him, lifted and settled over the thick stalk of his cock.

"Demons," she accused them as she felt it work inside her, spreading her, inflaming her nerve endings as she sent her magick to bind his erection the same as it bound Caise's. Dirty rat that he was thought he could protect himself, encase the area in his own magick and foil her attempts to succeed.

She stared into the pale blue of his eyes, watching the surprise, then the narrow-eyed promise of retribution as her power overcame it.

"Not without me," she panted. "You will… Aye gods." She tried to arch her back, tried to escape the fiery fingers of pleasure-pain tearing through her as she felt Caise began to ease slowly inside the overstretched entrance to her rear.

"Ah Consort, how sweet and hot you are." Kai'el drew her to him, his lips finding hers as his fingers speared through her hair to hold her still. They had released her from their magick, but their bodies held her more effectively than any power ever created. "You would make a Wizard weak with his need to fuck you."

"So fuck me already." She tore her lips from his, nipping at him when he would have taken them again, ignoring his chuckle as she fought to breathe.

She opened her eyes, staring into his, willing him to know she would not relent.

"With my heart and soul, I am bound to you," she whispered, licking her lips as she whispered a moan. Caise filled her fully now, flexing inside her ass, his cock throbbing with a heat and hardness that near broke her will. "See me, inside that part of me which is yours. I cannot lie to you, even for this. I will fight when and where I must." She nearly sobbed as need sizzled along her flesh. "Do not use this." She lifted her hand, her trembling fingers touching his cheek as his cock moved slowly inside her. "Do not take this from us."

They stilled.

Kai'el stared back at her, his gaze deep, filled with longing, slowly lighting with understanding.

"You will be the death of us." It was Caise, not Kai'el, who spoke behind her, regret, remorse, shadowing his voice.

Whatever they had shared between them remained private, but what came was for her alone. Kai'el captured the peak of her breast as they began to move, their cocks fucking her in unison, perfectly choreographed and stealing her mind as she felt the tension tighten.

Her pussy began to convulse, behind, her anus tightened, holding tight to the cock tunneling inside her as unexpectedly, violently, she began to shudder with her release. The command that held her warriors released at the explosion. She was only dimly aware of their desperate lunges inside her, the steady pounding force of their cocks fucking her past oblivion, sending them hurling into their own releases as Marina dissolved between them.

* * * * *

Coming to her senses, Marina found herself draped over Kai'el's chest as she lay beside him, Caise lay at her back, his fingers drawing tempting designs over her buttocks as she blinked to awareness.

"You are a very naughty witch," Kai'el grunted as she opened her eyes and stared, still slumberous, across the room.

"Keep it to yourself then." She fought the yawn that curved her lips. "Everyone else is convinced I'm the sweet princess. It is my sharpest weapon at the moment."

Kai'el grunted at the comment. "I must say, Consort, you may be right. Now, get up, we have much to discuss. The Veressi will be arriving within days, and we must plan for it. We must also try to figure out this dark magick amassing within your castle. That power is much different than that of our Keepers. We cannot accuse the warriors without proof. So if they are indeed involved, then we must prove it."

"And you intend to do this how?" She rolled to her back, watching as the two men left her bed and collected their clothing from the floor. "Even the well of magick below could not give me the answers I needed. What makes you believe you can accomplish what I cannot?"

Powerful Wizards they might be, but this was not Wizard lands.

"You can accomplish it, Consort." The answer surprised her. "It is simply not a battle you can undertake alone until you have learned the full scope of your awakening magick. Until the power you gain from us has built within yours, you haven't the strength to battle dark magick, no matter your belief that you can. Our power will combine with yours when we are close. That will be your true strength."

She watched, refusing to comment as they dressed, pulling on their pants and the soft linen shirts they had worn. They were perfectly confident that their will would be met, that she would obey them as though she were a pet faithfully padding at their heels. It was disappointing to see their lack of confidence in her. She had battled without them. For more than a year now she had faced the Seculars as they crossed the Covenani boundaries to attack at the small farms and villages. She had not been harmed, and until now, neither had the Sorceresses.

"Marina, I see well the anger brewing beneath that careful little expression of yours." Caise's hand gripped her chin, turning her eyes to meet his as he sat on the edge of the bed beside her. "Do not foolishly endanger yourself again or we will find measures to restrain your headstrong impulses."

Perhaps not a pet, she amended to herself. They saw her as a child.

She pulled her chin carefully from his grip and rose from her bed. Ignoring the Wizards, she donned a thick robe and pushed her feet into warm slippers before facing them once again.

"I am the Keeper of this land," she said, keeping her voice measured, quiet. "I will decide how I battle and if I need a Wizard's help." She stared at them both, restraining the need to rage, to allow her hurt and anger free. "You thought to weaken my will upon that bed." She waved her hand to the mussed covers. "Believed you could use my weakening passions for you against me." She tilted her chin, ignoring their glowering expressions. "I am no child to follow your every dictate, nor am I without a very conscious understanding of each strength and weakness I possess. I decide when and where I fight." She pointed to her chest, realizing she was trembling with her fury. "I decide who I fight with and who I do not. And I will be damned if you, The

Veressi or any other conceited, self-righteous Wizard will dare to dictate to me further."

With those words said, she stomped to the hidden doorway, waved her hand to once again move the stone door and headed for the bathing chambers. Let them stay or go as they willed it. She would not allow them to force a dependence upon them, nor would she allow her magick and her strengths to become weakened by her need of them.

"Consort, you try a Wizard's patience," Caise snapped behind her as she entered the grotto and slid the robe from her shoulders.

Stepping from her slippers, she sank into the warming waters, sighing in bliss as the mineral-rich liquid began to seep into her pores, to wash away the fatigue and weariness plaguing her.

"Do Wizards have patience?" Her voice was controlled as were her emotions as she sank beneath the surface, wetting her hair before coming up and dipping into the bowl of cleansing gel.

Heavy suds worked through the strands of her hair as she massaged the gel into it, cleaning away the drying perspiration and the dust of the earlier battle. She ignored Caise and Kai'el as they stepped into the waters with her.

"You cannot understand our worry for you, can you, Marina?" Kai'el asked then. "You can see only your determined independence and your fears that we would take from you, rather than give to you. Is it so farfetched to believe that we worry, that we beg caution, because of our feelings for you?"

She knew they were incredibly adept at making her feel childish.

"I can understand your worry," she admitted, refusing to face them as she bent back to allow the bubbling waters to rinse the long length of her hair. "I can even agree that if possible, I will not battle without you at my side." She rose and stared back at them evenly. "I will not agree to refuse to battle without you, nor will I agree to use your strength to aid my own unless I must. You forget, my Wizard Consorts, I am the Keeper of this land, and by rights, the ability to battle belongs to me."

Turning quickly from them, Marina rinsed her face, praying no trace of the betraying tears filled her eyes when she was finished.

"The Sentinel gods would not have aligned our magicks in such a way would you not need our strength as well, Marina." They stepped close to her, the warmth of their bodies wrapping around her, causing the pain in her chest to tighten, to burn brighter, hotter.

"They did not align them so you could control me," she whispered, raising her gaze to stare back at Caise, seeing in his eyes the pain she felt in her soul. "I will not forget the fears I had to face in finding the strength I possess. I will not be protected. No matter the reasons. I must protect…"

Instantly, her Wizards moved in close, Kai'el's hands clasped her hips as he kissed her shoulder gently. Caise held her head, his fingers weaving into her hair as he drew her to his chest.

"You make our hearts bleed," Caise whispered. "We would shelter you always, if we could. Have patience, my love, and understand our fears as well. Is this not what love is? Merging and understanding? We understand your need, I can only hope you would understand ours as well and find a common ground where we can live in peace."

"I will try, if you will do the same," she whispered. "I ask no more."

"And likely will push your limits at every chance," Kai'el murmured with no small amount of amusement.

"Enough of this." She pushed against Caise's chest, moving from them as she headed for the washing gel and began to cleanse her body quickly, determined to stand strong against the weakening need to allow them whatever they wished. "I must hurry and check on Serena before heading to the Griffon valley. You need to see to your warriors and the Wizards who await The Veressi."

She cleaned quickly, aware of the look Kai'el and Caise gave one another before following suit. Such emotionalism did not suit her. She had no idea how to handle it, how to accept what she could not change. And there was so much she wished she could change.

"Marina, hiding will not solve this problem." Kai'el and Caise followed, cleansing their bodies then following her to the wide stone ledge and the thick drying cloths folded there.

"I hide most effectively, Wizard," she sighed, burying her face in one of the thick cloths, holding back tears, need and hunger. "I will face what I must when I must."

She finished drying before jerking her robe back on and pushing her feet into the slippers once again before facing them.

"I cannot change the fact that you have overtaken my heart, any more than I can change the Joining or what is to come. I know only that I will not regret, at any time, what we have shared, my Wizard. That vow I truly can make."

Before they could speak, she turned and quickly left the chamber, nearly running in her haste to reach her rooms and to evade any emotion they would bring should they follow her.

For now, there was much work to be done.

Caise watched as Marina stomped from the bathing chamber, his head lowering at the defiant straightening of her shoulders, the lift of her head. She was a stubborn, independent woman, refusing to take direction as a woman should, demanding instead the same explanations and respect they would give one of their own counterparts. It was vexing.

Protecting her would have been much easier and definitely less harrowing on their souls.

"Loving her may well be the death of us," Kai'el sighed as he knotted the towel at his waist and stared into the dimly lit tunnel she had taken.

"Aye." Agreement wasn't needed, but Caise gave his anyway.

"I do not know if my heart can take seeing her in such danger again. I cannot prove The Veressi were there to hurt her, for their magick is much different than that of the dark magick I sensed there. And learning if they were there to protect or to harm is proving to be a most difficult task." Kai'el had spent precious time tracking the dark strands of power that still lingered in the chamber beneath the castle after he and Caise had brought Marina back to her room.

It was malevolent, jeering as he attempted to follow it, leading him in directions he knew it could not have ventured from.

"What of Garron—was there time to question him?" Caise asked as they moved slowly to the tunnel, giving their Consort time to compose herself and to escape, as she needed.

"None. He will not leave Serena's side, and the Sorceresses protecting her room will not request an audience of him. We must wait."

"We cannot wait much longer," Caise growled. "The Veressi arrive soon, when they find their way barred by that damned dragon, they will search all of Sentmar to learn his identity and his weaknesses. They will not falter in their determination to have the Princess Serena."

"Then we must do what we can to stand in their way." Kai'el paused, facing his brother fully, determination stamped across his features, filling his soul as he made his own vow. "We cannot let them take her."

"Aye." Caise nodded. "Just as we cannot claim what we believe to be our own. We have Joined with her, but can never truly possess her. How then, are our fates dissimilar?"

"Because we give her the choice," Kai'el growled, his voice fierce as unnamed, unfamiliar emotions surged within him. "Always, she will have the choice. I fear The Veressi will grant the heir to this throne much less."

Chapter Nineteen

ഇ

Serena had not yet awakened.

The wounds were healing, her physical self was nearly as well as it had been before the attack, but now, something else it seemed held her bound to sleep.

What?

Marina moved through the underground tunnels, her fingers trailing along the rough stone walls as she studied the level path she walked, a frown at her brow, her mind occupied by the knowledge that no matter what Garron tried, her sister had not wakened.

Garron has assured her all would be well. That ofttimes the mind needed to heal as well as the body after such magickal wounds, but Marina was not so certain. Perhaps it was the worry in the dragon's eyes. The pale, drawn features of her mother. She wasn't certain, but she sensed the lie for what it was. They feared Serena would not awaken at all.

And even more disturbing, as Marina had leaned down to kiss her sister's cool brow, she had felt something familiar. A darkness, a hint of malevolent power that she had felt only once when she had faced The Veressi in the Well of Magick.

Sweet merciful Sentinels, surely the Wizards had not somehow managed to hold Serena in thrall. It was nearly impossible to do. Even the Justices had been unable to learn that power or that of searching the mind for truth. Even their most powerful Justice was at a loss.

Wrapping her arms over her breasts, Marina grimaced as she entered the outer cavern, guarded by the large male unicorns that bore the Sorceresses through the forests.

Several were missing. She stopped, counting the proud beasts, wondering at the three unaccounted for. They must of course be in the Griffon Valley, with Selectra and Solara, but that left the third unaccounted for.

It wasn't unheard of for one of them to leave the caves that surrounded the base of the castle within the protected boundaries, but it was rare enough that she made note of the one missing and began searching the land for it. The call she sent was tentative, there was no sense in upsetting the forces that governed Sentmar, she merely sought an old friend, nothing more.

Yet, she could not sense him.

Saddling her own mount, she continued to feel for the unicorn's presence, certain he must be somewhere near. The creatures were very loyal to the Sorceresses and rarely strayed far in case they were needed. Yet, she could not find him, though admittedly, ofttimes it took a much more powerful call to the land to track farther from the castle. A call that would set the Sorceresses to arms and would risk awakening a Sorcerer. That she did not want. She had avoided awakening whatever resident Sorcerer had been assigned to their land for years. Keeping her magick contained, her power focused on a particular area rather than sweeping through the entire province of Covenan. The very thought of awakening the powerful male being said to be sleeping until needed, and rousing in fury if needed, was enough to make her shudder with dread.

Patting the unicorn's neck after securing the saddle, she mounted quickly, turned him to the entrance of the sheltered cave and sent him at a brisk run toward the Griffon valley.

She had not heard from either Selectra or Solara in hours, and since the visit from The Veressi, the magick around the castle seemed in chaos, as though it could not make up its mind if friend or foe faced it. It was odd, unsettling. Marina considered discussing it with Caise and Kai'el before leaving, but for the gods' sake she did not have the patience for more of their protectiveness. They were beginning to smother her, to make her feel faint with their constant watchfulness.

It was a relief to leave the castle and to allow them whatever the time they needed to conduct their own, so they thought, secretive investigations. As though she were unaware of what they tracked, within her own castle. Unlike her Wizards, she did not doubt The Veressi were the enemy. They were definitely not their allies, that left only one choice.

As the unicorn made his way through the forest, his legs stretching out, eating the distance, Marina allowed the magick building inside her freedom. She sent out tentative echoes of power, feeling them bounce back, identifying what was ahead and what may be behind her. She could sense no danger, yet she could feel it.

Her magick could pinpoint no direction, no obstacle or impression of Seculars, Sorceresses or Wizards, yet, she could feel the taint of danger carried back to her. She urged the unicorn faster, leaning over the long neck for greater speed as she allowed her body to relax, to flow with the animal and make the burden of her weight lighter.

The closer she drew to the Griffon Valley, the stronger it became. Yet no call to arms had been sounded by Solara and Selectra. No warnings, no calls from the griffon. Nothing to alert her that there could be trouble.

As the unicorn skidded to a stop within the entrance, she understood why.

A gray mist hung over the valley, dark magick filling it like an ominous fog as she slid from the animal's back then ordered him silently home. When he did not respond, she turned back slowly, horror filling her at the graying, stone image she encountered. The same as those of the griffon which once called happily to her.

She found Mustafa, a snarl on his silent lips, his eyes grayed, as still as the stone his body had become. Working herself farther through the mists that covered the valley, she stumbling against an obstacle, falling to her knees as a whimper of enraged pain left her lips.

One of the babes, so small, so fragile, had been broken apart, the lumps of stone revealing its broken wings and limbs.

"Sweet Mercy..." Agony blazed through her, trembling through her body as her breath hitched with tears, with rage.

It was Tambor, one of the priceless males so needed to revive the pride. A newborn, barely able to tumble about the ground in play, let alone to pose a risk to even a Secular child. Yet, he lay before her, destroyed, broken.

She reached out, fingers trembling as she breathed roughly, holding back the tears that filled her eyes as she touched the cool stone of a dismembered wing.

How had this happened?

She lifted her eyes, staring into the darkened gloom, the black clouds rolling ahead, and wondered what dark magick had hid the violence which had risen here. Struggling to her feet, she stared about her, fighting to get her bearings, to make her way to the small cave where the babes had been sheltered with their mother.

She could make out little except the tendrils of gray magick filling the valley, could sense nothing with her power except the violence moving through the sheltered area. She slid the sword carefully from the scabbard at her back, relishing the hiss of steel sliding over metal as she reached out to the land for the magick she needed.

Yet all she found was the dark force, one she dared not pull inside her soul for fear of tainting her own powers with it.

She moved through the mists, straining to see, stepping carefully, praying she would find no more of the babes shattered as she had Tambor. The sweet disposition of the cub had always brought a smile to her face, cheer to her heart. Its loss pricked deep, searing a wound across her heart.

But what of Selectra and Solara? Samara had returned to the castle hours ago with the report that all was well within the valley. What could have changed so quickly?

She found the wall of the cliff face leading to the cave and followed it slowly. Eerie, haunting moans filled the valley, a low cry of rage at the molestation of the land evil covered, a cackling hiss of glee as the clouds thickened overhead.

As she entered the shadowed cave, she came to a full stop, the breath stopping in her throat, fear ricocheting through her soul. Solara and Selectra were there, stripped of their clothing, bound spread-eagled, their bodies stone. At the back of the cave the remainder of the cubs and their mother, petrified with unnatural magick, gray, as cold as the form she had found Mustafa in.

"*Keeper...*" She heard the call on the unnatural wind flowing through the valley. Gleeful, jeering, it sent shivers of fear chasing up her spine as she fought to find a way to warn Caise and Kai'el.

She placed her palms against the wall of the cave, praying the evil had not managed to settle into the stone, and sent a call racing through her. She sent every shred of magick she possessed and that she knew they had given her, racing through dirt and rock, praying it would reach the castle.

There was no help for her as long as evil covered the ground, but here, within the very bowels of the cave, were small pockets still untainted by the dark fog. It was within one of those pockets that she sent the call flowing forth.

"*Keeper...surrender to me... I will show mercy...*" The voice, neither male nor female, reached her ears like the hiss of a deadly asp. There would be no mercy found within it, and it was growing steadily closer.

She couldn't allow herself to be trapped within the cave. Her chances of survival were greatly reduced here. The dark fog beyond yielded little hope, though.

Pulling back from the wall, she caught her sword back in her hand, commanded her magick, that which was personal to all magickal beings to shield her, and headed back into the jaws of the dark forces.

In the sky above, the form of a skull moved across the clouds. Whatever force sought her was powerful, strong. Never had Marina heard of such acts as what she witnessed now.

Her Sorceresses accosted, given no time to even send a mental cry for help. Her griffons turned to stone, her precious valley, once protected by the very land itself, overcome. How was it possible that this had happened and she had felt not even a sliver of awareness?

Keeping herself shielded, she moved through the tendrils of searching malevolence, knowing that somewhere within the valley, the owner of the dark power awaited. It wasn't possible that such a thing could occur from a distance, surely?

"Keeper, you cannot hide. I will find you, just as I found your valley, just as I found your sister. You cannot find victory here. I claim this land for my own."

Marina stilled, staring through the shrouded mists, feeling the presence now. It didn't feel like Wizards, surely The Veressi could not cloak themselves so effectively? But then, she had believed any of this could be possible before.

She refused to answer the taunting voice, staying silent, she crouched behind a tree which had once been thickly limbed and filled with leaves. It was now a merely skeleton of itself.

"Brianna escaped my plans for her. Escaped to the lands of her Wizards. You cannot escape me, Keeper. You are bound here, always within my grasp, too weak to fight me or to reclaim what I have taken. Always mine."

Marina's eyes narrowed at the gloating sound. Perhaps whoever possessed this magick wasn't as certain of themselves as they would like her to believe. If it were possible for the threads of magick filling the valley to penetrate her shield, then it would have. Instead, it flowed around her as though she did not exist, never probing at the almost colorless magick protecting her.

And she would be damned if anyone would claim this land. Whoever or whatever had brought such horror to this valley would pay. If she lived, they would pay.

She moved slowly from tree to tree, working closer to the presence she could only feel, keeping a wary eye out around her, glancing often to the skies and the skull staring down to the darkness below.

"*Reveal yourself, bitch!*" the voice snarled. "*I will bare you before me and see your magick taken by the very demons of the shadowhell, just as your cohorts who lie in yonder cave. They screamed for you, Keeper, they begged for mercy.*"

Marina tightened her lips, refusing to respond as she searched, moving with wraith-like silence through the valley.

She had no doubt her Sorceresses had not begged even if faced with the demons of the shadowhell. They were not visions of truth or light, but gruesome, unholy images of death and carnage. Gods help them all if Solara and Selectra had been raped by such creatures. There would be no healing them, no repairing the damage to their souls or to their magick.

She could only pray to the Sentinels that they had escaped such a fate.

Keeping her sword ready before her, she slid through a break in the fog, moving with deliberate silence to the dark form she glimpsed ahead.

There was but one. If her enemy was truly The Veressi twins, then she would die here.

"There you are." The form turned, the heavy cowl of the thick robe falling from a face well-known, and well-loved.

"Justice Layel." She stopped in shock as the woman's twisted smile and gold and gray eyes stared at her mercilessly.

One of the Justice Sorceresses, revered for her wisdom, stood before her like an evil caricature, her eyes glinting demonically as red lights flickered with the gray, and her twisted sneering smile revealed her triumph.

"Did you think you could take me, Keeper?" She nodded to the sword Marina carried, throwing back her cloak and bringing her hands before her.

Marina was unprepared for the blast of magick leveled at her, only the shield she had kept strong between them deflected the worst of the blast to her chest. It knocked her back, throwing her across the ground and stealing her breath as the sword went flying from her hand.

"Call upon the land you love so well, bitch," the Justice snarled. "I have watched you grow, tracked your magick, and made certain you never obtained the strength you needed to detect me, to find me. Do you believe your paltry magick will defend you now? That the magick of those whoresons you Joined with can shield you for long?"

Marina rolled as another fiery ball of power sped toward her, avoiding it by only inches as it slammed into the ground where she had once lain. Coming quickly to her feet, she watched the Justice warily, moving defensively to avoid the magick glowing at the woman's hands.

"Layel, what has happened to you?" she whispered, unable to believe the demon staring back at her. She had loved this woman, had gone to her often for advice.

"Nothing happened to me, sweet," she sneered once more, throwing another powerful flare of power directly toward her. "You just never knew the enemy living among you."

Marina threw herself to the side, knowing that to use the last measure of strength she possessed to retaliate would endanger the shield she may need to save her life. Her only hope was to find her sword, for surely there would be no other form of help.

Blast after blast fired toward her, barely missing her, weakening the shield Marina fought to keep before her. She screamed out to the land, to the Wizards, to Garron, but there was no answer. There were only the eerie screams of evil echoing around her as another flash of power erupted, catching her side and throwing her powerfully to the ground.

Marina gasped at the pain, fighting to find her breath as Layel moved closer, smiling with demonic intent as she lifted her hands once again.

Lightning ripped into the ground at Marina's feet, geysers of steam erupting around her as the ground itself split asunder, releasing a rainbow burst of magick that whipped around her, filled her, infused her as the Justice screamed in rage. The horrifying dragon's roar erupted from the dark as the screech of owls were heard above.

A kaleidoscope of power began to fill the valley, brilliant rays of color coalescing around her as she glimpsed Garron's white power barreling toward the Justice.

"Bastard dragon, whoreson Wizards," she screamed in rage as the dark tendrils of magick began to diffuse within the grip of the dozens of Wizards and Sorceresses now filling the valley.

Marina surged to her feet, using the escaping power of the land to fill her being, lifting her hands to infuse it, to allow it to twine within her as she delved into the very bowels of the ground beneath her to aid those who fought above.

It filled her, surged lightning-fast within her as she turned, raised her hands and directed it into the ominous skull lingering in the cloud-darkened skies. Her eyes closed, her senses, her being focused on the battle as she felt Caise and Kai'el surround her, adding their strength, their magick, until the battle that raged in the sky was as furious as the battle waging between Justice and dragon.

"Focus, Keeper. The dragon defends himself well and is aided by the magick of Sorceresses and Wizards. The skull is the true power. It is that which you must defeat. Center yourself…" The unfamiliar voice, dark, deadly, called out to her from beyond the Wizards protecting her. "Center yourself, damn you!" it ordered harshly. "You are the Keeper, if it defeats you, it defeats your land and the magick of the Covenani. If it defeats you, Serena dies, Keeper. All you hold dear is gone."

Rage burned inside her. She knew the voices now, knew The Veressi and knew they spoke the truth.

She opened herself completely. No hesitation, no fear, no remorse. She pulled in the strength of Caise and Kai'el, centered, allowed her body to become the weapon, the magick building within her the lance.

It built until she burned, until she felt the surging boiling cauldron of it ripping at her insides, tearing through her mind. She stroked the flames hotter, stronger, screaming out at the pain until finally it shot from her, a fiery burst of white light, so intense, so violent it rocked the ground at their feet as it hurtled toward the horrifying image overhead.

The power streaked through the skeleton's face, blazing through the eye sockets, striking at the weakest point as a scream of such horrendous evil, as though the combined demons of the shadowhell were being burned in the darkest pits until an explosion rocked the skies, a shower of magick, blinding in its color, and triumph filled the sky instead.

Marina collapsed. Her strength seeped from her body as Caise caught her in his arms, as she heard the joyous triumphant roars of her griffons mixing with the agonized, defeated screams of the Justice Layel.

"Selectra, Solara…" she gasped weakly, fighting to find her feet, to rush to assure herself of their safety.

"Get her to the Well of Magick," one of The Veressi snapped. "Her valley is once again free of evil and her Sorceresses unharmed. Get her from here, now."

She felt herself being lifted from Caise's arms, Garron's cool leathery skin a welcome balm against her burning flesh as she felt the fast, disorienting ride through the shadow planes.

Within seconds she was within the Well of Magick, sighing in bliss as she was eased into the cooling stream of magick which ran through it.

"You did well, my child," Garron whispered at her ear as she heard Caise and Kai'el cursing, their voices low, almost angered. "You are now truly the Keeper."

She was released as her eyes opened, but it wasn't the dragon she saw, it was her Wizards. Tears filled her eyes as they eased into the waters beside her, their bodies singed, much as she feared hers was as well.

"Keeper," Caise sighed as he pulled her into his arms. "I fear we are doomed."

She snuggled against his chest, moaning in pleasure as Kai'el smoothed her hair aside to scoop the liquid magick over her burning back.

"We are saved." She kissed his chest, feeling his erection rising to press into her stomach as a weak chuckle left her lips. Why was she not surprised?

"But doomed in the end," he growled, pulling her head back, staring down at her with laughing gold eyes, eyes filled with love, with thankfulness. "It is more than apparent that you cannot stay out of trouble. There is only one answer to this."

She gasped as she was lifted, impaled and shuddered in pleasure.

"Not fair," she gasped, clenching on the thick, heated cock now filling her.

Liquid magick infused them, raised their passions, their hungers, just as it did hers.

"Fair or no, there is only one answer to our problem." Kai'el moved behind her, his erection nudging at her anus, working into the suddenly slickened little entrance as the power flowing around them prepared her easily.

"We have a problem?" She breathed out roughly as he surged hard and deep inside her, sending quaking streams of pleasure tearing through her.

Ah Sentinels, she had never imagined such pleasure as these Wizards brought her.

"Aye, a dilemma of the most vexing sort," Kai'el growled as he began to move, fucking her in tandem to Caise's movements, filling her body, her mind with pleasure rather than pain, with need rather than fear. "How to keep our Consort safe."

She shook her head. She did not wish to hear it. If they must leave her soon then she did not wish to know. Not now. Not here. She knew The Veressi could call them from her before the Joining ceremony if they wished it. Knew that she could be separated from them, perhaps not forever, but far longer than she could bear. And though she hadn't voiced the fear, had refused to let it raise a thought within her mind, still, the shadow of it haunted her.

"There is only one way." Caise's voice was strained, his muscles tight as he thrust inside her, stroking flesh more sensitive for the magick washing over them, stretching her, invading not just her pussy but her soul, just as Kai'el filled her. Body and soul. Her Wizards.

"You cannot leave," she cried out then, shaking in their grip as she felt the pleasure building, her cunt tightening, her clit swelling with impending release. She should not have been ready so soon. She should not be nearing climax so quickly after near-death.

"Aye, my love." Kai'el's teeth raked her shoulders as they began to move harder, stronger within her. "We cannot leave. Ever. How do you leave your soul?"

Rapture surged within her, exploded, erupting through her heart, her soul, her very being as her climax tore through her body, shook her, locked them to her then milked their release just as violently from their bodies.

She felt the hard, heated blasts of semen filling her, just as she felt their magick whipping into her. Ecstasy, bright, consuming, miraculous.

She collapsed against them, her eyes fluttering closed, exhaustion taking her, sleep filling her. Held safe in her Wizards' arms.

Epilogue
Sellane Castle
One week later

ဢ

When Wizards Rule, power flows, builds and burns… Enemies'
ancient art revealed, power foretold, art awakened. When Wizards
rule… Heed your Wizards, Keeper… Heed your Wizards, Keeper…

Marina came awake with a gasp, fury screaming around
her, magick whipping through the castle, echoing even into the
land as she felt a dragon's rage piercing the stone. The sound,
a roar of menace, of retribution, had her jumping from the bed,
barely a second behind the Wizards who, with a wave of their
hands, clothed themselves then her, before gripping their
swords and rushing from the room, one behind her, one before
her.

"Garron guards Serena," she yelled as they raced through
the rapidly filling hallway, racing for her sister's rooms.

The enraged howls sounded again, shaking the very walls
of the castle a second before Marina felt grief singe her soul.
The echo of her mother's pain, Brianna's terror as the magick
of it was released.

"Serena!" Her own scream echoed around her as they tore
into Serena's wing of the castle, pushing their way into her
bedroom to stare in shock at what awaited them.

Brianna stood within her Wizard Kings' arms, having
only newly arrived at the castle that morning. Their magick
weaved through the room, searching through the almost
undetectable molecules of the very air itself, searching
for…something.

Garron stood beside the empty bed, his black eyes now
glowing orange as the powerful aura of his magick whipped

through the room, racing from corner to corner, screaming out his rage as he stood at her sister's empty bedside. Her mother was no place to be seen.

"Brianna," she ran to her sister, gripping her shoulders, pulling her back from Drago's chest and staring into her fear-filled eyes. "Where are Mother and Serena? What has happened?"

"Gods, they are gone, Marina." Her voice was hoarse, fear and anger filling it as Drago and Lasan shouted orders to the warriors and sorcerer guards rapidly filling the room.

"They are taken!" Garron's voice was a harsh, vicious growl as she turned to him, staring in surprise at the sparks of fury that leapt from his eyes when he faced her. "Those mother-dracas have stolen past my magick and taken them both. By the gods they will pay."

"Taken?" Her voice was a thread of sound as horror filled her.

"We felt them, Marina." Brianna sobbed then. "Drago, Lasan and I. I heard Serena cry out and Mother's curse a second before they were just...gone." Her eyes were awash in tears, her face pale. "They just disappeared before our eyes and we could not track them."

"Who would dare?" She moved back from her sister, automatically sending a surge of magick through the floor to the caverns beneath where magick flowed. Sentmar was magick, the very air they breathed was filled with it. Magick could track magick. Or so she had believed.

There was no trace of her sister, no sign of her mother. There was only emptiness.

"Kings Veraga, you will return to your own lands and guard this one there," Garron ordered as a clawed finger stabbed in Brianna's direction. "We can afford no other such loss." His voice rasped with his fury, sending a chill down her spine as he turned then to Kai'el and Caise. "You will stay here and should you allow aught to take this child then I will see to it myself that you are stripped of all you are," he snarled in their stoic faces. "Do you hear my words?"

"Our lives are hers, Dragon," Caise responded, his voice dark with his deepening anger. "I need no threat from you. From here, we will search for what information may be found. Do not deceive yourself in believing either of these sisters will pace uselessly and await Wizards or dragons to give them permission to aid their family."

"You are all forgetting, without Mother or Serena, these lands are undefended," Brianna reminded them all. "I cannot rule, for I have bonded with the Veraga lands and its people there. Marina cannot rule, for she is the Keeper. It is forbidden that she take the throne."

"But it is not forbidden that her Wizards rule." Garron turned to them slowly, suspicion filling his expression as he regarded them.

"Nay, I will not hear such a thing," Marina snapped furiously. "They had no part in this. Think you that I would not know if they had? Our Joining assured they can never hide such things from me."

"Enough Marina," Caise growled. "One dragon's suspicions do not affect us one way or the other. Not more than his Wizard magick would. If any practices deceit, he should look to himself first."

"Enough!" She waved her hand, standing between the dragon and Wizards as the tension began to escalate. "There is no choice. As the Sentinels warned me within the stream of magick, the Wizards will rule."

Her furious announcement had everyone in the room staring back at her in shock.

"And you did not inform your mother of this, why?" Garron's voice lowered dangerously.

"Because I had no idea of the warning it appears it was," she snapped back. "You forget, Dragon, I have not your endless years of experience in deciphering the riddles of magick. Now enough. They will take the throne until Mother and Serena's return, which will be right quickly if you would head your Dragon rage to The Veressi castle."

The Sentinel's riddle was now clear within her mind. What had made no sense before, now rose clear within her. Whatever or whoever worked against them would learn that the dark arts would never be enough to protect them. The Sentinels had assured her of that.

Garron stared at her for long moments, the fiery glitter in his eyes a terrible, frightening thing to see. When he opened his mouth, she expected the cruelty of his fury to descend upon her head.

"Think you my magick cannot penetrate The Veressi lands," he snarled furiously. "That I would not know were they the ones to steal the rulers of this land? Do you see me as such an inept worker of my own magick, Keeper?" His sneer was a terrifying sight to see.

"Then we are doomed," she whispered. "If The Veressi do not hold her, then only the darkest of magicks could have taken them, Garron."

"And if this were true, again, I would know," he raged, his lip curling with rage. "Whoever has taken them has learned the forgotten arts of 'shielding', magick only the greatest of Wizards once knew. A magick even I cannot perfect. Finding them will not be as easy as your innocence would convince you it is."

She turned to Caise and Kai'el, fighting back her tears as they moved to her, enfolding her in their arms.

"You did not tell us of this riddle, Keeper," Kai'el growled as she felt his and Caise's magick strengthening hers protectively. It appeared they intended to take no chances that she would be stolen as easily. She recognized the homing spell that suddenly weaved within the very core of her magick.

"I did not know it for the riddle it was." She fought her cries, leaning against him wearily then, the worry and fears assailing her now. "Pray to the Sentinels that I can remember exactly the words they whispered now. For I fear it will be our only strength."

"I will find your Queen Mother and the heir I groomed for this throne," Garron snarled. "And may the Sentinels have mercy on whoever has taken them, for they shall find shadowhell a comfort after they meet my fury."

* * * * *

Shadowhell
The Underworld of Sentmar

The realms of Shadowhell were far-flung, a dimension reserved only for the hapless souls too lazy, too filled with malevolence and evil to attain the realms of paradise. It was said in Shadowhell, you quickly learned regret for even the slightest misdemeanor committed in life, and that the souls wailed in endless agony against their end.

Perhaps some did. Others were more suited to the darkened, fiery realms, though. They coursed through the landscape, still preying on others, forever seeking the key to freedom. Certain that it could be found.

But there were those, not truly deserving of the darkest fates, yet neither were they pure enough for paradise. For those, there was the Tribune. A place not of pure misery, but neither was there much good to redeem it. Still, they did not hunger, they did not thirst as those in the deepest reaches were known to do. They found shelter from the showers of fiery rains and eked out a meager existence within the caves and caverns that led to the lakes of fire farther within the shadowy dimension.

Garron popped into the dimension with a swirl of heated wind and growling anger as the newcomers to Shadowhell stepped into the caverns. These men deserved the deepest pits, not this more comfortable, though darkened realm.

As his form materialized within the largest of the caverns, the scattered inhabitants scurried quickly out of the way, whimpers of fear leaving their cracked lips as eyes filled with terror. They moved to hunch protectively into the chipped-away depressions of the stone walls, staring back at him with envy, with fear as the dust swirled at his feet.

His eyes narrowed on the three straggling into caverns, urged forward by the Hell warrior at his back and the staff of magick used to control the new inhabitants leveled at his spine. They were the three killed with the warriors who attacked Serena. Those who died by his magick.

"This is wrong," one of them sobbed, the oldest, a burly light-haired Secular who led the raid on the Princess Serena, whose dagger had found her tender flesh and nearly stolen her life.

Garron's fists clenched in fury, the power clenched at his abdomen, fighting for freedom.

"We were to attain paradise." Tears leaked down weathered cheeks as dull gray eyes stared around in horror. "We were promised paradise."

The warrior grunted. "Someone, it would appear, has lied," he drawled, moving around the three to take his place at the back of the cavern, his dark eyes narrowed on the dozen or more who hid within the darkness before frowning as he stared back at Garron.

"Who promised you paradise?" Garron moved forward from the shadows, keeping his voice low, his head covered in the concealing cowl of his cloak. "Perhaps we could petition the gods in your favor, were you truly deceived."

Of course, this was not possible. The gods had already judged them unworthy; there were no second chances after death.

"We were deceived." The Secular nodded fiercely as he drew the other two to him. "These are my sons, they were murdered by those bedamned Sorceresses. We were deceived by the one who came to us, swearing the gods protected us." He stared back at Garron in uncomprehending misery. "The sun goddess herself came to us, urging us to her battle. She would not lie. Some terrible mistake has been made."

The boys at his side did not shed tears. Boys, men truly, though their adulthood had not long been achieved. They glared around the caverns, their intentions obvious. The strength of their souls for the moment appeared impressive. Soon, it would wither away to the hunched and fearful demeanor most of Shadowhell's denizens knew well.

"The goddess herself, huh?" Garron shook his head slowly. "'Tis a shame she seems to have forgotten your deal. Perhaps 'twas not the goddess who came to you as you believe. Was she accompanied by another perhaps?"

Of course she was. A male always accompanied the deceptive form of the goddess who preyed upon the evil that manifested within the Seculars.

"Aye, her warrior always travels at her side, this is known well." The man nodded. "He did not speak, though. The goddess promised us paradise," he sobbed again. "This is no paradise."

"This is your punishment," Garron growled, stepping forward as he stared at the boy to his side. "It could be worse, old man. You could be as wicked, as evil as this whelp of yours."

Magick lifted the young man, twining about him, throwing him into the wall as watery blue eyes bulged and widened in alarm. Within his palm he carried a sharpened stone, one of the many that dropped from the cavern ceilings on a regular basis.

Garron chuckled as he struggled, fighting to free himself as inhuman growls left his throat and the power sent shards of agony through his form.

"I could kill you again, whelp," he sneered. "You who sought only to debase and degrade a Sorceress protected by the Sentinels themselves. One whose purity and magick knows such greater worth than your stinking form and has not yet cursed your existence within this realm. Do you know, whoreson, what happens if such words cross her lips?"

The Secular fought, his feet kicking, hands clutching at his throat as the magick tightened about it. Garron snarled with fury, wishing he could kill him yet again. He would have shaken him until his bones rattled and burned his weak little body with the fiery breath his dragon powers commanded.

"Garron. Enough."

His head whipped around, the cowl falling free to his shoulders as gasps and screams of fear echoed around him. He knew the image he presented and lifted his lip in contempt at their sorrowful cries.

He released the soul form slowly, the bands of magick relaxing, slowly easing back to him.

"Nemesis, my dear. Slumming?"

She was the most beautiful of the Sentinel Priestesses. A vision of light and creamy flesh, and wicked stormy eyes. Dressed in a gown of dark silk, cinched by a red corset, her long, long black hair falling around her form like veils of silken threads.

"Garron, you were forbidden to come here," she sighed, her silver eyes staring back at him with solemn chastisement. "There are no answers for you here. This realm." She extended her arms slowly, the wide, deep sleeves falling back from her slender wrists as she looked around once more. "It knows enough misery, enough foul fury. There is no need to add your own."

Her voice held patience, sympathy. He had no need for either. She was but a fledgling to the true power Sentmar possessed, and had no idea the problems he could cause her precious realm.

"I have been forbidden many things throughout my lifetimes," he snapped then. "When have such commands affected me?"

"Each time you disobeyed the will of the gods," she told him, her voice gentle, piercing the dark souls with pain each time she spoke. Their howls and whimpers of misery echoed around them. "Have you not lost enough, Garron, must you lose more because of your refusal to heed their will? You cannot seek vengeance in this realm, no more than you may seek answers. You are of the living, not of the dead. You have no place here."

He felt her magick weaving about his, attempting to find his weakness, to force him back to the upper lands. He crossed his arms over his chest, tilted his head and smiled as a flash of frustration filled her eyes.

"Fledgling," he grunted. "Your Sentinels send a lamb to confront the griffon. Really, Nemesis, you should discuss with them their attempts to do you harm, for that could be their only wish to so foolishly send you against me."

"I would never fight against you, Garron," she sighed. "Leave this place, my friend, heed my words before more is lost. The gods know mercy, strength and love, but you yourself know their chastisements are often harsh, and never forgotten. Do not tempt their anger upon your head once again."

"Their anger," he snarled, his arms lifting to his sides as he faced her. "Look upon me, Nemesis, they have not changed my form, nor do they command it. I will learn who leads these bedamned Seculars and I will learn it soon. And warn me not of our gods' so-called loving ways. From the womb I have known the lash of their fury, as no more than a babe, I knew the fire of their rage. I, my dear Priestess, am an example of their failures, nothing more."

"Garron, I beseech of you." Her crimson lips turned down with a saddened curve. "You have many powers, abilities none of our kind has ever known. You will tempt the gods to strike you down do you not cease this battle. The one you seek does not exist."

He drew himself to his full height, his arms falling to his sides. "Oh, he exists, little sister," he drawled. "And well you know it. You prefer to believe the lies rather than the truth. I..." He laid his fist to his chest. "I will know the truth, and I will exact payment for the past. This I vow."

As quickly as he materialized into the realm, he was gone. As the dust settled in his wake, Nemesis lowered her head, clasping her hands before her as another form wavered into being.

"Watch him close, little sister," the voice laughed, mockery and sarcasm filling it with a thick undertone of evil. "Aye, watch him close and do not fail me again. Next time, it may be your soul trapped within this realm."

* * * * *

Veressi Castle
Cauldaran Lands

Serena stared around her at the enclosure she was confined within. The magick was rainbow-hued, though dark, as though each color of the wondrous spectrum had been tainted with black. There were no iridescent hues of pastels or brilliance, though she was forced to admit the darker colors were exceptional in their beauty. Just as their masters were said to be.

She knew where she was, deep beneath the most powerful castle in the lands bordering the Raging Seas. She could hear the crash of the waves, feel the power of the magick being blocked by the shield that hovered around the room. She was defenseless, unable to call out to her mother or her sisters, confined in a way she had never known before. And she was naked.

She leaned her head against the smooth wood of the headboard of the bed she sat upon, staring at the dark gray of the walls outside her prison, searching, ever searching for a weakness within the power swirling around her, the ever-shifting colors hampering her ability to penetrate it.

She clutched a thin sheet to her bare breasts, her eyes narrowing as anger once again burned inside her. She had no idea how long she had been trapped within this room. Opulent as it was, it was still little more than a cave and it sure as shadowhell wasn't her mother's castle.

"Dracas!" She screamed out the hateful word. "Stinking, slimy whoresons. Garron will have your heads for this infamy. You will not escape his fury."

Her hands balled into fists as she fought back the tears of fury. Garron would find her and when he did, he would present their heads to her upon a platter of gold. No one dared harm those within the Sellane castle without feeling his wrath.

"Your language leaves much to be desired, Princess." Where there had been only silence, only the furnishings of the room, there now stood one of The Veressi. Which one, only the gods knew for both were identical to the other even in ways unfamiliar to the Cauldaran Wizards. And he was alone.

A howl of fury left her lips as he waved his hand, and the sheet disintegrated between her fingers, leaving her bare to his gaze, utterly defenseless before him.

"Bedamned bastard whoreson," she screamed, shaking her head and pulling her hair around her to shield her nudity. Cursed Wizards. Somehow the bastards had even managed to have her prepared for Joining. The soft curls she had carried between her thighs were gone, magickally shorn to remove the protection against the magicks which could align with her own.

"Naughty girl." His wicked smile sent her rage burning higher. Eyes as black as the pits of shadowhell were said to be twinkled with small shimmering lights. His black hair fell long to his shoulders, framing a face of such male beauty and arrogance as to set a female's teeth on edge.

"You dare to kidnap me," she fumed, maintaining her place on the bed rather than flying at him in rage as she longed to do. "You block my power and think to get away with this? Do you intend to kill me? Do you mean to, do it now, dracas, for if I escape I shall see your heads gracing the doors of Sellane Castle."

He slid his hands into the pockets of his breeches, shaking his head as he tsked mockingly. The pure white, fine linen of his shirt stretched across the width of his chest, tucking into the low-slung pants and cinched with a wide black belt. Calf-high boots graced his feet, and he wore no weapon for her to attempt to steal.

"You are a most ungracious guest, Serena." His voice seemed to croon her name. "And quite insulting to the accommodations we prepared for you."

"Bastard," she muttered again, huddling against the headboard, certain she would shatter if he dared to touch her.

Was this to be her fate? Would she be raped, her body and her magick taken at the hands of these dark Wizards?

A frown jerked between his brows as he waved his hand toward the bed. Instantly a robe materialized, thick, warm. She jerked it to her, spreading it around the front of her body as she glared at him furiously.

"I do not take unwilling women," he growled as though he knew her thoughts. "But you will not stay unwilling for long. Heed my words, you will not leave this castle, and you will not escape. You refused the Rite of Reception or Courtship, therefore, you will stay within this room until alignment has been decided by the gods. Reluctant or willing, you will be our Consort."

Serena stared at him in shock, her eyes widening at the cold words which seared into her brain.

"You cannot be serious," she whispered. "No such Joining would be recognized by the Sentinel Priests or Priestesses. You will not get away with this. And should you try, Garron will make certain you regret it."

"Infidel Wizard that dragon is." His lip curled contemptuously. "He must first find you, and within this cavern, you will be completely hidden. Should the time come that you settle within yourself and accept this Consortship, then you will know at least partial freedom. Until then, this place you shall call home." He waved his hand to encompass the magick-protected area.

She sneered in kind.

"I am no weak-kneed witch or easy strumpet for you to so threaten." She rose to her feet, jerking the robe around her, ignoring the flaring lust in his gaze as she did so. Belting the robe, she allowed her gaze to rove insultingly over the tall, strong contours of his body. "Handsome you are, but dark villains were never to my taste, Veressi. Seek another, for to me you are the vilest of creatures and I would rather seek my death than to lie between such cursed Wizards as yourselves. Speaking of which, where is your other half? Off tormenting other unsuspecting Sorceresses, I have no doubt."

He watched her broodingly, and aye, the feel of those cold eyes moving over her vulnerable form brought a spurt of fear that she dare not let him see. Then his eyes narrowed, his lips flattening in anger as his magick suddenly snapped around her. They curled about her wrists, jerking them straight out from her sides as her ankles were pulled apart similarly. The belt of the robe uncurled as she screeched in rage.

"Lying whoreson," she raged as the robe fell away, leaving her naked before him, her body open, undefended. "You swore you would not."

"Do you feel my cock within you?" he snarled as he neared her. "Do you lie between my brother and I, impaled as you should be? I spoke no lie, Sorceress, neither did I swear I would not punish you for the unknowing ignorance of your words."

The robe tore from her body as she fought the magick holding her still before him.

"There is no ignorance in my words, you are but dark Wizards intent only upon your own power and greed. I will have no part of you."

She screamed as his fingers touched her, the tips only smoothing across her heaving breasts as he stared down at her in fury.

"Garron will see you destroyed."

"He must first find you," he murmured, his fingertip glancing her nipple as fire seemed to lance from the sensitive tip to the flesh between her thighs. Shock held her rigid for one second and no more before she bucked against the touch, curses raining from her lips as she screamed in fury.

He would not release her. By the gods she could find no way to escape his touch and did he not stop soon, then she was lost. She could find no pleasure in this touch, in such evil. She refused to allow it.

"You will be ours," he whispered, his head lowering to her ear as he breathed the words, his fingers trailing down her breast before caressing her abdomen, moving ever closer to the bare flesh of her pussy.

"I refuse you. By magick bound, and strength betrayed, I say nay." She screamed out the words, calling upon the only defense she knew, and only then if the Wizard held enough honor to obey the words the Sentinel Grace herself had given the Sorceresses to refuse an unwilling Joining.

He paused, sighing deeply before removing his touch. Moving back, he shook his head slowly, his firm lips quirking into a mocking, cold smile as he watched her.

"You had only to find no pleasure in the touch, Princess," he informed her coolly. "I would have gone no further should the silken flesh of your soft cunt not hold the dew of your lust. But…" he glanced farther down. "Perhaps it does."

She was doomed. She could feel her own dampness, feel the prickle of sensation within her deepest core as she stared back at him, refusing to speak.

"If the alignment is possible, then all the protestations within this world will not save you." He shrugged carelessly as he called back his magick with a flick of his fingers.

Instantly she was free, jerking the tatters of the robe from the floor to hold against her.

"I do not wish this," she whispered then, suddenly terrified, aware that her magick, aye, her body, could well be her downfall.

"Wishes do not matter at this time, Princess," he answered her, his voice sounding weary, resolute. "A time comes to all of us when we must do even those things we abhor to achieve what must be done. You will learn this soon."

He moved to the barrier of magick, his palm outstretched, feeling the power within it.

"I will not accept this. Ever. Whatever trickery you might play upon my body matters not, Veressi. It is my heart which will defeat you."

He glanced over his shoulder, his expression so damned emotionless as to have her gritting her teeth at the sense of defeat that filled her. He did not care. All that mattered were his own objectives.

"I will return later," he said quietly. "We will bring your dinner, and some clothing if you can mind your language. Continue to heap such curses upon our heads and you will eat naked before us, accepting each morsel from our fingers as your punishment." He flashed her a dark smile. "To our great enjoyment. It is your choice."

Before she could speak he stepped through the swirling magick, moving with no haste across the floor to the barred door on the other side of the room.

"I will not allow this," she yelled at his back, her fists clenching in fury. "Do you hear me, Veressi? I will not submit to such deceit. Ever."

There was no reply. The door opened as he neared it, closed and rebarred itself as he passed through the doorframe, leaving her alone, uncertain, and suddenly terribly frightened that The Veressi Twins would indeed have her. If not willingly, then eventually, in other ways.

Why an electronic book?

We live in the Information Age—an exciting time in the history of human civilization, in which technology rules supreme and continues to progress in leaps and bounds every minute of every day. For a multitude of reasons, more and more avid literary fans are opting to purchase e-books instead of paper books. The question from those not yet initiated into the world of electronic reading is simply: *Why?*

1. *Price.* An electronic title at Ellora's Cave Publishing and Cerridwen Press runs anywhere from 40% to 75% less than the cover price of the exact same title in paperback format. Why? Basic mathematics and cost. It is less expensive to publish an e-book (no paper and printing, no warehousing and shipping) than it is to publish a paperback, so the savings are passed along to the consumer.

2. *Space.* Running out of room in your house for your books? That is one worry you will never have with electronic books. For a low one-time cost, you can purchase a handheld device specifically designed for e-reading. Many e-readers have large, convenient screens for viewing. Better yet, hundreds of titles can be stored within your new library—on a single microchip. There are a variety of e-readers from different manufacturers. You can also read e-books on your PC or laptop computer. (Please note that Ellora's Cave does not endorse any specific brands.

You can check our websites at www.ellorascave.com or www.cerridwenpress.com for information we make available to new consumers.)

3. *Mobility.* Because your new e-library consists of only a microchip within a small, easily transportable e-reader, your entire cache of books can be taken with you wherever you go.

4. *Personal Viewing Preferences.* Are the words you are currently reading too small? Too large? Too... ANNOYING? Paperback books cannot be modified according to personal preferences, but e-books can.

5. *Instant Gratification.* Is it the middle of the night and all the bookstores near you are closed? Are you tired of waiting days, sometimes weeks, for bookstores to ship the novels you bought? Ellora's Cave Publishing sells instantaneous downloads twenty-four hours a day, seven days a week, every day of the year. Our webstore is never closed. Our e-book delivery system is 100% automated, meaning your order is filled as soon as you pay for it.

Those are a few of the top reasons why electronic books are replacing paperbacks for many avid readers.

As always, Ellora's Cave and Cerridwen Press welcome your questions and comments. We invite you to email us at Comments@ellorascave.com or write to us directly at Ellora's Cave Publishing Inc., 1056 Home Avenue, Akron, OH 44310-3502.

erridwen, the Celtic Goddess of wisdom, was the muse who brought inspiration to storytellers and those in the creative arts. Cerridwen Press encompasses the best and most innovative stories in all genres of today's fiction. Visit our site and discover the newest titles by talented authors who still get inspired - much like the ancient storytellers did, once upon a time.

Cerridwen Press

www.cerridwenpress.com